CH00705229

AN OLD ADAGE T
CAN'T JOIN 'EN

G-M-L Homes, manufacturers of bubble houses, the greatest advance in the history of architecture, had become the biggest and most powerful corporation in the history of commerce. Unfortunately, power, greed, and rampant criminal activity had taken over corporate principals. Charles Mundin, just a criminal lawyer, had unwittingly been pulled into the thick of things, when Norma Lavin—a very beautiful client of his—had been kidnapped by corporate operatives. With grim resolve Mundin, along with the help of a shrewd accomplice, Harry Ryan, laid the plans to get the girl back and expose the massive corruption of a giant corporation. But never had there been a more one-sided battle—a handful of nobodies, armed only with ingenuity and audacity, against the greatest concentration of financial and economic power in all history! The stakes, though, were larger than money or influence; they were the fulfillment of a dead man's dream!

FOR A COMPLETE SECOND NOVEL TURN TO PAGE 161

CAST OF CHARACTERS

CHARLES MUNDIN
This criminal lawyer's associates had grossly underestimated him, but with some ingenuity he was going to rip their scam wide open.

NORVELL BLIGH
This company man eagerly organized the bloody spectacles that kept his boss in business—a business ripe with office politics.

VIRGINIA BLIGH
Sold by her parents, she was lucky to be merely a shill in a pickpocket operation instead of a brothel.

HARRY RYAN
He was an old-time corporation lawyer, but his once-sharp brain had been dulled by years of addiction to yen pox.

DON LAVIN
There was a fortune in stock certificates waiting for him, but an unfortunate brainwashing left him no memory as to where they were.

NORMA LAVIN
Norma, spitfire that she was, wasn't going to take being swindled lying down, but what could she actually do about it?

LANA
As boss of the juvenile Belly Rave gang known as the Wabbits, she would do practically anything—for a price,

SHEP
Big and beefy enough to survive on the streets of Belly Rave, he wanted nothing more than to paint.

GLADIATOR AT LAW

By
FREDERIK POHL & C. M. KORNBLUTH

ARMCHAIR FICTION
PO Box 4369, Medford, Oregon 97504

For more information about Armchair Books and products, visit our website at…

www.armchairfiction.com

Or email us at…

armchairfiction@yahoo.com

CHAPTER ONE

THE accused was a tallow-faced weasel with Constitutional Psychopathic Inferior stamped all over him. He wailed to Charles Mundin, L1.B., "You got to get me off! I've been up twice and this time, they'll condition me!"

Mundin studied his first client with distaste. "You *won't* plead guilty?" he asked again, hopelessly. He had been appointed by the court and considered that the court had played him a low trick.

His stubborn client's pore patterns were all over Exhibit A, a tin cashbox fish-hooked from a ticket window at Monmouth Stadium. Modus operandi coincided with his two previous convictions. An alleged accomplice, who had kept the ticket clerk busy for almost all of the necessary five minutes, was ready to take the witness stand—having made his deal with the prosecutor. And still the fool was refusing to cop a plea.

Mundin tried again. "It won't be so bad, you know. Just a couple of days in a hospital. It's quite painless, and that's not just talk. I've seen it with my own eyes. They took us around in junior year—"

"Counselor, you just don't understand. If they condition me, my God, I'll actually have to go to *work!*"

Mundin shrugged. "I'll do what I can for you."

BUT the trial was over in a matter of minutes. Mundin objected that the moral character of the witness made his testimony inadmissible in a condition able offense. The prosecutor, a grandee from Harvard Law, haughtily smacked him down by pointing out that the essence of the conditionable offense lay in the motivation of the accused, not in the fact of commission, which was all the accomplice had testified to. He then cited a series of precedents.

GLADIATOR AT LAW

By FREDERIK POHL & C. M. KORNBLUTH

PART 1 OF A 3-PART SERIAL

The authors of Gravy Planet again tour the future—this time a world of bubble houses and Belly Raves!

The Judge's eyes went blank and distant. Those inside the hall could hear confirmation of the precedents droning faintly into his ears through the headphones under his elaborate wig. He nodded and said to Mundin, "Overruled. Get on with it."

Mundin didn't even bother to take an exception.

Illustrated by EMSH

The prosecution rested and Mundin got up, his throat dry. "May it please the Court," he said. His Honor looked as though nothing had pleased that court, ever. Mundin said to the jury box, "The defense, contending that no case has been made, will present no witnesses." That, at any rate, would keep Harvard Law from letting the jury know of the two previous convictions. "The defense rests."

7

Harvard Law, smiling coldly, delivered a thirty-second summation which, in three razor-sharp syllogisms, demonstrated the fact that defendant was guilty as hell.

The court clerk's fingers clicked briskly on the tape-cutter, then poised expectantly as Mundin stood up.

"May it please the Court," said Mundin. That look again. "My client has not been a fortunate man. The product of a broken home and the gutters of Belly Rave, he deserves justice, as does every citizen. But in his case, I am impelled to add that the ends of justice can be served only by an admixture of mercy."

Judge and prosecutor were smiling openly. The devil with dignity! Mundin craned his neck to read the crisp yellow tape that came clicking out of the clerk's encoding machine. He could read jury box code, more or less, if it were simple enough.

The encoded transcript of his summation was simple enough. The tape read—

$0=0...0=0...0=0...$

"Defense rests," he mumbled, ignoring a despairing croak from his client.

THE Judge said, "Mr. Clerk, present the case to the jury box."

The clerk briskly fed in the two tapes. The jury box hummed and twinkled. If you could only fix one of those things, Mundin thought savagely, staring at the big seal on it. Or if you could get one of those damned clerks to cut the tape—no, that was out, too. The clerks were voluntarily conditioned. Traded freedom for a sure living.

The red window lit up. GUILTY AS CHARGED.

"Work!" the thief bleated.

The Judge said, shifting his wig and showing a bit of earphone under it, "Mr. Bailiff, take charge of the prisoner. Sentencing to-morrow at eleven. Court's adjourned."

The thief moaned, "I hate them damn machines. Couldn't you have got me a human jury, maybe get an injunction?"

Mundin said wearily, "A human jury would have crucified you. Why did you have to steal from the Stadium? Why not pick on something safe, like the Church, or the Judge's piggy bank?" He turned his back on the defendant and bumped into Harvard Law.

"Nice try, young man," the grandee smiled frostily. "Can't win them all, can we?"

Mundin replied rudely, "If you're so smart, why aren't you a corporation lawyer?" and stamped out of the courtroom.

He was on the street before he regretted the crack. Harvard's face had fallen satisfactorily, but the jibe was 0=0 if ever there was one. Why, indeed? For the same reason Mundin himself wasn't, of course. He hadn't inherited one of the great hereditary corporation law practices. Even grinding through Harvard Law School couldn't get you conveniently reborn into the proper families. And Mundin hadn't gone to Harvard. Not for Harvard—or for Charles Mundin—the great reorganizations, receiverships and debenture issues. Not for them, the mergers and protective committees. For them—the mechanical jury box and the trivia of criminal law.

A morose, fifteen-minute walk through Monmouth's sweltering, rutted streets brought him to his office building. Some cluck from the sheriff's office was going to pick him up at 1400 for the rally. Besides being a member of the Criminal Bar, Charles Mundin, L1.B., was foredoomed candidate for the Monmouth City Council on the Regular Republican ticket in the 27th Aldermanic District.

His wallet-nerve twinged at the thought, then twinged again as his eye fell on the quietly proud little plaque beside the door of building. It announced that its rental agents were sorry, but could offer no vacancies. Mundin hoped rentals would stay that way, at least as far as his own office was concerned.

HE GOT an elevator to himself. "Sixteen," he told it. He was thinking of his first client. At least he would get a fee—you got one on conditionable cases. The crook was terrified that he'd find himself unable to steal. Maybe Counselor Mundin himself might soon be driven to dangling a hook and line over the wall of a ticket window at Monmouth Stadium.

Or he might get really desperate and find himself one of the contestants in the Field Day inside.

His mail hopper was empty, but his Sleepless Secretary—he was still paying for it—was blinking for his attention. The rental agents again? Law book salesman? Maybe even a client? "Go ahead," he said.

In its accurate voice, the machine reported, "Telephone call, 1205 hours. Mr. Mundin is out, madam. If you wish to leave a message, I will take it down."

Del Dworcas' outraged baritone shouted, "Who the hell are you calling madam?"

The secretary: "Gug-gug-*gug*—ow-*wooh*. Sir."

Dworcas: "What? Oh, one of those damn gadgets. Well, listen, Charlie, if you ever get this. I sent somebody over to see you. Named Bligh. Treat him right. And look me up at the rally. Something to talk about with you. And you better get that lousy machine fixed unless you want to lose some business."

The secretary, after a pause: "Is that the end of your message, madam?"

Dworcas: "Yes! And stop calling me madam!"

The secretary: "Gug-gug-*gug*—ow-*wooh*." And click.

Oh, fine, thought Mundin. Now Dworcas was sore at him, no doubt, and Dworcas was chairman of the Regular Republican County Committee. And the secretary's confusion between the sexes and its banshee howl weren't covered by the service contract.

The mail tube popped while he was blaspheming the salesman who had flattered him into buying the secretary. He eagerly flushed the letter from its hopper, but when he caught sight of the return address, he dropped it unopened. It was from the Scholarship Realization Corporation. He knew he owed them the money and he knew, as a result, of the law course they had paid for, that they couldn't attach his hypothetical income.

THERE was nothing to do until someone showed up—this Bligh or the man from the sheriff's office. Trying hard to think of the priceless publicity and contacts he was getting from his flier in politics, he took his account book out and added it up. It made him wince. The price of the priceless publicity and contacts to date was $854.32.

Of course, he reminded himself, the Party had laid out money, too. That TV time, for instance, when he was right there on the platform, must have cost a hunk of change. Of course, he hadn't actually *spoken*.

But his end included postage, stationery, truck rental, PA system rental, direct-mail fees, carfare, banquet tickets, fight tickets, Field Day tickets, fund-raising lottery tickets, charities, dues and entertainment. Then the rivers of beer, which he didn't enjoy, drunk with people he didn't like. And the bhang, which scared hell out of him, sipped with the teetotal Muslims of the 27th District. There was the way his doctor had tsk-tsked when he last stood in front of a fluoroscope with a barium meal coursing sluggishly through him.

And, of course, the certainty that he would be crushed like a bug on Election Day. And that The Boys—Dworcas was only one of The Boys—had played him for a sucker.

Sing *"Hey"* for the life of a lawyer, gabbling at machines that, he naggingly suspected, thought him not as bright as they were.

The Sleepless Secretary said, "Sir or madam, as the case may be. Gug-gug-*gug*. Regret to advise." Mundin kicked it savagely. It burped and said: "A gentleman is in the outer office, Mrs. Mundin."

"Come in!" Mundin yelled at the door.

The man blinked at him and came in cautiously. He looked around and picked out a chair. He wore a hearing aid, Mundin noticed. Perhaps that was why he cocked his head a little.

He said, "My name's Norvell Bligh. I—uh—asked Mr. Dworcas if he could recommend a first-class attorney and he—uh—he suggested you."

Mundin asked aloofly, "What can I do for you?"

BLIGH'S eyes roamed nervously around the room. "My wife—that is, I would like to get some information on adoption. I have a stepdaughter—my wife's daughter by her first marriage, you see—and, well, my wife thinks we should arrange about adopting her."

Good old Del Dworcas, Mundin thought savagely. He *knows* I belong to the Criminal Bar, yet he goes right ahead... He said, "I'm sorry, Mr. Bligh. I can't help you. You'll have to find a civil attorney to handle that for you."

Bligh touched the control of his hearing aid.

"Beg pardon?"

"*I—can't—do—it!*"

"Oh, I know *you* can't," Bligh said. "Mr. Dworcas explained that. But he said that the civil attorneys would charge an awful lot, while you… That is, since you're a friend of his and I'm a friend of his brother, it could be done on a friendly basis. All I need to know, really, is what to do. I don't think I'd have to have a lawyer in court, do you?"

Mundin pondered hopefully. "Maybe not." It was questionable practice, no doubt of it, and small thanks to Dworcas for getting him into it. Still, if it was just a matter of advice and information— thank God, the corporation boys didn't have *that* sewed up.

He leaned back, covertly looking Bligh over. Tolerably well dressed, certainly not a deadbeat. He'd be some kind of contract worker, no doubt, getting his regular pay; living in a G-M-L house, suffering his wife's obvious nagging.

Mundin said, "Tell me the story. First of all, the court will want to be sure you can earn enough to support the child."

"Well, I've *been* supporting her for three years. Excuse me, Mr. Mundin, but can we keep this short? I'm on my lunch hour and Mr. Candella is very fussy about promptness."

"Certainly. Just give me the facts."

NORVELL BLIGH coughed self-consciously. "I'm an associate producer for General Recreations, in charge of Field Day procurement, mostly. My wife is named Virginia. She was married before I met her to a man named Tony Elliston. They didn't get along too well—it was a pretty rough experience for her. They had one daughter, Alexandra. Virginia's first husband died. I have the papers here. Alexandra is 14 now. Anything else?"

Mundin scribbled rapidly—purely pretense, since the Sleepless Secretary was recording the whole thing automatically. On second thought, he told himself, maybe not pretense at that, considering the way it was acting. He put down his pencil.

"That's enough for the time being," he said. "I'll have to look up—have to discuss this matter with one of my colleagues. Come back Friday at this time."

As Bligh left, looking vaguely alarmed, the Sleepless Secretary said, "Pending the receipt. Ow-*woooh*. Mrs. Mundin is out of town."

Mundin turned it off.

Two clients in one day, he thought wonderingly. Anything was possible. Perhaps he would even win the election. Perhaps he wouldn't, after all, have to let the finance company reclaim the secretary and the Scholarship people garnish his income and the landlord toss him out on the street.

Perhaps.

THE RENTED sound truck, with the man from the sheriff's office driving, rolled slowly past glowering, red brick fronts and stone stoops crowded with liquid-eyed women and their skinny, brownish kids. Mundin didn't like this neighborhood. It was on the outskirts of the city, too close to Belly Rave for safety, too close to the factories and the yards for comfort. But he didn't have to *live* here, even if the miracle should happen and he got elected.

He chanted wearily into the mike at the indifferent Ay-rabs of the 27th. "My friends, don't miss the big free rally tonight at Republican Hall. Learn the truth, don't be misled. The Regular Republican Party promises inside plumbing for every family. We promise stockyard workers paid time off for noon prayers and doubling the bonus for handling pork. My friends, don't miss the big free rally. Don't fail to miss the big free—"

"*Hey!*" the driver cried.

Mundin put his hand over the mike. "*Damn!* Right out of my subconscious, that one." He uncovered the mike and said, "Don't *miss* the big free rally. The Regular Republicans are the party of Lincoln, the party of Eisenhower. We stand for inside plumbing. Learn the truth at the big free rally..."

The liquid eyes stared entirely without interest. Mundin subsided and turned on the sound tape. The speaker horns began to blare, *you and me and the moon*. Apathetically, he noted that one of the older Ay-rab women wore a veil. Unusual, nowadays.

The driver leaned over and nudged him. "You'll never get anywhere with the Ay-rabs, Mr. Mundin," he said confidentially. "We had a good crowd in the 27th before the war. Poles and Irish.

The Poles voted Republican—you only had one Republican Party then, you know. And the Irish voted Democrat. But then the packers began flying in the Ay-rabs and now you don't know where you stand."

Mundin nodded indifferently.

They passed somebody's G-M-L bubble house, obviously an early model, before the corporation figured out the bubble-city plan, and it was showing its age. Mundin could see the family taking their ease in the living room. He chuckled. Their polarizer was out of order and they didn't know it.

But the driver was shocked. He stopped the truck and honked, pointing indignantly through the wall. The man heard the honking and hastily strode to a manual control. The wall opaqued.

The truck rolled on. The driver muttered something about goddam fishbowls. "I'm a married man," he added indignantly and irrelevantly.

"Yeah," said Mundin. "Say, the hell with 85th Street. Turn around—let's go back to the club."

He flicked off the speakers in mid-chorus. It made no difference to the dark, liquid eyes: they followed the silent truck as uncaringly as they had the blaring horns.

"My friends," Mundin said to the dead microphone, "vote for my opponent. He's as big a liar as I am, but he can afford this and I can't."

Which was also irrelevant, for he was stuck with it now.

CHAPTER TWO

THIS fellow Mundin might not be much of a lawyer, Norvie Bligh told himself on the way back to his office, but at least he probably wouldn't charge much. Arnie Dworcas had as much as promised him that.

Anyway, who needed a legal eagle to put adoption papers through? The whole thing was downright silly. If only Ginny weren't so touchy lately, you could explain to her that it was just an unwarranted expense, that nobody was going to take Alexandra away from them, that there wasn't any question about who'd inherit his contract status and bubble house if he died.

He considered that for a moment. Virginia had certainly seemed to take that part of it seriously, he thought. She had mentioned it half a dozen times. "Don't forget to ask him about inheriting." And, of course, he had forgotten. Well, there would be another chance on Friday.

You couldn't really blame Virginia if she felt a little—well, insecure. Life with that Tony must have been pure hell, living in Belly Rave from hand to mouth. That was why she was such a devoted wife.

Of *course*, she was a devoted wife, he told himself.

Right now, though, the important thing was whether Candella was going to say anything about his being fifteen minutes late. Candella was pretty difficult lately. Naturally, you couldn't blame him for being jumpy, with the big Fall Field Day coming up and all.

Of course, you couldn't blame Candella. Of course, you couldn't blame Virginia, or Arnie Dworcas when his promises didn't jell, or Alexandra when she was a little touchy, like any 14-year-old, of course.

Of course, you couldn't blame anybody for anything. Not if you were Norvell Bligh.

Fortunately, Candella didn't notice what time he came back from lunch. But in the middle of the afternoon, the boss's secretary came hurrying out to Norvie's desk and said, "Mr. Candella would like to discuss your Field Day program with you."

He went in with a feeling of uneasiness.

Old man Candella slapped the papers down and roared. "Bligh, maybe you think a Field Day is a Boy Scout rally, where kids shoot arrows and run footraces around a tennis court. Maybe you think it's a Ladies' Aid pink tea. Maybe you just don't know what a Field Day is supposed to be. Is that it?"

NORVIE BLIGH swallowed. "No, sir," he whispered.

" 'No, sir,' " Candella mimicked. "Well, if you *do* know what a Field Day is, why isn't there at least one good, exciting idea in this whole bloody script? I take back that word 'bloody.' There might be some complaints in the other direction, but I guarantee there wouldn't be any complaints that there was too much blood."

He jabbed at the program with a hairy forefinger. "Listen to this. 'Opening pageant—procession of jeeps through gauntlet of spearmen. First spectacle—fifty girl wrestlers versus fifty male boxers. First duet—sixty-year-old men with blowtorches.' Ah, what's the use of going on? This is supposed to be the big event of the year, Bligh. It isn't a Friday-night show in the off-season. This is the one that counts. It's got to be *special.*"

Norvie Bligh shifted miserably. "Gosh, Mr. Candella. I—I thought it *was*. It's a classical motif, don't you see? It's like—"

"I can tell what it's like," Candella bellowed. "I've been producing these shows for fifteen years. I don't need anybody, to tell me whether a script will play or it won't—and I'm telling you this one won't!"

He stabbed a button on his console.

Norvie felt the seat lurch warningly underneath him and barely managed to scramble to his feet as it disappeared into the wall.

"Take this script away," Candella growled. "We've got to start casting on Monday. Let's see if we can have something by tomorrow night." He didn't even look up as Norvie cringed out the door.

Norvie dictated and erased five tapes. He sent his three assistants on three different errands of research, to find the best spectacles on the highest-rated Field Days in every major city. Nothing they brought back was any help.

When Miss Dali came in to pick up the afternoon's dictation and he had to face the fact that there was no afternoon's dictation, he grumbled to her, "What do they expect in that moldy gym they call a stadium here? Look at Pittsburgh—we're twice as big and *they* have armored halftracks."

"Yes, sir," said Miss Dali. "Mr. Stimmens would like to see you."

"All right," he replied ungraciously and dialed a chair for his junior scriptwriter.

"Excuse me, Chief," Stimmens said hesitantly. "Can I see you for a moment?"

"You're seeing me," Norvie had picked that bon mot up from Candella the week before.

STIMMENS hesitated, then blurted much too rapidly, "You've got a great organization here, Chief, and I'm proud to be a part of it. But I'm having a little trouble—you know, trying to get ahead, hah-hah—and I wonder if it wouldn't be better for you, Chief, as well as me if…" He went on through a tortuous story of a classification clerk's mistakes when he had finished school, and an opening in Consumer Relations, and a girl who wouldn't marry him until he got a Grade Fifteen rating.

Long before Stimmens had come anywhere near the point, Norvie knew what he wanted and knew what the answer had to be. But Candella's bruises were fresh on his back and he let Stimmens go on till he was dry. Then, briskly, "Stimmens, *if* I'm not in error, you signed the regular contract before you joined us."

"Well, yes, sir, but—"

"It has the usual provision for cancellation. I believe you know the company's policy in regard to selling contracts. We simply cannot afford to sell unless the purchase price is high enough to reimburse us for the employee's training time—which, in your case, is all the time you've spent with us, since you have clearly failed to master your job. I'm surprised you should come to me with such a request."

Stimmens stared at him. "You won't let me go?"

"I can't. You're at liberty to cancel your contract."

"Cancel! And go back to Belly Rave? Mr. Bligh, have you ever been in Belly Rave?" He shook his head like a man dispelling a nightmare. "Well, sorry, Mr. Bligh. Anything else for me to do today?"

Norvie looked at his watch. "Tomorrow," he growled. As Stimmens slumped away, Norvie, already feeling ashamed of himself, petulantly swept the chair back into the wall.

It was almost quitting time.

He made a phone call. "Mr. Arnold Dworcas, please…Arnie? Hello, how're you? Fine. Say, I saw that attorney, Mundin, today. Looks like everything will be all right… Uh-huh. Thanks a lot, Arnie… This evening? Sure. I was hoping you'd ask me. All right if I go home first? Ginny'll want to hear about the lawyer… About eight, then."

ARNIE Dworcas had a way of chewing a topic interminably and regurgitating it in flavorless pellets of words. Lately he had been preoccupied with what he called the ingratitude of the beneficiaries of science.

At their frequent get-togethers, he would snarl at Norvie, "Not that it matters to us Engineers. Don't think I take it personally, just because I happen to be essential to the happiness and comfort of everybody in the city. No, Norvie, we Engineers don't expect a word of thanks. We Engineers work because there's a job to do, and we're trained for it. But that doesn't alter the fact that people are lousy ingrates."

At which point, Norvie· would cock his head a little in the nervous reflex he had acquired with the hearing aid and agree, "Of course, Arnie. Hell, fifty years ago, when the first bubble cities went up, women used to burst out crying when they got a look at one. My mother did. Coming out of Belly Rave, knowing she'd never have to go back——"

"Yeah. Not that that's evidence, as we Engineers understand evidence. It's just your untrained recollection of what an untrained woman told you. But it gives you an idea of how those lousy ingrates settled down and got smug. They'd change their tune damn fast if we Engineers weren't on the job. But you're an artist, Norvell. You can't be expected to understand." And he would gloomily drink beer.

Going home from work and looking forward to seeing his best friend that night, Norvie was not so sure he didn't understand. He even felt inclined to argue that he wasn't an artist like some crackpot oil painter or novelist in a filthy Belly Rave hovel, but a technician in his own right. Well, kind of—his medium was the emotional fluxes of a Field Day crowd, rather than torques, forces and electrons. He had an important job, Norvie told himself— Associate Producer, Monmouth Stadium Field Days. Of course, Arnie far outstripped him in title. Arnie was Engineer Supervising Rotary and Reciprocal Pump Installations and Maintenance for Monmouth G-M-L City.

Not that Arnie was the kind of guy to stand on rank. Hell, look at how Arnie was always doing things for you—like finding you a lawyer when you needed one, and… Well, he was *always* doing things for you.

It was a privilege to know a man like Arnie Dworcas.

CHAPTER THREE

CHARLES Mundin, L1.B., just parked the truck for the sheriff's man—he was too busy—and entered Republican Hall through the back way.

He found Del Dworcas in the balcony—the Hall was a slightly remodeled movie house—telling the cameramen how to place their cameras, the soundmen how to line up their parabolic mikes, the electricians how to use their lights.

Mundin stood on the sidelines, faintly hoping one of the cameramen would extract a few of Dworcas' front teeth with a tripod leg, but they kept their tempers admirably. He sighed and tapped the chairman on the shoulder.

Dworcas gave him the big hello and asked him to wait in the manager's office—he had to get these TV people squared away, but it wouldn't take more than a few minutes. "Did you see that fellow Bligh?" he asked. "Yeah? Good. Soak him, Charley; you got to make a living, you know. Some friend of my brother Arnie's. Now go on down to the office. Couple of people there for you to talk to." He looked annoyingly mysterious.

Mundin sighed again. At the foot of the stairs, he yelled in astonishment, "Great God Almighty! Prince Wilhelm the Fourth!"

William Choate IV jerked around and looked confused, then stuck out a hand for Mundin to grasp. He was a pudgy little man of Mundin's age, a classmate from John Marshall Law School, heir to a mighty corporate practice, a tidy dresser, former friend, solid citizen and four-star jerk. "Why, hello, Charles," he said uncertainly. "Good to see you."

"Likewise. What are *you* doing here?"

Choate made a mighty effort and produced a shrug. "Oh," he said, "*you* know."

"Meaning that even a corporation lawyer has political dealings once in a while?" Mundin helped him out.

"That's it exactly!" Choate was pleased. It was just like old times. Mundin had always helped him out, all the way through John Marshall Law.

Mundin looked at his former protégé with emotions that were only distantly related to envy. "It's a pleasure to run into you, Willie," he said. "They keeping you busy?"

"Busy? *Whew!* You'll never know, Charles." That was a very unfortunate remark, Mundin thought. "You know the I.G. Farben reorganization?"

"By reputation," Mundin said acidly. "I'm in criminal practice right now. Incidentally, I had an interesting case today—"

"Yes," Choate said. "Well, you might say I've won my spurs. The old man made me counsel for the Group E Debenture Holder's Protective Committee. Old Haskell died in harness, you know. Think of it—forty years as counsel for the Protective Committee! And with a hearing before the Referee in Receivership coming up. Well, I won *my* spurs, as you might say. I argued before the referee this morning, and I got a four-year stay!"

"Well," Charles Mundin said. "To use a figure of speech, you certainly won your spurs, didn't you?"

CHOATE beamed. "I thought you'd see it that way. I simply pointed out to old Roseheaver that rushing through an immediate execution of receivership would work a hardship on the committee and I asked for more time to prepare our suits for the trust offices. Old Roseheaver thought it over and decided it would be in the public interest to grant a stay. And, Charles, he congratulated me on my presentation! He said he had never heard the argument read better!"

"Well done," said Mundin. It was impossible to resent this imbecile. A faint spark of technical interest made him ask, "How did you prove hardship?"

Choate waved airily. "Oh, that was easy. We have this smart little fellow in the office, some kind of distant cousin of mine, I guess. He handles all the briefs. A real specialist—not much at the Big Picture, you know, but he could prove old man Winthrop was starving in the gutter if you told him to. I'm joking, of course," he added hastily.

Poor Willie, thought Mundin. Too dumb for Harvard Law, too dumb for Columbia, though he was rich enough to buy and sell them both. That was how he wound up at John Marshall, which had carried him for eight years of conditions and repeats until memorizing had worn grooves in his brain that carried him through his exams. Mundin compassionately had written most of his papers.

And poor dumb Willie glowed: "You know what that little job is worth? The firm's putting in for two hundred and twenty-five thousand dollars, Charles! And as counsel of record, I get half!"

That did it. Poor Willie thought he was just letting good old Charles know that the protégé at last was a success on his own. But his kindly idiocy broke Mundin.

"Willie," he begged hoarsely, "give me a job. You know I've got the brains. You know you never would have got through school if it hadn't been for me, and I never asked for a nickel. There were plenty of sharks around who would have soaked you plenty and still not got you through. Please, Willie, I can be a smart little fellow in your office just as well as somebody's cousin. Give me a chance. Law clerk. The bottom. Anything!"

WILLIE said dismally, "Gosh, Charles, I don't think we can do that. The old man wouldn't understand at all if I asked for somebody who wasn't in the family. Be fair, Charles. What would you do in my place?"

Mundin hopelessly knew what he would do. He would keep the lucrative practice of corporate law right in the grip of the family. He would sit on top of his practice with a shotgun in his lap.

"I understand, Willie," he said heavily.

Willie glowed. "I knew you would, Charles. After all, it's got to be a family affair. Why, with any luck, I'll hand the Group E Debenture Holders' Protective Committee down to William Choate the Fifth!"

"Thank you, Willie," Mundin said gently. "Must you go now?"

"Must I? Oh. I guess I must. It's been good seeing you, Charles. Keep up the good work."

Mundin stared impotently at his pudgy back. Then he turned wearily and went on to Dworcas' office.

Dworcas had still not arrived. The manager's office, behind the closed-up ticket booth, was tiny and crowded with bales of literature in Arabic and English. Two people were waiting there—a young man and a young woman—obviously brother and sister. Big sister, kid brother; they were maybe twenty-eight and twenty-two.

The girl got up from behind one of the battered desks. No lipstick, cropped hair, green slacks, a loose plaid shirt.

"I'm Norma Lavin," she said. "Mr. Mundin?"

"Yes." Why was good old Del passing this screwball on to him?

"This is my brother Don."

Don Lavin had something weird and something familiar about him. His eyes drew the attention. Mundin had often read of "shining eyes" and accepted it as one of those things you read that don't mean anything. Now he was disconcerted to find himself looking into a pair of eyes that actually did shine.

"Please sit down," he invited uneasily.

The girl said, "Mr. Dworcas tells us you're a lawyer, Mr. Mundin, as well as our next councilman from the 27th District."

Mundin automatically handed her one of his fancy cards. Don Lavin looked a little as if he had been *conditioned.* That was it! Like a court clerk or one of the participants in a Field Day—or, he guessed, never having seen one, a criminal after the compulsory third-rap treatment.

"I'm a lawyer," he said. "I wouldn't swear to that part about being councilman."

"You're the best we can do, Mundin. We got nowhere in Washington, nowhere in Chicago, nowhere in New York. We'll try local courts here. Dworcas passed us on to you. We have to start *somewhere.*"

"Somewhere," her brother very dreamily agreed.

"Look, Miss Lavin—"

"Just Lavin."

"Okay, Lavin, or Spike, or whatever you want me to call you. If you're through with the insults, will you tell me what you want?"

Del Dworcas stuck his head in the door. "You people getting along okay? Fine!" He vanished again.

The girl said, "We want to retain you for a stockholders' committee—G-M-L Homes."

G-M-L Homes, Mundin thought, irritated. Why, that meant the bubble houses. The bubble cities, too. It meant real estate in practically continental lots. It meant the private roads, belt lines, power reactors...

It wasn't a very funny joke.

The shiny-eyed boy said abruptly, "The 'L' stands for Lavin. Did you happen to know that?"

Mundin tried to glower. He couldn't. Suppose—just suppose—that maybe it wasn't a joke. Ridiculous, of course, but just suppose—

G-M-L Homes.

Such things didn't happen to Charles Mundin, L1.B. "I'm not licensed to practice corporate law," he said flatly. "Try William Choate the Fourth."

"We just did. He said no."

They made it sound real, Mundin thought admiringly. Of course, it couldn't be. Somewhere it was written—*Charles Mundin will never get a fat case.* Therefore, this thing would piffle out.

"Well?" demanded the girl.

"I said I'm not licensed to practice corporate law."

"Did you think we didn't know that? We dug up an old banger who still has his license. He can't work, but we can use his name as attorney of record."

"Well," he, began hazily, "it's naturally interesting—"

"Yes or no?"

Dworcas stuck his head in again. "Mundin, I'm awfully sorry, but I've got to have the office for a while. Why don't you and your friends go over to Hussein's for a cup of coffee?"

"Sure, Del," Mundin said dazedly. "Thanks. Ah—will I get any broadcast time?"

"Afraid not this time, Charlie. They cut us down to fifteen minutes and old man Ribicoff showed up and we had to give him five. You know how he is."

"Yeah. Thanks for trying, Del."

HUSSEIN'S place, across the street, was pretty full, but they found a low table on the aisle.

The old-timers in fezzes stared at the strange conditioned face of Don Lavin. The kids in scat hats with five-inch brims looked once and then away, quickly.

Norma Lavin got no stares at all. Young and old, the Ay-rabs looked coldly through her. Mundin suddenly realized that he was doing his political chances no good by being seen in public with her. The Ay-rabs blamed modem women—quite wrongly, as it happened—for the disconcerting way their own women were changing.

Hussein himself came over. "Always a pleasure, Mr. Mundin," he beamed. "What will you have?"

"Coffee, please," Mundin said. Don Lavin shook his head absently. Norma said nothing.

"*Majun* for the lady?" Hussein asked blandly. "Fresh from Mexico this week. Very strong. Peppermint, raspberry, grape?"

Norma Lavin icily said, "*No.*" Hussein went away, still beaming. He had delivered a complicated triple insult—by calling her a lady, offering her a narcotic and, at that, one traditionally beloved by Islamic women denied love by ugliness or age.

Mundin masked his nervousness by studying his watch. "We have about ten minutes," he said. "If you can give me an idea of what you have in mind—"

Somebody coming down the aisle stumbled over Don Lavin's foot.

"I beg your pardon," Lavin said automatically.

"What's the idea of tripping me?" asked a bored voice. It was a cop—a big man with an intelligent, good-humored face.

"It was an accident, Officer," Mundin said.

"Here we go again," Norma Lavin muttered.

"I was talking to this gentleman, I believe." The cop asked Don Lavin again, "I said what's the idea of tripping me? You a cop-hater or something?"

"I'm really very sorry," Lavin answered dreamily. "Please accept my apology."

"He won't," Norma Lavin whispered angrily to Mundin.

"Officer," Mundin said sharply, "it was an accident. I'm Charles Mundin, candidate for the Council in the 27th, Regular Republican. I'll vouch for this gentleman."

Ignoring him, the policeman said to Lavin, "Suppose we show some identification, cop-hater."

LAVIN took out a wallet and spilled cards on the table. The cop inspected them and growled, "Social Security account card says you're Donald W. Lavin, but Selective Service registration says you're Don Lavin, no middle initial. And I see your draft registration is with an Omaha board, but you have a resident's parking permit for Coshocton, Ohio."

Lavin said somnolently, "I'm extremely sorry, Officer."

The cop decisively scooped up the cards and said, "You'd better come along with me, Lavin. Your career of crime has gone far enough. It's a lucky thing I tripped over you."

Mundin noted that he had dropped the pretense of being tripped. "Officer, I'm taking your shield number. I'm going to tell my very good friend Del Dworcas about this nonsense. Shortly after that, you'll find yourself on foot patrol in Belly Rave—the two-to-ten shift—unless you care to apologize and get the hell out of here."

The officer shrugged. "What can I do? When I see the law broken, I have my job to do. Come along, Dangerous Don."

Lavin smiled distantly at his sister, and went along.

Mundin's voice was shaking with anger. "Don't worry," he told Norma Lavin. "I'll have him out of the station house right after the meeting. And that cop is going to wish he hadn't been born."

"Never mind. I'll get him out," she said. "Five times in three weeks. I'm used to it."

"What's the angle?" Mundin exploded.

Hussein came up with coffee in little cups. "Nice fella, that Jimmy Lyons," he said chattily. "For cop, that is."

"Who is he?" Mundin snapped.

"Precinct captain's man. Very good to know. The uniform is just patrolman, but when you talk to Jimmy Lyons, you talk right into precinct captain's ear."

Norma stood up. "I'm getting my brother sprung before they start shunting him around the precincts again." Her voice was weary. "I suppose this is the end of the road, Mundin. But if you still want to take our case, here's the address. Regrettably, there's no phone." She hesitated. "I hope you'll—" It was almost a cry for help.

She bit off the words, dropped a coin and a card on the table and strode from the coffee shop. The Ay-rabs looked icily through her as she went.

Mundin sat at the little table, bespelled, turning her card over in his fingers. G-M-L Homes, he thought. Corporate practice. It's not generally known that the "L" stands for Lavin.

And a cry for help.

The card said *Norma Lavin*, with an address in Coshocton, Ohio, and a phone number. These were scratched out, and written in was *37598 Willowdale Crescent*.

An address in Belly Rave! Mundin shook his head involuntarily. But there had been a cry for help.

THE big free rally, attended by perhaps eighty-five voters, went off on dreary schedule. Mundin managed to see Dworcas for a moment after things broke up. "Del, what's with these Lavin people? What do you know about them?"

"Not a hell of a lot, Charlie. I thought I was throwing some business your way. They mentioned a stockholder's suit. Are they phonies or crackpots?"

"Maybe. I don't know. But some cop named Jimmy Lyons picked the kid up in Hussein's. No reason that I could see."

"Jimmy Lyons? He's the captain's man. I'll call and see what I can do about that, Charlie."

He called and came back, smiling. "The sister identified him. They held him a couple of hours to cool him off and let him go. Lyons just got sore because the kid gave him some lip. What the hell, cops are human. Charlie, maybe you'd better forget about these people. The desk man said the kid was conditioned or doped up or something."

"Conditioned, I think. The wise kids at Hussein's kind of eyed him fast, if you know what I mean."

"Sure, Charlie, sure." Del was beginning to look uncomfortable. Mundin let him go.

CHAPTER FOUR

IT HAD been a trying evening for Norvie Bligh. When he walked in on Virginia and her daughter, they had been perfectly normal—sullen. His news about the lawyer, Mundin, and the prospects of adopting Alexandra had produced the natural effects. "You forgot to ask about the *inheritance!*"

Before he finished dinner, he was driven to the point of shrieking at his wife, slapping the girl and slamming out of the house.

But there was always Arnie Dworcas.

He killed time for half an hour—Arnie didn't like it if you got there too early—and then hurried. He was almost out of breath as he got to Dworcas' door.

And Arnie was warmly friendly. Norvell began at last to relax.

It wasn't just a matter of plenty of beer and the friendly feeling of being with someone you liked. Arnie was going out of his way, Norvell saw at once, to get at the roots of Norvell's problem. As soon as they had had a couple of beers, he turned the conversation to Norvell's work. "They must be really beginning to roll on the Field Day," he speculated.

Norvell expanded. "Sure. I've got some pretty spectacular things lined up for it, too. Of course, Candella hasn't given me the final go-ahead—" he frowned at a submerged memory "—but it's going to be quite a program. One gets a big charge out of doing one's best on a big job, Arnie. I guess you know that. I remember a couple of years ago—"

Dworcas interrupted. "More beer?" He dialed refills. "Your place has quite a good reputation," he said with sober approval. "This afternoon, in the shop, we Engineers were talking about the technical factors involved."

"You *were?*" Norvell was pleased. "That's interesting, Arnie. This time I was talking about—"

"Especially the big shows," Dworcas went on. "The Field Days. You know what would be interesting, Norvell? Getting a couple of the fellows to go to one, to see just how the thing looked from the engineering viewpoint. I'd like to go myself—if I could get away, of course. We're pretty busy these days. Might invite a few of the others in the shop to come along."

"You *would?*" Norvell cried.

"Say, that would be fine. There's a lot of engineering connected with a Field Day. Like this time a couple of years—"

"Excuse me," Arnie interrupted. "Beer. Be right back."

WHILE Dworcas was gone, Norvell felt actually cheerful. Arnie was concerned with his work. You didn't find many friends like Arnie. Warmed by the beer, Norvell re-examined his recent blinding depression. Hell, things weren't too bad.

He had almost decided to have a swift cup of black coffee and go home when Arnie came back, beaming. "Well, what say, Emotional Engineer? Want a couple of real, live slide-rulers to look over your show?"

"What? Oh, sure, Arnie. Just let me get this Field Day out of the way. We'll throw a real party—one of the Friday-night shows. There's a lot of complicated stuff under the stadium. You'd be interested—"

"I don't know," Dworcas said doubtfully, "whether the fellows would be interested in one of the second-rate shows. Maybe we ought to skip it."

"No, no! The regular shows are just as interesting technically. Why, just last week, we had a broken-field run—barbed wire and maimer mines—and half an hour before the show started, the director came around, crying that he didn't have enough men for the spectacle. Well, Candella—that is, we put in a quick call to the cops and they sent a squad down to Belly Rave. Got twenty-five volunteers in fifteen minutes. The orderlies lined 'em up and gave them million-unit injections of B1." He chuckled. "Arnie, you should have seen some of those guys when they sobered up. We had to…"

Arnie was shaking his head. "That sort of thing isn't what We Engineers are interested in. It's the big effects."

"Oh! You mean like in the Field Day next week." Norvell thought vaguely about the Field Day. "Yeah," he said uncertainly, "there certainly are plenty of headaches when you run a Field Day. Can I have another beer, please?"

AS he dialed another glass, Dworcas said sunnily, "Suppose you fit us in, then. After all, you've got eighty thousand seats. There ought to be five somewhere that the man who runs the whole damn thing can give to a friend."

"Sure," Norvell mumbled. "Uh—my turn. Excuse me, Arnie."

When he came back, the room wasn't spinning quite so dizzily, but the warmth in his body wasn't so gratifying, either. He stared so long at the glass of beer by his chair that Arnie thought it was flat and pressed a replenishment button.

"Oh, thanks," Norvell said, startled. He picked up the glass and took a sip, then put it down hard. Half of it slopped over. Above the whistle of the suction cleaners draining the spilled beer, Norvell said with sudden misery, "Arnie, I'm in trouble."

Dworcas froze. He said carefully, "Trouble?"

"I swear to God, if it weren't for people like you—if it weren't for you *personally*—I don't know what I'd do!" He told Dworcas about the grisly dinner with his wife and stepdaughter, about the countless run-ins with Candella, about all the fights and frustrations. "The worst was this morning, just before I went to that lawyer. I was chewing out that little punk Stimmens when Candella walked into the room. He must've heard every word I said, because when I turned around and saw him, he said, 'Excellent advice, Mr. Bligh, I hope you'll follow it yourself.' And Stimmens just stood there, laughing at me. I couldn't do a thing. For two cents, I would have gone in and asked for my contract."

Dworcas nodded precisely. "Perhaps you should have."

"What? Oh, no, Arnie, you don't understand. General Recreations is lousy on that. They won't sell unless they can get their pound of flesh, and plenty more besides. We had a vice president once, a couple of years ago, got in Dutch with the board and wanted out. Well, they set a price of *four hundred thousand dollars* on his contract. He killed himself. It was that or cancel."

"That's a point to remember, Norvell. In any engineering problem, there are always at least two components to any vector."

"I see what you mean. There's no way out."

"No, Norvell, there are *always* two ways out, sometimes more."

"Well—"

"At the shop," Arnie said, leaning back, "these problems don't arise, of course. Not like with you temperamental artists. But when I was a journeyman, I... Well, it was rough. I know just what it's like. And, of course, I know what I would do."

"What?"

"If it were my decision, I'd cancel."

Norvell goggled. He was suddenly sober. "You'd *cancel?*"

"That's right," said Arnie. "I'd cancel."

Norvell looked at him unbelievingly, but Dworcas' gaze was calm and benign.

"It's a tough decision to make, Norvell. Heaven knows, I'd find it a hard one to make myself, without half an hour or more of serious thought. But what's your alternative?"

Norvell shifted uncomfortably in his chair. He put his beer down. Neither man said a word for a long time, while Norvell's mind raced from Candella to Dworcas to the lawyer, Mundin, to Virginia, to Stimmens, to a fire-red mystery marked "Belly Rave," to the old man who had sat weeping while he waited for the broken-field event to start.

"I don't think I ought to," Norvell said faintly.

Dworcas inclined his head. "It's your decision."

"I just don't see how I can, Arnie. I'd lose the house, Virginia would raise holy—"

Arnie stopped him. "You may be right. Who knows? There's certainly no security in the world for a man without a contract job. You'd have to leave your home, true, and move to the suburbs—" Norvell blinked—"at least temporarily. It's a hard life there, a constant challenge to prove yourself—to make your way in spite of hell or high water—or fall by the wayside." He looked speculatively at Norvell and dismissed the subject. "I just wanted to give you the benefit of my thinking on the point. You do as you see fit. I guess you'll want to be getting home."

"Sure," Norvell said. "Oh, I meant to thank you for steering me to that lawyer. I don't know what I would have—"

"Think nothing of it. I'm always glad to do anything I can for you, you know that. You won't forget about the tickets?"

"Tickets?" Norvell asked vacantly.

"The tickets for the Field Day. Not general admission, you know. As close to the Master's box as you can get them."

Norvell's eyes opened wide. He said in a thin voice, "Arnie, you were bragging to your boss that you could get tickets, even though they've been sold out for six weeks. Isn't that it?" They stared nakedly at each other; then Norvell's eyes fell. "Just kidding," he mumbled. "I'll get them."

VIRGINIA was still awake, but there was only a minor squabble over the music coming from behind Alexandra's locked door. Norvell made the mistake of commenting that it was past midnight and a 14-year-old should be asleep.

His wife said furiously, "Should be this, and should be that, and should do everything Mr. Bligh wants her to. This whole house isn't organized around you. It's our home, too, and—"

Norvell had had all he could take. "It's the *company's* house and one more word out of you and I give it back to them. Then you two prize packages from Belly Rave will be right back where you belong."

Virginia's face stiffened in shocked surprise. Norvell stalked downstairs to the bar and poured himself a drink.

He sat with it in his hand and looked in sudden wonder at the room around him.

Was there so much difference between a G-M-L bubble house and Belly Rave? He decided he'd have to visit Belly Rave one of these days. Just to get a look. But what could the difference be?

A house was a house. If you didn't like the floor warm, you dialed it to cool. If you didn't like the wall color or pattern, you turned the selector wheel to something else. If you didn't like a room plan, you clipped the wall somewhere else.

Norvell dialed a bed and set the house to full automatic. As he lay down, his pillow chimed softly, but he didn't need sleepy music that night. He reached over his head and turned it off.

In the copper plexus at the house's core, transistors pulsed, solenoids barred the doors, micro-switches laid traps for intruders, and thermocouples dried the incoming air and cooled it. Commutator points would boil the water for the coffee in the morning; heat the griddle for the eggs, set their breakfast dishes.

Naturally—Norvell thought sleepily—that's what a house was.

CHAPTER FIVE

FOUR taxi drivers flatly refused to take Mundin to Belly Rave. The fifth was a reckless youngster. "Just took this job waiting for the draft call," he confided. "How can I lose? You're paying plenty and maybe I'll get beat up so bad in this here Belly Rave place that they won't draft me." He laughed. "Fact is, I've never been out there, but I figure it can't be as tough as they say."

Mundin did not contradict him, though he felt a lot less certain, and off they went.

There was no sizable city that did not have the equivalent of Belly Rave. Festering slums that had once been respectable suburban residential sections, like Belle Rave Estates, they had been abruptly made obsolete by the G-M-L bubble houses—good enough for derelicts to live in, not good enough to keep in repair. The battered streetlights, Mundin noticed, didn't light; the yards were weed-grown; roofs were rotted through, walls sagging.

To one who had always lived in bubble houses, the place was shocking. He had thought the early bubble houses were ludicrous because the automatic controls sometimes went out of order and manual ones had to be used temporarily. But these primitive structures—even someone like himself, with no more than a layman's knowledge, saw instantly that this old-style architecture must have taken an incredible number of man-hours just for upkeep.

He asked himself indignantly why this architectural jungle wasn't torn or burned down and bubble houses put up. He knew the answer, of course—G-M-L Homes. They could manufacture the units, but their advertising explained why they didn't. Living in a bubble house was a mark of success. And so they limited production, maintained an artificial scarcity value...and doomed people to Belly Raves, or whatever the local name was, in every city.

Hell with it, Mundin thought in annoyance; he had his own troubles. He hadn't come out to Belly Rave to worry about it; he was there on a job. If he was lucky and it turned into a real, honest-to-God case.

There was life in Belly Rave—a furtive, crepuscular life called into being by the unpoliceable wilderness of tall weeds, wrecks of homes, and endless miles of crumbling pavement. Scatty little cars prowled the cracked roads, occasionally pulling to the curb when a dim figure swung a phosphorescent handbag.

THE taxi passed one block of houses that was a blaze of light and noise. A doorman trotted alongside the cab, urging, "Anything goes, mister. Spend the night for five bucks, all you can drink and smoke included. Why pay taxes, mister?"

Sometimes, though not often, the Alcohol & Hemp Tax Unit raided such joints.

The driver asked, "We anywhere near 37598 Willowdale Crescent?"

"What you need is a guide," the doorman said promptly. "Jimmy!" Somebody yelled out of the dark. Mundin heard a fumbling at the cab door.

"Step on it!" he yelled at the driver, snapping the door lock. The driver stepped on it.

Ambush left behind, they cautiously approached bag-swingers for directions and before long were on the 37,000 block of Willowdale Crescent, counting houses.

"This must be it," said the driver, no longer devil-may-care.

"I guess so. Wait here, will you?"

"No, sir! How do I know you ain't going to slip through a back door? You pay me what's on the clock and I'll wait."

The meter read a whopping eight dollars. Mundin handed over a ten and started up the crumbled walk.

The taxi zoomed away before he had taken half a dozen steps. Mundin cursed wearily and knocked on the door. He studied the boarded-up picture window while he waited. Like all the others, it was broken, boarded up. Inevitably, in the years that had gone by since they were eased and puttied carefully into place, the rock had been flung, or the door had been slammed, or the drunk had lurched into the living room.

The man who came to the door was old and visibly sick.

"Is this the Lavin place?" Mundin asked, blinking against a light haze of wood-smoke. "I'm Charles Mundin. She asked me to call in connection with a legal matter. I'm an attorney."

The old man started at the word. "Come in, Counselor," he said formally. "I am a member of the bar myself—"

He broke off into a fit of coughing that left him leaning against the door.

MUNDIN half carried him into the living room and eased him into a sagging, overstuffed chair. A Coleman lamp, blowing badly, cast a metallic blue-green glare into every corner of the room. A fire smoldered in the hearth, billowing against a closed register. A tinny radio was blaring, "—was kept from spreading, though the four houses involved in the arson attempt were totally destroyed. Elsewhere in Belly Rave, warfare broke out between the Wabbits and the Goddams, rival junior gangs. One eight-year-old was killed instantly by a thrown—"

Mundin clicked it off and opened the register. The smoke began to clear from the room and the fire to flicker. The old man was still folded up in the chair, his parchment face mercilessly bleached by the flaring light. Mundin fiddled aimlessly with the valve and somehow got it to stop roaring. There was a green glass shade; he put it on and the room was suddenly no longer a corner of a surrealist hell, but simply a shabby room.

"Thank you," the old man muttered. "Counselor, would you please see if there is a small, round tin in the bathroom cabinet?"

The bathtub was full of split kindling and the cabinet shelves loaded with the smaller household staples—salt, spices and such. There was an unmarked tin, which Mundin pried open. Small, gummy-looking pills and an unmistakable odor—yen pox! He shuddered and brought it out.

The old man took it and slowly swallowed five of the opium pills. When he spoke, his voice was almost steady. "Thank you, Counselor. And let this be a lesson to you. It's weakening, humiliating. You said you had an appointment with Norma? She should have been here hours ago. Naturally—this neighborhood—I'm worried. I'm Harry Ryan. Member of the S.E.C. Bar and other things. Of course—" he stared at the tin of yen pox—"I'm retired from practice."

Mundin coughed. "Miss Lavin mentioned you, though not by name. You would be attorney of record and I'd do the legwork in some sort of stockholder's suit, right?"

Ryan nodded. Mundin hesitated, then went on to tell the old man about the arrest in Hussein's place.

"YES," Ryan said matter-of-factly. "I told her it was a mistake to go to Mr. Dworcas. It is inconceivable that Green, Charlesworth would neglect to have an understanding with the Regular Republican Central Committee."

Green, Charlesworth was the name of an investment house usually mentioned in hushed and tremulous tones. Mundin said, "She told me it was connected with G-M-L Homes. How does Green, Charlesworth come into it?"

Ryan chewed another opium pill. "Not in more than two dozen ways—that I know of." He actually smiled. "Raw materials, belt transport patents, real estate, insurance, plant financing—" He heaved himself from the overstuffed chair as the doorknocker rattled. "I'll get it," he said. "It was just a temporary indisposition. You needn't mention it to..." He jerked his chin at the door.

He came back into the living room with Norma and Don Lavin.

"Hello, Mundin," she said tonelessly. "I see you found us. Have you eaten?"

"Yes, thanks."

"Then excuse us while we have something. The Caddy broke down five times on the way out here. I'm beat."

She and her brother morosely opened a couple of self-heating

cans of goulash. They spooned them down in silence.

"Now," she said to Mundin, "the background. I'll make it short. Don and I were born of rich but honest parents in Coshocton, Ohio. Daddy—Don, senior—was rather elderly when we came along. He spent the first fifty years of his life working. He started out as a plastics man with a small factory—bus bodies, fire trucks, that kind of thing. He happened to have gone to school with a man named Bernie Gorman, who happened to have specialized in electronics and electrical stuff. The two of them worked together, when they could find time, dreaming dreams and weaving visions. They were dedicated men. They invented, designed and, constructed the first pilot model of the G-M-L Home, otherwise known as the bubble house."

Mundin said frostily, "I happen to know a little about G-M-L, Miss Lavin. Wasn't there a man named Moffatt involved?"

"Not until later—much later. For almost thirty years, Daddy and Mr. Gorman starved themselves, gave up everything for their dream. Mother said she scarcely saw Daddy from month's end to month's end. Mr. Gorman died a bachelor. They had designed the bubble house, they had built it, but they didn't have the capital to put it on the market."

Mundin objected, "They could have leased the rights."

"And had them bottled up," she said. "Didn't I tell you they were dedicated men? They had designed a home that was cheaper than the cheapest and better than the best. It was a breakthrough in housing, like nothing that had gone before, except perhaps, the revolution in synthetic textiles. Don't you see that even a millionaire could not have owned a better house? Daddy and Mr. Gorman wanted to give their dream to the people at a reasonable profit. They weren't big businessmen, Mundin—they were dreamers. They were out of their field. Then Moffatt came along with his plan."

Ryan stirred himself. "Most ingenious, really. By leasing manufacturing rights to large corporations, G-M-L avoided capital outlay; the corporations gave their employees what could not be had elsewhere—and good-by to labor troubles. At first, G-M-L leased the rights for money. Later, when they got bigger, the consideration was blocks of stock, equities in the leasing firms."

The girl nodded soberly. "Within ten years, it owned sizable shares of forty corporations, and Daddy and Mr. Gorman owned half of G-M-L. Then Daddy found out what was happening. He told Mr. Gorman and I think it killed him—he was an old man by then, you see. Contract status. One word of backtalk and you get thrown out of your G-M-L house. Get thrown out of your G-M-L house and you find yourself—here."

Mundin said wonderingly, "But if your father was one of the owners of the company—"

"Only twenty-five percent, Mundin. And Mr. Gorman's twenty-five percent went to distant cousins. So there was Daddy, at sixty-five. His vision was a reality—his bubble homes housed a hundred million people. But they had become a weapon and he was frozen out of the firm."

Don Lavin said dreamily, "They gave the plant guards his picture. He was arrested for drunk and disorderly when he tried to go to the stockholders' meeting. He hanged himself in his cell." He stared absently at Mundin's shoe.

Mundin cleared his throat, "I'm sorry. Wasn't there anything to be done at all?"

RYAN said, with a touch of professional admiration, "Very little, Mr. Mundin. Oh, he still had stock. They impounded it. A trumped-up creditors' committee got an order on his safe-deposit box against dissipation of assets when he died. They kept it impounded for twelve years. Then somebody got careless, or somebody quit or got fired, and the new man didn't know what the impoundment was for. Anyway, the order expired. Norma and Don Lavin are twenty-five percent owners of G-M-L."

Mundin looked around the shabby room and said nothing.

"There's just one little thing," Norma said bitterly. "Don got the stock out of the box and put it away. Tell us where it is, Don."

The brother's dreamy eyes widened. His face worked wildly. He said, "K-k-k-k-k-k" in a convulsion of stammering. The terrified stutter went on and on, and then Don Lavin began raspingly to cry. Norma, stone-faced, patted him on the shoulder.

SHE said to the appalled lawyer, "When we began making trouble, as they called it, Don was snatched. He was gone for three days. A doctor he went to says he must have got more than fifty hours of conditioning."

"That's illegal! Private persons can't use conditioning techniques!"

"You're our lawyer now—just straighten that out for us, will you? Get an injunction against G-M-L."

Mundin sat back. Habitual criminals—like his client earlier in the day—were conditioned in twenty hours of treatment spread over a week or more. Good God, fifty hours in three days! But proving it against G-M-L or anyone else—that was the hard part. The conditioned person was naturally conditioned against taking any action of the sort.

He felt ill. "Sorry I was so stupid. So now you want to find the stock and Don doesn't know where he put it."

Ryan looked at him with disgust. "I could manage to get duplicate certificates. Unfortunately, our position is not that simple. Donald, as the male heir, was the obvious person to conduct a suit, so Norma signed an irrevocable proxy of interest to him. That was an error, as it turned out. Donald can't bring suit. He can't tell us where the stock is. He can't even discuss it."

Mundin nodded sickly. "I see. You're stymied."

Norma made a contemptuous noise. "Now that it's established that we're licked, we might as well lie down and die."

"I didn't say that, Miss Lavin. We'll do what we can." He hesitated. "For instance, no doubt we can have your brother undergo a de-conditioning course somewhere else. After all—"

" 'Private persons can't use conditioning techniques,' " she quoted derisively. "Didn't you say that just a moment ago?"

"Well, yes, but surely *someone* will—"

Norma seemed to collapse. She said to Ryan, "*You* tell him what he's up against."

Ryan said, "G-M-L's assets are not less than fourteen billion dollars, comprising cash in the bank, negotiable securities, plant and properties and equities, as of their last statement, in eight hundred and four corporations. I don't say that they can break the law with impunity, Counselor, but they can sure as hell keep *us* from breaking it."

FOURTEEN billion dollars! Mundin, trudging apprehensively through Belly Rave's dark streets, felt very small, pitted against fourteen billion dollars.

A mournful hooting from the shadows made him quicken his step, but no lurking thugs showed up. Mundin shivered uncomfortably and turned up his coat collar. It had begun to rain.

Luck was with him. He was neither mugged nor lured into one of the clip joints. The footpads were stalking other streets; the roving gangs of armed adolescents plotted in their cellars instead of braving the rain; the cab Mundin spotted, ran after and hailed was a legitimate cab, not a trap.

The ride gave him time to think. But the thinking came to very little. The Lavins, he was convinced, had a legitimate claim. He had promised them he would work on it; he had tried to reassure them that things were not as hopeless as they seemed. He felt uncomfortably sure that the girl had seen through his empty words.

The cab came at last to territory he recognized and he stopped it at an all-night restaurant. Coffee might help, he thought. While he was waiting for it, he invested in a call to his office—you could never tell, maybe someone had phoned.

Someone had. The Sleepless Secretary groaned and came across with the record of a familiar, scared voice: "Mr. Mundin—uh—this is Norvell Bligh. Can you come and get me out of jail?"

CHAPTER SIX

NORVIE woke up with a start. They were joggling him, with identical, contemptuous smiles. Even in the fog of sleep, he felt a little stab of pride at Virginia's beauty, a twitch of unhappiness at the same lean beauty smothered beneath the adolescent fat of her daughter.

"What's the matter?" he croaked.

His voice sounded odd and he realized he wasn't wearing his hearing aid. He groped for it beside the bed. It wasn't there. He sat up.

He yelled at Alexandra, "Where is it? If you've hidden it again, I'll break your neck!"

Alexandra looked smugly shocked. She mouthed at him, "Goodness, Norvell, you know I wouldn't do that," though he had repeatedly told her that exaggeration made it impossible to read lips.

Virginia tapped him on the shoulder and said something, stiff-lipped. He caught an "eep" and a "larm."

"What?"

"I said you must have come in too drunk to set the alarm before you went to sleep. Get up. You're an hour late for work now."

He leaped from bed. An hour late on this day, of all days!

He found the hearing aid on the floor in the entrance hall, where he couldn't have left it, any more than he could have failed to set the alarm. But he didn't have time to take up these minor points. He depilated in ten seconds, bathed in five, dressed in fifteen and shot out of the house.

Fortunately, Candella wasn't in. Norvie sent Miss Dali to round up his staff and began the tooling-up job for the integrator keyboard, while the production men busied themselves with their circuits and their matrices, and the job began. This was the part of Norvie's work that made him, he confessed secretly to himself, feel most like God. He fed the directions to Stimmens, Stimmens fumblingly set up the punch cards, the engineers translated the cards into phase fields and interferer circuits…and a World That Norvie Made appeared in miniature.

He had once tried to explain his feelings to Arnie. Arnie had snarled something about the presumptuous conceit of a mere pushbutton. All he did, Arnie explained over many glasses of beer, was to decide what forms and images he wanted to see; it was the Engineers who, in their wisdom, transmuted empty imaginings into patterns of light and color, that magically took the form and movement of tiny fighters and wrestlers and spear-carriers. The original thought, Arnie explained severely, was nothing; it was the tremendous technical skill, that transformed the thought into visual reality that was important. And Norvell, perforce, humbly agreed.

EVEN now, he was deferential to the production men, those geniuses so well versed in the arts of connecting Circuit A to Terminal IV, for they were Engineers. But his deference extended only to the technical crew. "Stimmens!" he barked. "Hurry it up! Mr. Candella will be here any moment!"

"Yessir," said Stimmens, hopelessly shuffling the stacks of notes from Norvell's hands.

Stimmens was coming along, Norvell thought. A touch of the whip was good for him.

It took twenty minutes and a bit more, and then Norvell's whole design for a Field Day was on punch cards. While Stimmens was correcting his last batch of cards, the production men began the run-through. The little punched cards went through the scanners; the packed circuits measured voltages and spat electrons; and in the miniature mockup of the Stadium, tiny figures of light appeared and moved and slew each other and left.

They were Norvell's own, featureless and bright, tiny and in-substantial. Where Norvell's script called for the bodies of forty javelin-throwers in the flesh, the visualizing apparatus showed forty sprites of light jabbing at each other with lances of fire. No blood spilled; no bodies stained the floor of the Stadium; only the little bodiless fire-figures that disappeared like any other pattern of excited ions when the current went off.

Somehow, Norvell thought of the Field Days themselves as taking place here. He had heard the cries of the injured and seen the drawn faces of the next of kin; but it was as mannequins that he thought of them, always.

One of the production men said approvingly, "Looks like a good show, Mr. Bligh."

"Thanks," said Norvell gratefully. It was always a good sign when the technical crew hung over the miniature stadium this way, watching the mockup figures go through their paces.

Now the question was, what would Candella say?

"BLIGH, the upcoming Field Day is important," was what Candella said to Norvie. "At least, it seems to *me* that everything we do is important. Don't *you* think so?"

Norvell said, "Well, of course!"

"Our work *is* important, Bligh. It is a great and functional art form. It provides healthful entertainment, satisfying the needs of every man for some form of artistic expression. It provides escape—escape for the hardworking bubble-house class, escape for the masses of Belly Rave. It siphons off their aggressions. Allotments and Field Days—our society is built on them! You might call our work the very foundation of society. Do you agree?"

"Yes, sir," Norvie almost whispered.

Candella looked politely apologetic. "I beg your pardon?"

"*Yes, sir!*" Norvell, too late, found he was almost bellowing.

Candella looked pained. "You needn't shout. There is nothing wrong with my hearing." Norvell winced. "Foundation of our society, but also an art form. The cultured classes appreciate our efforts on the artistic plane. The rabble of Belly Rave—with all respects, my dear Bligh, to the origin of your charming wife—need it on the glandular level. *Every* show we can produce is important. But the Field Day—"

His thick brows came down like the ragged anvils of thunderclouds. "The Field Day, you tin-eared fumbler, is the biggest day of the year! *Not* just because it draws the biggest audience—but because that's the one *I* am Judged by! The Board attends. The Mayor attends. The men from G-M-L attend. If they like it, good. If they don't—that's *my* neck on the line, Bligh!"

Norvell opened his mouth.

"Not a word! I want no excuses. Your notion of what constituted a Field Day was, of course, uninspired. But I thought that, with patching and improvising, we might get by. I no longer think so—not since examining the superb presentations that was handed me this morning—by a member of your own staff, Bligh! A brilliant boy whom you have evidently been holding down. Thank God he had the courage and sense to come to *me* with this masterpiece instead of permitting you to destroy it!"

Norvell was able to croak, "Who?"

"Stimmens."

Stimmens? Wet behind the ears, untried, simple research. Who didn't even want to stall with the firm, who had the infernal gall to ask for a contract release? *Stimmens?*

NORVELL'S hand stretched out for the punched card and then he stopped.

"Go ahead," Candella said coldly.

Bligh scanned them in astonishment. Why, he thought, this is impossible—and this bit here, we can't—

"Mind if I play these, Mr. Candella?" he asked and, getting an ironic nod, fed the punch cards into Candella's machine. The circuits scanned the punches and built a scene of electronic slaughter for him. He watched the little fire-figures in growing apprehension.

When he looked up, he said, so bemused that he hardly remembered to be fearful, "Why, it's good!"

"Of course it's good!"

"*Really* good, Mr. Candella." He shook his head wonderingly. "Stimmens, eh? I never would have believed it. Of course, the emotional values need bringing out. The comedy stuff with the vitriol pistols ought to follow a tense thriller like Man Versus Scorpions, instead of another comedy number like the Octogenarians with Flame-throwers. But that's easy enough to fix. Race against Manmade Lightning is out, too. Stimmens told me himself we couldn't get the equipment from Schenectady. I suppose he forgot."

Candella was looking at him with an indescribable expression, but Norvell raced on. "Real originality, Mr. Candella. I—I must say I admire him. Piranhas in the aquatic meet—wonderful. And the octogenarians are a terrific switch. Number after number I've never heard of! I have to admit it, Mr. Candella, that boy has talent."

"What the hell are you babbling about?"

"Why, the—the *originality,* Mr. Candella. The *freshness.*"

"Originality! Bligh, do you think I'm crazy enough to run untried novelties in a show like this? *Every one* of these features has been a smash success somewhere in the country within the last ninety days."

"Oh, no! I've been getting all the reports—and none of this stuff—Stimmens was doing the research himself. He ought to know!"

Candella exploded. "Look, you fool!" He tossed a sheaf of reports at Norvell.

They were all there—names, dates, places. Norvell looked up in horror. "It's a double-cross! He wants a fifteen rating. Just yesterday, he tried to get me to recommend remission of his contract. I wouldn't do it. This is his way of getting even."

"Bligh, that's a serious charge!"

"Oh, I'll prove it, Mr. Candella. I've got the copies of his reports locked in my desk."

Candella stood up. "Show me," he ordered.

Ten minutes later, he was saying grimly, "Thought I wouldn't call your bluff, eh?"

Norvell stared unbelievingly at the reports, face white as a sheet. They had been in his desk, locked with his key. And they were not the reports he had seen. They sparkled with novelties—all the magnificent new concepts in Stimmens' outline and more, much more.

How? He couldn't have left the desk unlocked. Nobody had a key but him and Miss Dali—and she had no reason to do such a thing. Had he gone mad? Was it some chemical prank, the reports he saw in disappearing ink, the substituted ones then coming to light? *How?*

Over Norvell's desk set, Candella was calling Stimmens in. The boy appeared, looking awed and deferential.

Mr. Candella said, "Congratulations, Stimmens. You're the head of the department as of now. Move into your office whenever you like—*this* is your office. And throw this bum out." To Norvell: "Your contract is canceled *for cause.* Don't ever try to get a job in this line again; you'll waste your time." He left without another word.

Stimmens said uneasily, "I didn't have the heart to go through with it. I had to give you a chance—you turned it down."

Norvell just stared.

Stimmens went on defensively, "It isn't as if I just walked into it. Believe me, I earned this. What do I know about Field Days? Sweat, sweat, sweat—I haven't had a moment's peace."

Miss Dali walked in and kissed Stimmens, burbling, "Darling, I just heard! You wonderful Grade Fifteen, you!"

"Oh," said Norvell in a sick voice.

They said more, but he didn't hear. It was as if his hearing aid were turned off, though, in, this instance, the switch was not in his pocket, but in his mind. He was out on the street before he realized what he was doing—and what had happened to the contract career of Norvell Bligh.

Norvell came up to the problem of Virginia in his thinking and, like a thousand times before, he backed away from it. He ordered another drink.

No contract status meant no bubble house. It also meant Belly Rave. Norvell took a deep swallow. Still, what was so bad about Belly Rave? The allotments would take care of eating. His extra work—whatever it turned out to be—would give him a chance to save a little money, make a fresh start, maybe get back on contract and into a bubble house again. After all, he was a trained man—an Engineer, in a way.

He wished once again that he knew a little more about Belly Rave. Funny, considering that Virginia had been born there. But she had never wanted to talk about it.

And there he was, back on the subject of Virginia.

How would she take it? He really couldn't guess. She had been so resolutely silent on the subject of Belly Rave and all it concerned. Her childhood, her parents, even her husband—the power-cycle stunter whose crash in a long-ago Field Day had left young Norvell Bligh with a tearless widow to jolly out of filing a claim. He had married her instead and Candella had made an unforgivable joke... No, he hadn't married her—*she* had married, not Norvell Bligh, but a contract job and a G-M-L house.

He dialed another drink. Well, there was still Arnie. He wasn't the kind of friend to look the other way when you were a little down on your luck—not even that, really, just temporarily the victim of a professional misunderstanding and a double-cross. Good old Arnie, Norvell thought sentimentally.

He caught a glimpse of the time. Maybe he ought to have it out with Virginia, and then go over and spend some time with Arnie. The thought braced him.

He swallowed his drink and slipped his wallet into the bar slot. Having it out with Virginia might not be so tough at that. The fact that she had been born in Belly Rave was an advantage, if he could only make her see it that way. She'd have friends there. She'd have some ideas about pleasant, useful work he could do to supplement the allotment until he got on his feet again—

Something crushed his shoulder and spun him around. "Whaddya think you're up to?" the policeman demanded. He shook the wallet under Norvell Bligh's nose. "You know the penalty for passing a bum penalty card? You Belly Ravers are all alike—find a lapsed card and a front and try to get a free load. Come along. The Captain wants to talk to you."

BLIGH spent a long time trying to make them believe him down at the precinct, before he realized they did believe him—believed him and just didn't care.

It was close to dinnertime and they put him in something they called "the Tank" until the desk sergeant got back from his meal. Norvell didn't like the tank and he didn't like the looks of the half-dozen other persons who occupied it with him.

Still, it was only a question of his lapsed credit card—they could easily have added drunk and disorderly to the charge—or even no visible means of support, which meant getting a job instantly or being jugged for quite a while. And there was only one kind of job a man in police trouble could pick up a phone and get, every time.

Usually you didn't have to phone. The cops would drive you down to the Stadium's service entrance themselves. Norvell knew the process, having seen enough "volunteers" delivered.

"Hey, Bligh."

Norvell said, "Yes, sir?"

The cop opened the door. "This way." They came to a dingy room. There was an embarrassing process of holding your hands over your head while someone searched you. You couldn't blame them, Norvell told himself; they must have had plenty of desperate criminals here. There was a curiously interesting process of inking the fingers and rolling them across a piece of paper. There was a mildly painful process of looking into what seemed to be a binocular microscope; a light flashed, and Norvell had a little trouble seeing.

While Norvell was blinking at the halo in his field of vision, the cop said something. Norvell said, "What?"

"I said do you want to call your lawyer?"

Norvell shook his head automatically. Then he remembered—he *had* a lawyer. "Why, yes," he said. He found Mundin's phone number in the book with some difficulty. It was after hours, but he was lucky enough to get an answer—though Mundin himself wasn't there and the person who answered seemed to be drunk or something. But Norvell left a message, and then there was nothing to do but wait.

Curiously, the waiting was not unpleasant. Even the thought of what Virginia would say or do about this was not particularly terrifying. What worse could happen than had already?

CHAPTER SEVEN

"THANK you very much, Mr. Mundin," Norvell said. He looked back at the precinct house and shuddered.

Mundin said, "Don't thank me. I just put in a word with Del Dworcas and he put in a word with the precinct. Thank him."

Norvell brightened. "Oh, I intend to! I've wanted to meet Mr. Dworcas for a long time. His brother Arnie is a very close friend of mine."

Mundin shrugged. "Come on, then. I'm going to the Hall any-how."

Mundin stalked sourly ahead of his client, his mind on G-M-L Homes. The hope kept hammering at his good sense—*maybe* he could pull it off. Maybe...

Norvell followed contentedly enough through the rain. Everything was being ordered for him. He was out of a job, he had been *in jail,* he was hours and hours late for Virginia without a word of explanation—but none of it had been his own decision.

Decisions would come later. That would be the hard part. Norvell stared around the Hall curiously. It wasn't as impressive as one might expect—though maybe, he thought, you had to admire the Regular Republicans for their common touch. There was certainly nothing showy about the place.

Norvell stopped, politely out of earshot, as Mundin spoke to a dark, sharp-featured man in shirtsleeves. Some kind of janitor, he guessed. He was astonished when Mundin called him over and introduced the man as Del Dworcas.

Norvell said, "I'm really delighted to meet you, Mr. Dworcas. Your brother Arnie is very proud of you. He and I are very good friends."

Dworcas asked irrelevantly, "Live around here?"

"Oh, no. Quite some distance away, but—"

Dworcas seemed to lose interest. "Glad to meet you. You want to see Arnie, he's in Hussein's, across the street. Now, Charles, what was it you wanted to see me about?"

Norvell was left standing with his hand extended. He blinked a little, but—after all, he reminded himself, Mr. Dworcas was a busy man.

On the way downstairs, he caught a glimpse of the time. It was after eleven!

ARNIE was at a table by himself reading. He looked up as Norvell came close and hastily put the magazine away.

Norvell smiled and slipped into a vacant seat. "Surprised to see me?"

Arnie frowned. "What are you doing here?"

Norvell lost his smile. "Can—can I have some coffee, Arnie? I came out without any money."

Arnie looked mildly outraged, but beckoned the grinning waiter.

Then Norvell told him—about the jail, and Mundin, and Del Dworcas.

"You've had a busy day," Arnie said humorously. "I'm glad you met Del, though—he's a prince. Incidentally, I've taken the liberty of asking a couple of associates to the Field Day. So when you get the tickets—"

"Arnie—"

"When you get the tickets, will you pick up three extras?"

"Arnie, listen to me. I *can't* get the tickets."

"You *what?*"

"I got fired today. That's why I didn't have any money."

There was a pause. Dworcas began looking through his pockets for a cigarette. He found the pack and put it absently on the table in front of him without lighting one. He said nothing.

Norvell said apologetically, "It wasn't my fault, Arnie. This rat Stimmens—" He told what had happened at the office, concluding, "It's going to be all right, Arnie. Don't worry about me. It's like you said—maybe I should have canceled long ago. I'll make a fresh start in Belly Rave. Virginia can help me; she knows her way around there. We'll find some place that isn't too bad, you know, and get it fixed up. Some of those old houses are pretty interesting. And it's only a question of time until—"

"I see. You've taken an important step, Norvell. Naturally, I wish you the best of luck."

"Thanks, Arnie," Norvell said eagerly. "I don't think it'll be so bad. I—"

"Of course," Arnie went on meditatively, "it does put me in kind of a spot."

"You, Arnie?" Norvell cried, aghast.

DWORCAS shrugged. "It doesn't matter, I suppose. It's just that the fellows at the shop warned me that you were probably stringing me along about the tickets. I don't know what I'll tell them that won't make you look pretty bad, Norvell."

Norvell squeezed his eyes shut. Loyal Arnie! Concerned about *his* status in the eyes of the other engineers!

"Well, that's the way the ball bounces, Norvell," Arnie went on. "I can't blame you for putting your own problems first." He looked ostentatiously at his watch. "I'd better be getting back to the Hall. My brother has something he wants to consult with me about." He dropped a bill on the table and piloted Norvell to the door.

Under the dingy marquee, he patted Norvell's shoulder. "Drop me a line once in a while, won't you?" he urged. "I'm the world's worst letter-writer, but I'll always be glad to hear how you're getting along."

Norvell stopped. "Write you a letter, Arnie? I'll be seeing you, won't I?"

"Of course you will." Dworcas frowned at the rain. He said patiently, "It's just that you naturally won't want to make that trip from Belly Rave too often. For that matter, I'll be kind of tied up evenings myself until I get this thing for my brother over with... Look, Norvell, no sense standing here. Drop me a line when you get a chance. And the *best* of luck, fellow!"

Norvell nodded blankly and walked into the rain. With his credit card canceled and no cash-money in his pockets, it was a long, wet way home. After the second block, he thought of going back and borrowing cab fare from Arnie.

He decided not to.

He needed plenty of time to rehearse what he was going to say to Virginia.

FORTUNATELY, Virginia's daughter was asleep. Norvell changed his sopping clothes without a word to his wife, came down, looked her in the eye and told her—directly and brutally.

Then he waited for the explosion. Virginia sat there, blank-faced, and ran her fingers caressingly over the soft arms of the chair. She rose and wandered to the wall patterner. Typical of her sloppy housework, the morning-cheer pattern was still on. With gentle fingers, she reset the wall to a glowing old rose and dimmed the lights to a romantic, intimate amber. She drifted to a wall and mirrorized it, looking long at herself.

Norvell looked, too. Under the flattering lights, her skin was gold-touched and flawless, the harsh scowl lines magicked away.

She sat on the warm, textured floor and began to sob.

Norvell found himself squatting awkwardly beside her. "Please, honey. Please don't cry."

She didn't stop. But she didn't push him away. He was cradling her uncomfortably in his arms, talking to her in a way he had never been able to before. Being without contract status would be hard, of course, but weren't thousands of people standing it right now? Maybe things had been physically too easy for them, maybe it took pressure to weld two personalities together, maybe their marriage would turn into shared toil and shared happiness and...

Alexandra giggled from the head of the stairs.

Norvell sat straight up. The girl tittered, "Well, excuse *me!* I didn't dream there was anything *intimate* going on."

Virginia got quickly to her feet.

He swallowed and made the effort. "Sandy," he said gently, using her almost-forgotten pet name, "please come down. I have something to tell you."

Virginia stood tensely. Norvell knew she was trying and loved her for it.

THE girl came down the stairs, her much too sophisticated dressing gown fastened with a careless pin.

Norvell began firmly, "Sandy—"

Alexandra's face was ancient and haughty. *"Please,"* she interrupted him. "You *know* how I feel about that *humiliating* nickname."

"I didn't mean—"

"Of *course* you didn't mean *anything*. You didn't *mean* to wake me up with your drunken *performance* on the stairs, did you? You didn't *mean* to keep Virginia and me in *terror* when you didn't *bother* to let us know you'd be out late." She shot a sly glance at her mother, fishing for approbation.

Virginia's hands were clenched in a tight knot.

Norvell said hopelessly, "I only wanted to tell you something."

"Nothing you can say *now* would help."

"No?" Norvell yelled at her, restraint gone. "Well, listen anyway, damn it! We're going to Belly Rave! All of us—tomorrow! Doesn't that mean anything to you?"

Virginia said at last, with a wiry edge to her voice, "You don't have to shout at the poor child."

That was the ball game. He knew perfectly well she had meant nothing of the kind, but his glands answered for him. "So I don't have to shout at her—because she isn't deaf like me, is that it? My loyal wife! My loving family!"

"'I didn't mean that!" Virginia cried.

"You never do!" Norvell bellowed over Alexandra's shrill contribution.

Virginia screamed, "You *know* I didn't mean it, but I wish I had! You call yourself a husband! You can't even take care of a family!"

It went on and on almost until dawn.

CHAPTER EIGHT

CHARLES Mundin said, "Thanks for springing Bligh, Del."

Dworcas answered affably, "Hell, any time. Besides, he's a friend of Arnie's. Now what's on your mind?"

"G-M-L Homes. Del, I think you've put me onto something. If it works out—well, I won't forget."

"Sure, Charles. Look, it's getting late and I've got a couple of things to do."

"I'll make it quick. This election, Del—let me out of it, will you? I mean I'll take my licking at the polls and all that, but I want to get right on this G-M-L thing, not spend my time on a sound truck or waiting for a broadcast that never happens. Besides— honestly, Del, I can't afford it. I'm busted."

"What's the matter, Charles? The going getting rough?"

Mundin said stubbornly, "You don't give a damn whether I run or not and you know it. I've got no hard feelings. Just let me off the hook."

Dworcas made his decision. He grinned. "Why should I get in your way? Hop on this deal if it looks so good. I'm not saying it won't leave me short-handed— I've even got Arnie helping out, though God knows he won't be good for much. So you think this G-M-L deal is actually on the level?"

Charles opened his mouth to answer, but one of Dworcas' handymen stuck his head in the door.

He whispered to Del.

Dworcas apologized, "Sorry, Charles, but Jimmy Baker is here. Excuse me a minute."

It really wasn't much more than a minute, even though, when Dworcas came back, he was walking slowly and he didn't look at Mundin. "What was I asking? Oh, yeah—if you think the G-M-L deal is actually on the level."

"Yes, I do. At any rate, I'm going to give it a whirl."

"Wonder if you're doing the right thing."

Mundin was startled. "How do you mean?"

Dworcas shrugged. "It's a pretty serious business, practicing a kind of law you aren't trained for. It's *your* affair, though. I just don't want to see you getting into trouble."

"Wait a minute! What's this about? It was your idea, wasn't it?"

Dworcas said coldly, "Worried, Mundin? Trying to hang it on me?" He picked up his phone in a gesture of dismissal. "Take off, will you? I've got work to do."

IT bothered Mundin all the way home, and it bothered him the next morning when he woke up.

It bothered him even more at the County Courthouse. He walked in with a nod to the duty cop and the cop looked right through him. He said to the assistant clerk at the counter, "What do you say, Abe? How are the kids?" And the clerk mumbled something and closed his window with a bang.

By then, Mundin began to catch on. He got sore and he got determined. He waited in line at the next window and asked for the records he wanted. He sent back the wrong folder they gave him first. He pointed out that half the papers were missing from the right folder when he got it. He sat in the County Clerk's waiting room for two hours, until the secretary wandered in and said, with aggrieved hostility, "Mr. Cochrane has gone to lunch. He won't be back today."

He wrote out a formal complaint on the sheet of paper she grudgingly gave him, alleging that he was being illegally and improperly hampered in his attempt to examine the corporate public-records files of G-M-L Homes, Inc., and he doggedly left it with her, knowing what would happen to the paper as soon as he got out of the door.

It fluttered into the wastebasket *before* he got out of the door and he turned angrily to object.

The duty cop was standing right beside him, looking eager.

Mundin went back to his office to think things over.

Fourteen billion dollars…

BUT how the devil did they know so fast? Not from Dworcas, Mundin told himself. He could swear that Del hadn't known the heat was on until Jimmy Baker had called him out of the room. And Dworcas had sent Mundin there in the first place. Because— Mundin flushed angrily at the thought, almost certain that it was right—because Dworcas was pretty sure that a two-bit ambulance chaser like himself wouldn't do them any good? Then what had changed his mind?

Mundin kicked the Sleepless Secretary and went on pacing. In bell-like tones, the Secretary told him that Mrs. Mundin would remit the full balance due by Friday.

He sat down at the desk. All right, so the going was going to be tough. That figured. What else could you expect? And the harder G-M-L Homes made it, the more scared they were—didn't that figure, too? And the more scared they were, the more chance that this whole impossible thing was on the level, that Charles Mundin, Ll.B., stood on the threshold of corporate law.

He took out a piece of paper and began to figure. They could make it rough, but they couldn't stop him. He could get court orders to see the records. That was the obvious starting place, if only to make sure for himself that the Lavins were on the level. As long as Norma Lavin was willing to call him her attorney—in fact, they couldn't keep him out.

There would be a slowdown in court, naturally, but it couldn't take more than a couple of days. Meanwhile, he could get started on some of the other angles. Don's conditioning—there might be a criminal charge in that somewhere, if he could manage to get names, dates and places.

He reached for his model-forms book and began drafting a power of attorney for Norma Lavin to sign. She'd sign it, of course—she was an independent and difficult person, but she didn't have much choice. Besides, he thought absently, a lot of that hardness was undoubtedly protective armor. In circumstances like hers, what could you expect?

The phone rang. He cut out the Sleepless Secretary hastily and picked up the receiver. "Mundin," he said.

The voice was ancient and utterly lost. "This is Harry Ryan," it quavered. "Better come out here, Mundin. I think they've snatched Norma!"

CHAPTER NINE

NORVELL was lying on a cake of ice. He kept trying to explain to someone enormous that he was sorry for everything, that he'd be a good and dutiful son or husband or friend or whatever he was supposed to be, if only the someone would leave him alone.

But that enormous someone, who couldn't have been Norvell's father, because Norvell didn't even remember his father, only put his hand before his mouth and tittered and looked down from a long flight of stairs, and then, when Norvell was least expecting it, reached out and swatted him across the ear and sent him skidding across the enormous cake of ice into the tittering face of Alexandra and the jagged, giant teeth of Virginia—

Norvell woke up.

He was very cold, very stiff. He looked dazedly around him. The living room. But—

Yes, it was the living room. With the wall pattern off and no light, except a sickly dawn from outside. All the walls were on full transparent and he was lying on the floor. The bed he had dialed out to sleep in had folded into the basic cube, dumping him on the floor. And the floor was cold.

No heat—no power—the house was cold.

He got up, wincing, and sidled hopelessly to the window control. It didn't respond. The windows remained full transparent.

He knew what had happened and swore between clenched teeth. The skunks! Turning off the place without a word of warning, at daybreak, without even giving him a chance to...

Wearily, he began picking up his clothes from the floor where a rack had dumped them when it had folded back. Through the indecently transparent windows, he saw the other bubble houses, all respectably opaqued, with only their nightlights and entry lights.

By the time he was dressed, he began to hear a clamor upstairs. His wife and daughter charged down in negligees, commanding him to do something about it.

"Get dressed," he said and pointedly disconnected his hearing aid.

He rambled about the house while they did so. Absently, he tried to make coffee and gave up with a half-laugh when the water would not flow. The closets, drawers and dressers had rejected all their contents, upstairs and down. Pushers had calmly shoved them out and the doors had closed and locked—to him, forever. He contemplated the disordered piles of clothes and kitchenware and began to pack a traveling case.

Two bored policemen wandered in; the door, of course, was no longer on lock. He plugged in his hearing aid, taking plenty of time about it.

"Well?" he asked.

They told him he had plenty of time—they weren't in any hurry. "Take an hour if you need it, bub." They'd tote him and his family and their stuff out to Belly Rave, help him pick out a good place.

The moving had a golden moment. One of the cops helpfully picked up a suitcase. Alexandra told him to remove his *filthy hands from*—

The cop clouted her and explained they didn't take none of that off Belly Rave brats.

The police car handed Norvell a jolt.

It was armored.

"You—you get a lot of trouble in Belly Rave?" he guessed.

The friendlier of the cops said, "Only once in a while. They haven't jumped a squad car in six months, not with anything but pistols, anyway. You'll be okay."

They pulled away from Monmouth G-M-L Unit W-97-AR. There was no sentiment to the parting. Norvell was sunk in worry, Alexandra was incandescent but still. And Virginia had not said two words to anyone that morning.

THE car paused at the broad beltway circling the bubble-city, its motor idling, its driver impatiently talking into his radio. Finally, two more police cars rolled up and the three of them, in convoy, left the city roads for the cracked asphalt that led to Belly Rave. Once the road they traveled had been a six-lane superhighway, carrying a hundred thousand commuters' cars, morning and night. Now it wound through a scraggly jungle and the tollbooths at the interchanges had crumbled into rock piles and rust.

They bumped along for a couple of miles, then turned off into a side road that was even worse.

The first thing that hit Norvell was the smell.

The second thing was worse—the horrible feeling of betrayal. Belly Rave, in its teeming ruin, was worse than anything Norvell had dreamed.

The convoying cars pulled up ahead and behind. A cop got out of each and stood ankle-deep in weeds and refuse, a hand idly resting on his gun.

Norvell's driver said, "This one will do. Let's go."

The act of moving their possessions into the house in the driving rain, ringed by an audience of blank-faced Belly Ravers, was mercifully blurred in Norvell's mind. At one moment, he was sitting in the police car, staring in disbelief at the wretched kennel they were offering him. The next, the police cars were gone and he was sitting on a turned-up suitcase and Alexandra was whining, "Norvell, I've *got* to have something to eat before I absolutely *die*. It's been—"

"Shut up," Virginia said levelly to her daughter. "Norvell, help me get the big suitcase upstairs."

She kicked a heap of rattling cans out of her way and headed for a flight of steps, ignoring her daughter.

Norvell followed her up the narrow broken stairs. The upper floor—Expansion Attic for Your Growing Family, the billboards had said—was soggy with rain, but Virginia found a spot where no water was actually dripping in. He dropped the suitcase there.

"Go on down and watch the other stuff," she ordered. "I'm going to change my clothes."

Before she got down, they had company—three men in ragged windbreakers.

"Police," one of them said, flashing something metallic in Norvell's face. "Just a routine check. You people got any valuables, alcoholic beverages, narcotics or weapons to register?"

Norvell protested, "The police just left."

"Bubble-town police, buster," the man said. "They got no jurisdiction here. Come on, what've you got to register?"

NORVELL shrugged feebly. "Nothing, I guess. Unless you count our clothes."

The men moved purposefully toward the bags. "Just clothes? No guns or liquor?"

Virginia's high, clear voice came down from the stairs. "You're damned right we have guns! You bums scram before you find out the hard way!"

Norvell, eyes popping, saw an old-fashioned revolver in her hand.

"Just a minute, sister," one of the men objected.

"Beat it!" she snapped.

They were gone, swearing.

Virginia handed the gun to Norvell. "Keep it," she said coldly. "Looks better if you have it. Just in case you were wondering, there aren't any cops in Belly Rave."

Norvell swallowed. He hefted the gun cautiously. It was far heavier than his unskilled imagination would ever have estimated. "Where did you get this thing?"

"Used to be Tony's, before he died. There's lesson one for you—you don't live in Belly Rave without a gun."

Alexandra came forward with shining eyes. "You were *wonderful!*" she breathed. "Those detestable *brutes*—heaven only knows *what* would have happened to me if just *Norvell* had been here!"

She started to plant a wet kiss on her mother's cheek. Virginia shoved her daughter away. "We'll have no more of that cack. From now on, you're going to level with me—and with Norvell, too. Hear me? We can't afford lying, faking, double-crossing or temperament. The first bad break you make, I'll sell you like a shot."

Alexandra's face was a study in terror.

"Sink or swim—you're in Belly Rave now. You don't remember, but you'll learn. You'd better—fast. Now get out of here. If you can't scrounge something to eat, go hungry. But don't come back until sundown."

The child stood blankly. Virginia took her by the shoulder, pushed her through the door, slammed it behind her.

Norvell looked through a chink in the boarding of the cracked picture window and saw Alexandra plodding hopelessly down the battered walk, weeping.

Uncertainly, he asked Virginia—the *new* Virginia—"What was that about selling her?"

"What I said. You can always find a fagin or a madam for a kid. I don't know how prices are now—when I was thirteen, I brought fifty dollars."

Norvell, his hair standing on end, said, *"You?"*

"I guess I was lucky—they sold me to a fagin, not into a house. He ran a tea pad. I helped him roll the clientele. That's where I met Tony. Now, if there are no more useless questions, help me unpack."

HE helped her, his head whirling. Without shame or apology, she had demolished the story he had painstakingly built up from her "accidental" hints and revelations over the years. The honest, industrious parents. The frugal, rugged life of toil. The warmth of family feeling, drawn together by common need. The meeting with Tony Elliston—glamorous, advantage-taking cad from the Field Day crowd. Not a bad fellow. "But not love, Norvell—not what *we* have."

He had thought himself clever. He had pieced it together into a connected tale, chuckling privately because she couldn't know how much she had "unwittingly" revealed.

And all the while, she had been a pickpocket in a dope joint, sold into it by her parents.

There was a knock on the door.

Virginia said, through her teeth, "If that brat's come back, before I told—" and swung it open. She screamed.

Norvell found he had the revolver in his hand, pointing it at the middle of the hulking, snaggle-toothed figure in the doorway.

The figure promptly raised its enormous hands over its shock-haired head, grinning.

"Don't shoot, mister. I know I'm not pretty, but I'm harmless. Came here to help you out. Show you where to register and all. The name's Shep. I'll give you a fair shake. Show you the best places for firewood, wise you up on the gangs. Hear you have a little girl. You want to sell her, I'll get you a price. You want to go into business, I can put you next to a guy who'll start you out with hemp seed. If you got real money, I know a sugar dealer and a guy with a still to rent. I'm just Shep, mister. I'm just trying to get along."

Virginia said, "Keep the gun on him, Norvell. Shep, you come in and sit down. What do you want?"

"Surplus rations," the giant said with a childlike smile. "Cash, if you have any. I'm always desperate, but right now I'm out of my mind." His arm swept at the open door. "See the rain?" It's the front end of the rainbow, mister. See it? I have to catch it. And to catch it, I've got to have some crimson lake. Some other things, too, but the crimson lake. You don't see crimson in it, do you? Well, you won't see crimson in the canvas, but it'll be there—in the underpainting—and, because it's there, I'll have the pot of tears, the bloody, godawful rainsweep caught gloomdriving down on two hundred thousand desolations."

Norvell, lowering the pistol, said stupidly, "You paint."

"I paint. And for fifty bucks I can get what I need, which leaves me only the problem of getting fifty bucks."

VIRGINIA said, "With your build, you could get it."

"Not like you mean. Not since I started painting. So I run errands. Any errands? I've got to raise the fifty before the rain stops."

Virginia appeared to come to a conclusion. "Norvell, give Shep fifty dollars." He shot his wife a horrified look. That would leave them with eighteen dollars and sixty-five cents. But she wasn't even looking at him. She told Shep, "You'll work for it. One week's hard work. The outhouse is probably afloat. The chimney looks like it's blocked. We need firewood. This place needs patching all around. Also, my husband doesn't know the ropes and he might get in trouble. You'll watch him?"

"For fifty, sure. Want me to watch the kid?"

"No," she said shortly.

"You know what you're doing, lady. It'll be rough on her. Can I have the fifty now? It'll take ten bucks for the kid who does the running. *I can't miss this rain.*"

Norvell counted out fifty dollars and handed them over.

"Okay!" Shep boomed happily. "We'll get my crimson lake out of the way, then registration."

They walked through the driving rain to a tumbledown building guarded by a rat-faced boy of twelve. Shep told him cryptically, "Got a message for Monmouth."

The boy hooted mournfully, "Wa-wa-wa-wa-wabbit twacks!"

Norvell blinked. Kids—everywhere—from nowhere! Gimlet-eyed, appearing silently, from the rain shroud.

Shep told them, "Like last time, but with *crimson lake*, too. Got it?"

A haggard girl of perhaps thirteen said dispassionately, "Cack like last time. The Goddams joined up with the Goering Grenadiers. It'll be a busted-bottle job getting through the West Side."

"I'm in a hurry, Lana. Can you do it or can't you?"

Mildly, she told him, "Who said 'can't'—you or me? I said it'd be a busted-bottle job."

The rat-faced twelve-year-old said sullenly, "Not me. They know I was the one got Stinkfoot's kid brother. Besides, what about the Willowdale—"

"Shut your mouth about Willowdale," Lana blazed. The boy cowered away. "Bwuther wabbits, inspection—*harms!*"

Jagged glass edges flashed. Norvell gulped in horror.

"Good kids," Shep said approvingly and handed Lana the fifty dollars.

"Wa-wa-wa-wa-wabbit twacks!" she hooted and the kids vanished back into the shrouding rain.

TRUDGING after Shep through the floods, Norvell asked no questions. He had learned that much, at least.

The Resident Commissioner lived in an ordinary house, to Norvell's surprise. He had expected to see the man responsible for the allowances of thousands of people in a G-M-L. Certainly his rank entitled him to one.

Then Norvell saw the Resident Commissioner. He was a dreary old political hack. He told Norvell vaguely, "Carry your cards at all times. Be sure and impress that on your wife and the little girl. There's all kinds of red tape to getting duplicate cards, and you might go hungry for a week before they come through, if you lose these. As head of the family, you get a triple ration and there's a separate one for the wife. Is the little girl a heavy eater?"

Norvell guessed so.

"Well, we'll give her an adult ration then. Lord knows there's no shortage of food. Let's see, we'll make your hours of reporting on Wednesdays, between three and five. It's important to keep to your right hours, otherwise there's likely to be a big rush here sometimes and nobody at all others. Is all that clear? You'll find that it's mostly better to travel in groups when you come down for your allowance. Shep can tell you about that. It—prevents trouble. We don't want any trouble here." He tried to look stern. He added pathetically, *"Please* don't make trouble in my district."

He consulted a checklist. "Your ration cards entitle you and the whole family to bleacher seats at all bouts and Field Days?" Norvell's heart was torn by the words. The rest was a blur. "Free transportation, of course—hope you'll avail yourself—no use to stay home and brood—little blood clears the air—door always open…"

Outside, in the rain, Norvell asked Shep, "Is *that* all he does?"

Shep looked at him. "Is there something else to do?" He swung around. "Let's get some firewood."

CHAPTER TEN

As a disappearing act, it was a beaut. Mundin had tried everything. No Norma Lavin. After Ryan's phone call, the track was lost.

He went first to the police, of course. When he told them Norma Lavin was a Belly Raver, they tried not to laugh in his face.

"Look, mister," a kindly Missing Persons sergeant explained. "People are one thing—Belly Ravers are something else. Are these people on the tax rolls? Do they have punch-card codes? Do they have employment contract identification tattoos? No, they don't. So what can we do? We can find missing persons, sure, but this girl ain't a person—she's a Belly Raver. Maybe she just took a notion to wander off. Maybe she's got her toes turned up in a vacant lot. We just wouldn't know, see?"

But he took Charles Mundin's name, just in case. Mundin found himself making regular trips to the Lavin-Ryan home, loaded down with groceries. He also found that Ryan was tapping him for cash to buy drugs.

Don Lavin was sinking into a kind of catatonia without his sister. Ryan, alternately coldly confident with a bellyful of yen pox and devoured by the weeping shakes, begged Mundin to try something, anything. Mundin tried a doctor.

The doctor made one visit—during which Don Lavin, sparked by some flickering pride, rallied wonderfully and conversed good-humoredly with the doctor. The doctor left, with an indignant glare at Mundin, and Don lapsed back into his twilight gloom.

"All right, Ryan," Mundin said bitterly, "now what?"

Ryan shook the last pill out of the tin, swallowed it and told Mundin now what.

And Mundin found himself calling on his old schoolmate, William Choate IV.

POOR Willie's office was a little smaller than a landing field. He sprinted the length of it to embrace good old Charles.

"Gosh!" he burbled. "I'm so glad you could come and see me! They just put me in here, after old Sterling died. It used to be his office, see? So when he died, they put—"

"I see," Mundin said gently. "They put you in here."

"Yep. Say, Charles, how about some lunch?"

"Maybe. Willie, I need a little help."

Willie said reproachfully, "Now, Charles, it *isn't* about a job again, is it? Gee, that's an awful spot to put me in."

Well, Mundin thought, they had succeeded in beating one thing into Willie's head, though not two. "I just want a little advice. I'd like to know when and where the annual stockholder's meeting of G-M-L Homes comes off."

Willie said happily, "I don't know. Don't they have to publish it somewhere? In a newspaper?"

"Yes, they have to publish it in a newspaper, Willie. The trick is to find out what newspaper. There are maybe fifty thousand of them in the country and the law just says that it has to be published in one—not necessarily English language either."

Willie looked sorrowful. "I only speak English, Charles."

"Why don't you ask your Periodical Research Department?"

Willie nodded vigorously. "Oh, sure, Charles—anything to oblige. Anything at all!" Willie uncertainly asked his squawk-box whether they had anything like a Periodical Research Department, and the squawk-box said, "yes, sir," and connected him.

Half an hour later, while Mundin was deep in the intricacies of the preliminary pre-hearing of the Group E Debenture Holders' Protective Committee, the squawk-box coughed and announced that the G-M-L Homes meeting was advertised in the Lompoc, California, *Intelligencer*. Time, day after tomorrow. Place, Room 2003, Administration Building, Morristown, Long Island.

"*Whew!*" said Willie dubiously. "They won't get many people to come *there*, will they?"

"One too many," Mundin said.

THE next morning, Mundin was waiting at a two-dollar ticket window of the New York Stock Exchange when the opening bell rang.

He examined the crumpled instructions from Ryan nervously, as sweating and tense as any of the passionate throng of devotees pressing around him, but for other reasons.

Ryan's instructions were complete and precise, except for one thing—they didn't tell him what bets to make. Mundin swore under his breath, shrugged and swiftly punched Number 145. Anaconda Copper. He inserted his token, threw the lever and tore off his ticket. At 19,999 other windows in the gigantic hall, 19,999 other investors were doing the same. And outside, on the polychrome street, ten thousand latecomers were waiting for their turn inside.

The angular Big Board in the center of the hall flashed and twinkled—fast, then slow. The lights stopped. The pari-mutuel computers began to hum.

Mundin leveled his field glasses on 145, but it was hard to stay on it. His hands were trembling.

The gong rang and the line he was watching flashed:

145, up 3.

The great hall trembled with noise, of which Mundin's obscene monosyllable was only the twenty-thousandth part. A lousy six cents profit. Not worth taking to the cashier's window.

A passing broker, a grimy Member's button in his lapel, said intimately, "Hey, bud—watch metals."

"Beat it or I'll have you run in," Mundin snapped. He had no time to waste on phony touts. He swept his field glasses over the Big Board, trying to make some sense out of the first movement of the day.

Industrials were down an average of four, the helpful summary told him. Rails—meaning, mostly, factory-site land developments—were up three. Chemicals, up eight.

Mundin figured—that meant the investors would layoff chemicals because they would figure everybody would be on chemicals because of the rise—except for the investors, who would be on chemicals because they would figure everybody would lay off chemicals, because they'd figure everybody would be on chemicals. Because of the rise.

Thirty-second warning bell.

"Bud," said the broker insistently. "*Watch metals!*"

"Go to hell," Charles said hoarsely, his fingers shaking over the buttons. He punched Anaconda again, bought five tickets and waited.

WHEN he heard the great groan at last, he opened his eyes and swept the board with his glasses.

145, up 15

"Remember who told ya," the broker was saying.

Mundin gave him a dollar. "Thanks bud," the broker said. "Don't switch. Not yet. I'll tell ya when. This is a morning crowd— Tuesday morning at that. Not a crazy hysterical Monday-morning crowd that gets in fast and gets cleaned out fast. Look around and see for yaself. Little fellows taking a day off. The family men that play it smart—they think. Smart and small. I been watching them for twenny years. I tell you, don't switch."

Charles didn't switch.

He kept feeding a dribble of dollars to the broker, who was either lucky or a genius that day. By noon, Charles had a well-diversified portfolio of metals with a cash-in value of four hundred and eighty dollars.

"Now," the broker said hoarsely. He had borrowed Charles's field glasses to scan the crowd. "See? Some of them's leaving. Some of them's breaking out sanniches. The handle's dropping. They're getting not so smart now, not so small. I been watching them twenny years. Now they start doing the dopy things, because they're gettin' hungry and a hungry man ain't smart. Sell twenny points short. Jeez, I wish I had the nerve to say thirty!"

Two minutes later, he was pounding Charles on the back and yelling, "We made it, bud!"

Metals had broken—thirty-eight points. Charles, by now icy-calm, gave him five dollars. Step One in Ryan's instructions—build up a stake. He'd done that.

He turned the dial to the $500 range. "Give me a winner," he told the tout. "I'm in a hurry and this is taking too long."

The broker stammered: "Solid fuels ought to rise now. But—but please, bud, make it $250. One on solid fuels and one on—on…" He swept the board with his glasses. "Can's been sleepin' all day," he muttered. "A Tuesday crowd stays off Can, but after metals break…"

He said nervously, "Buy solid fuels and Can."

BY two in the afternoon, Charles had a cash-in value of $2,300 and the broker's pockets were bulging with small change. He was talking to himself in an undertone.

Charles said abruptly, "Okay. Now I want a share of G-M-L."

The broker blinked at him. "Old 333? You can't do that."

"I want it."

"Bud, you're new here; I been around for twenny years. They have an investor, see? All day long, he just punches 333. That's him over there, third tier, second aisle. Like Steel and P & A—they don't take no chances on anybody claimin' no stock."

"I want it," repeated Mundin.

"Ain't you made enough for one day? Come on, let's go get a drink. I'll buy. You fool around with the big boys, they *punish* you. Like G-M-L. You try to grab a share and you'll get hurt. Unlimited resources, see—un-*limit*-ed. Every movement, all day long, he has a 'buy' bid in. He bids *ten thousand bucks,* way over real value. You get a wild idea and bid over ten thousand and you'll get the stock, sure. So, next movement, what happens? He sells short, maybe. Maybe he waits. But sooner or later you're squashed. You know what they say, bud— 'Him who sells what isn't his'n must buy it back or go to prison.' And plenty have."

Mundin said coldly, "What's G-M-L par?"

"Two thousand. But ya can't claim it, didn't I just tell you? He's got a bid in, every movement."

Charles set himself to persuade the broker to do what Ryan had planned. At last, the broker, shaking, stumbled off toward the third tier, second aisle. Mundin followed him with the field glasses.

It was working. Sweating, Mundin saw in miniature, through the glasses, the greeting, the silent shove, the wordless rejoinder, the growing heat of the quarrel. The G-M-L investor was a small, elderly fat man. The broker was small, too, but lean and wiry.

The fight broke out as the thirty-second warning bell rang. Charles took his eyes off the fighters and the for-once-untended investor's window and punched four $250 tickets on Old 333.

ONE bid and no offerings did not constitute a transaction according to the electronic definitions of the New York Stock Exchange pari-mutuel machine. As it had all day, the Big Board said—

333, no change

One bid and no offerings. In a claiming movement, it meant a quick profit—the difference between the bid and the par value. An investor next to Charles, eying him respectfully, said, "What do ya like in Chemicals, bud?"

Mundin ignored him. He left his station, almost regretfully, and took the escalator up to the cashier's window marked: *Industrials— $1,000 and up.*

"Two thousand dollars," said the bored clerk, inspecting the tickets, glancing at his miniature of the Big Board, noting the no change. He began to count out hundred-dollar bills.

"I'm claiming," Mundin said through stiff lips.

The clerk suddenly awakened. "Old 333! How'd you do it?"

"I'm claiming two thousand dollars par value."

The clerk shrugged and tapped out an order on his keyboard. Moments later, one share of G-M-L Homes voting common stock fluttered from a slot in the desk. The clerk filled in Charles' name and home address and recorded them.

"You'll get that to the company's board of directors immediately?" the attorney asked.

"It's automatic," said the clerk. "It's in their files now. Say, mister, if you don't mind telling me how you pulled it off—"

He was being much too affable—and Charles, looking closer, saw the little ear plug of a personal receiver. He was being stalled.

He darted into the crowd.

The two gambles had paid off, Mundin realized, heading for the street and Belly Rave. He had the stake—and he had his single share of stock in G-M-L Homes, entitling him to a seat at the annual stockholders' meeting.

Now the real gambling would begin.

Mundin whistled for a cab. There was some commotion behind him, but the cab came before Mundin had time to notice that the man who was being worked over, in broad daylight, by three huskies, was a small, wiry man with a Member's button in his lapel.

CHAPTER ELEVEN

"GETTING on toward noon," Shep said. "Let's find a restaurant."

"A restaurant?" Norvie Bligh goggled. He followed Shep down the littered, filthy street, wondering. In a week, he thought he had learned something about Belly Rave under Shep's tutelage. But he had seen no neon-glittering, glass-fronted havens.

What Shep led him to was just another Belly Rave house. A wheezing old crone crept around the living room. There was a fire going in the fireplace and water bubbling in a blackened kettle. *Restaurant?*

Shep took a couple of rations from his pocket. He never seemed to be without a dozen or so. They were easy enough to get from the R.C.—you could claim you had a dozen dependents and he would apathetically list you for 273 rations a week. If you could lift them, they were yours. There was plenty of food.

And plenty of circuses.

Shep split the two-by-three-by-six plastic box with his thumbnail and Norvell clumsily followed suit. Things tumbled out. Shep tossed one of the "things"—an unappetizing little block of what looked like plastic-wrapped wood—to the crone. She caught it and gobbled it down.

"Business not so good?" Shep asked casually.

She glared at him, bailed water out of the kettle with a rusted can and slopped it into his plastic ration box. Shep popped open a little envelope and sprinkled a dark powder on the water.

Coffee! The magic smell made Norvell suddenly ravenous. He handed the crone a similar block from his own ration, got his water, made his coffee, and greedily explored the other things that had come out of the box.

Biscuits. A tin of meat-paste. A chewy block of compressed vegetables. Candy. Cigarettes. The combination was one he hadn't encountered before. The meat-paste was highly spiced but good.

Shep watched as he gobbled. "When you've eaten each menu ten thousand times—well, I won't discourage you."

OUTSIDE, Norvell asked shyly what in the world the old woman thought she was doing for a living.

"It's simple," said Shep. "She gets her rations and trades them for firewood. She uses the wood to heat water—for coffee, or bouillon, or tea, or whatever. She trades the water for rations. She keeps hoping that someday she'll come out ahead on the deal. She never has."

"But *why?*"

"Because it makes her feel like a human being."

"But—"

"But, hell! It's hard to starve to death in Belly Rave; in a bad week, though, she comes close to it. She's risking her capital in the hope of gain. What if she always loses? She's *doing* something— not just sitting and waiting for ration day to roll around again."

Norvell nodded. He could see how it would make irresistible, unarguable sense, after the ten-thousandth of each menu. Those who could do anything, anything at all, would try anything, anything at all.

It gave him a clue to the enigma named Shep. He said comprehendingly, "So she has her restaurant, and you have your art, and—"

The giant turned on him. "You little louse! If you ever say, or hint, or *think* that I'm just piddling around to kill the time, I'll snap you in two!"

In a clear, intuitive flash, Norvell realized that he had said the unspeakable. He managed to say, very sincerely, "I'm sorry, Shep."

His knees were shaking and his heart was pounding, but it was only adrenalin, not fear. He knew what torment had driven this placid hulk to rage—incessant, relentless, nagging self-doubt. Where leisure is compulsory, how can you tell the burning drive to create from its sterile twin, "puttering"? You can't. And the self-doubt must remain forever un-resolved, forever choked down, forever rising again.

Norvell added honestly, "I won't say that again. I won't even think it. Not out of fear of you, but because I know it's not so." He hesitated. "I—I used to think I was a kind of artist myself. I know what you must be going through."

Shep grumbled, "Bligh, you're just beginning to find out what you go through—but I'm sorry I blew my top."

"Forget it." They walked on.

AT last, Shep said, "Here's where we get some more supplies." The place was one of the inevitable picture window, fieldstone-chimney ruins, but with a fenced-in yard. The gate had a lock on it. Shep kicked the gate down, tearing out the hinges and the staples of the hasp.

Norvell said, "Hey!"

"We do this my way. *Stearns!*"

A grim, gray man threaded his way to them around stacks of plastic fittings, guttering and miscellaneous. "Hello, Shep," he said flatly. "What do you want?"

"You hijacked repair materials that a couple of friends of mine got through legitimate black-market channels. I want them back—with interest."

"Still on the protection kick, Shep?" the man asked, his voice ugly. "If you had any sense, you'd come in with me."

"I don't work for anybody, Stearns. I do favors for a few friends, they do favors for me. Trot out your team, Titan of Industry."

Shep, so fast to resent the slur himself, was insensitive enough to use it on others. With the same results.

Stearns' face went pasty with rage and Norvell knew what was coming next—unless he moved fast. *"Stearns!"* he yelled, and used the moment's delay to draw the pistol that Virginia had ordered him to carry. Stearns' hand stopped at his lapel and slowly, unwillingly, dropped to his side.

Shep gave Norvell a quick, approving glance. "Trot out your team, Stearns."

Stearns didn't look away from the gun in Norvell's hand. "Chris! Willie! Get the truck."

The truck was a two-wheeler stake job with one starved-looking teen-ager pulling between poles and another pushing against a canvas breast-band. Walking Stearns before him, Shep ordered him to pick up this or that article of building material and put it on the truck. He topped the load with a rusty pick and shovel from the tool shed, then told Chris and Willie, "Roll it, kids. It won't be far."

Norvell didn't pocket his gun until they had put three blocks between themselves and Stearns' final malevolent glare.

There were two stops before they headed for Norvell's home. At each of them, a part of the supplies was unloaded, to the tearful thanks of sober-looking citizens who had thought them gone forever—and, with them, the months of accumulation, gambling and wangling that had earned them in the first place.

Norvell, eying the heaving, panting teen-agers, suggested uneasily, "Let's give them a hand with the truck."

Shep shook his head. "Our job is convoying."

BUT there was no trouble. The kids rolled the cart to the door of Norvell's house and unloaded the firewood and building materials, stacking them on the shredded broadloom that covered the floor of the sunken living room.

Virginia cast an appraising eye over the neat heaps. "No tar paper, linoleum, anything like that?"

Shep guffawed. "No diamonds, either. You think your roof is the only one that leaks? You're lucky—you got two finished floors. Let the top one get soaked. You'll be all right down here."

"Cack," she said and Norvell winced. "If you can't get tar paper, see if you can find something else to make shingles out of. Sheet tin will do."

"So will the roof off a G-M-L," Shep said sourly, but he made a note. He tossed a couple of rations to the waiting kids, who took them and pushed their empty truck away. "Anything else?"

Virginia, suddenly a hostess, said, "Oh, I suppose not. Care for a drink?"

Norvell, for politeness' sake, took a sip of the bottle Virginia produced. "Ration-jack," she called it, obtained by trading firewood with the evil-eyed octogenarian in the house next door. It tasted like the chewy fruit bars he had enjoyed until then, when he found them in his ration pack. But the taste was overlaid with the bite of alcohol. Beer was what he really liked. They didn't seem to have any in Belly Rave, though.

Norvell let the conversation drift past him. He sat back, bone-weary. Physical weariness was a new thing to Norvie Bligh. He had never had it as a child, never had it at General Recreations. Weariness was not one of the fixtures that came with possession of a G-M-L bubble house, it seemed.

Why was it, that doing nothing, involved physical labor, while doing actual creative, productive work—running a Field Day, for instance—involved only the work of the mind? Norvie admitted it to himself: already he was taking on the coloration of Belly Rave. Like all its discouraged, hopeless inhabitants, he was living for the day and ignoring the morrow. Rations and a place to sleep. It would not be long, he told himself bitterly, before he would be one of the simians queuing up at Monmouth Stadium.

Unless he found something else to do.

But what was there to do? Work on the house? The essentials were done. The bars were up, the trash had been carted out into the street, where it would slump into a featureless heap like all the other middens along the road. The less urgent things couldn't be done. You couldn't fix the lesser roof leaks—no shingles. You couldn't fix the stairs—no materials, no tools. Above all, no skill.

HE said excitedly, oblivious to the fact that he was interrupting, "Virginia! How about starting a garden? A couple of fruit trees— orange, maybe. A few rows of—"

Virginia laughed almost hysterically. Even Shep chuckled. She said, "Orange trees don't grow around here, my dear husband. Nothing else does, either. You start digging out there and first you go through two feet of garbage and trash, then maybe six inches of cinder and fill. Then you hit the real pay dirt—sand."

Norvell sighed. "There must be *something* to do."

Shep suggested, "You could paint your dump, if you're feeling ambitious. I know where there's some house paint."

Norvell sat up, interested. He accepted the bottle of ration-jack and took a small swallow. "Why not? No reason why we can't keep the place looking decent, is there?"

Shep shrugged. "Depends. If you want to start some kind of a business, paint's a good advertisement. If you want to just drift, maybe you don't want to advertise. You make yourself too conspicuous and people get ideas."

Norvell said, dampened, "You mean robbers?"

Virginia reached for the bottle of ration-jack. "Cack," she said bluntly, taking a long swallow. "We aren't painting."

There was a long pause. In the G-M-L bubble house, Norvell reminded himself, Virginia had never let there be any doubt who was boss—but she had seldom shown it in front of outsiders.

They weren't in the bubble house any more, however.

I want Arnie, Norvell cried to himself, suddenly miserable. It isn't working out right at all, not the way Arnie said it would. He'd said it would be a chance for Norvie to express himself, to make something of his marriage, to be on his own. And it wasn't that at all!

He reclaimed the bottle of ration-jack. It still tasted quite disgusting, but he gagged down a long drink.

SHEP was saying, "...didn't do so badly today. Stearns gave me a little trouble. If Norvie hadn't held a gun on him, I might not have got the stuff so easy."

Virginia looked at her husband appraisingly. But all she said to Norvie was, "You better keep an eye on that gun. Alexandra tried to sneak out with my kitchen knife today."

"Eh?" Norvie was jolted.

"Put on quite a scene," her mother said, almost admiringly. "She's getting in with the Goering Grenadiers and it seems they pack knives and guns. They look down on the Wabbits and their busted bottles."

"Does she *have* to do that?" Shep said grimly.

"If she wants to stay alive, she does. Get it straight, Norvie—this is Belly Rave, not a finishing school. It's a permanent Field Day, only without rules."

Now *there* was something he knew about, Norvell thought, brightening. "You ever go in for a Field Day?"

"Nope. Just the weeklies."

"Oh, you ought to, Shep. That's where the real money is. And it's not very dangerous if you play it smart. Take spear carrying in Spillane's Inferno, for instance. Safe as houses. And from the artistic side, let me tell you from experience that—"

"Cack on spear-carrying, Bligh," Shep said, with a wire edge in his voice. "I don't do that any more. I've been there, sticking the poor slobs who fall off the high wire before they reach the blonde. I've even been on the wire myself—once." He reached for the ration-jack, his face blank. "She missed me with all eight shots. I fractured her femur with my first. And then I dropped the gun."

He took a huge drink. "They booed me. I didn't get the midriff bonus or the navel super-bonus. I didn't want them. All I wanted was some brushes, some canvas, some graphite sticks and some colors. I got them, Bligh, and I found out I couldn't use them. Not for six damned months. And then I couldn't paint anything except her face when the slug hit her thigh and she fell off the perch."

Norvell contemplated the ration-jack bottle with distaste. He got to his feet, weaving slightly. "I—I think I want some air. Excuse me."

"Certainly," said Virginia, not even looking at him. As Norvell went out the door, he heard her ask Shep, "This blonde you shot—was she pretty?"

CHAPTER TWELVE

MUNDIN was not followed from the Stock Exchange. He got to Belly Rave by late afternoon, his share of G-M-L Common securely tucked in a pocket.

"Ah!" exclaimed Ryan, coherently jubilant. "One share voting. The meeting is tomorrow—and accessory before the fact to simple assault. A good day's work, Counselor."

"I hope this share is going to be enough to get me in," Mundin said anxiously. "What if it isn't entered or they challenge it?"

"They can't. *Id certum est quid reddi potest*, Counselor."

"But *affirmantis est probatio*, you know."

Ryan grinned amiably. "Score one for your side. If they won't let you in, we'll have to think of something else, that's all."

"You've been right so far, though." Mundin stood up and took a turn around the dingy room, tripping over Don Lavin's feet. "Sorry," he said to the sprawling youth, trying not to look at the staring, shining eyes. There was an excellent chance, he realized, that what had happened to Don Lavin might, sooner or later, happen to himself if he persisted in sticking his nose into the corporate meat grinders.

Mundin asked, "Nothing new about Norma?"

Ryan shook his head. "You'll have to pry her loose from them tomorrow. Wish I could go with you…"

"Oh, by all means, come along," Mundin said sarcastically. "Love to have you. You'll like Morristown—it's so much like Belly Rave."

"I'd never stand the trip. You'll have to play it yourself, Counselor. I have confidence in you. Just keep your head and remember the essential nature of a great private utility corporation."

"A legal entity. A fictive person."

The old eyes were gleaming in the ruined face. "Forget that. Think of an oriental court, a battlefield, a government, a poker game that never ends. The essence of a corporation is the subtle flux of power, now thrusting this man up, now smiting this group low. You can't resist power, boy, but you can guide it. He reached shakily for the battered tin of pills. "Oh, you'll manage. The thing for you to do now is to vanish. Get lost. Don't be seen until you turn up at the meeting. And don't go to your office or apartment." He glanced meaningfully at Don Lavin and Mundin cringed.

"What then?" Mundin demanded. "You want me to stay here?"

"Anywhere out of sight.

Mundin looked at his watch. If he could only go to bed now and wake up just in time to start for the meeting! But he had nearly twenty-four hours to kill. Twenty-four hours in which to think and get nervous and lose the sharp edge of determination.

"I'm going out," he said. "I don't know if I'll see you before the meeting or not."

HE said good-by to Don Lavin, who didn't notice him, and wandered through the growing dusk of Belly Rave. He changed direction a couple of times when he caught sight of what looked like purposeful groups of men or children ahead, but there was actually small chance of attack before the Sun went down.

He found himself nearing the General Recreations recruiting station and felt somewhat more secure in the shelter of the inviting, pink-spun-candy-looking structure. General Recreations policed its area with its own guards.

Mundin studied the gaudy posters and the shuffling, gossiping men and women. It was the first time he had come really close to the raw material that Stadium shows were made of and he felt a little like an intruder. He had seen the shows themselves, of course—plenty of them. He had gone religiously to the Kiddies' Days back in Texas. As an adolescent, he had been a rootin', tootin' red-hot fan, as able as any to spout the logbook records on hours in combat, percentage of kills, survival quotients.

Naturally, his enthusiasm had quieted down when the Scholarship people approved his application and he entered law school and he had never picked it up again. Nothing against the games, of course, but an attorney was expected to go in for more cerebral forms of amusements.

Like dodging creditors, he told himself bitterly.

Somebody called from the mob, "Hey, Mr. Mundin!"

He started, half-ready to run.

But it was only whatsisname—Norvell Bligh—the client Dworcas had sent.

But so shabby!

Then Mundin remembered. Bligh had lost out on his contract—with General Recreations, ironically enough. But still, to find him here!

The little man panted up to Mundin and wrung his hand. "My God, it's good to see a friendly face! Were you—were you looking for me, maybe?"

"No, Mr. Bligh."

Bligh's face fell. "I—uh—thought perhaps you might have a message for me—as my attorney, you know—maybe the Company... But they wouldn't, of course."

"No, they wouldn't," Mundin said gently. He looked around. He couldn't stand the little man's misery, nor could he hurt him by walking away. "Is there any place we can have a drink around here?"

"*Is* there! Mr. Mundin, the things I've seen in the week I've been here!"

He led off, with Mundin following. It was only half a block to the nearest blind pig. Bligh knocked. "Shep sent me," he told a bitter-faced woman through a peephole.

INSIDE, the place reeked of alcohol. They sat at plank tables in the wretched living room and, through the sloppy curtains, Mundin saw the gleam of copper tubing and shiny pots. They were the only customers at that hour.

The woman asked tonelessly: "Raisin-jack? Ration-jack? Majun? Reefers? Gin?"

"Gin, please," Mundin said hastily.

It came in a quart bottle. Mundin gasped when she asked for fifty cents.

"Competition," Bligh explained when she had gone. "If it was just me, she'd have sold it for twenty-five. But, of course, she could tell you were only slumming."

"Not exactly," Mundin said. "Health!"

They drank. Mundin felt as if somebody had smashed him on the back of the head with a padded mallet.

Hoarsely, he asked Bligh, "How have you been getting along?"

Tears were hanging in Bligh's eyes. "It's been hell, only one day of hell after another, and no end in sight. I wish to heaven I—" He stopped himself, sat up straighter. "Sorry. Been drinking the whole afternoon. Not used to it."

"That's all right."

"Mr. Mundin, you can help me. *Please!* A big lawyer like you, candidate for the council and everything—I don't expect a contract and a G-M-L. I had them and I was a fool—I threw them away. But there must be some kind of a job, any kind, enough so I can get out of Belly Rave before I split right down the middle and—"

Mundin, thinking of his appeal to Willie Choate, said sharply, "I can't, Bligh. I don't have a job to give."

"Nothing I can do for you here, Mr. Mundin? I know the ropes—*ask* me!"

It was a new thought. Mundin said uncertainly, "Why—why, as a matter of fact, there just *might* be something, at that. I've been trying to locate—a friend here in Belly Rave. A girl named Norma Lavin. If you think you could help me find her…"

Bligh looked at him expressionlessly. "You want me to find you a girl?"

"A client, Bligh."

"I can do it, I bet! I've got friends—contacts. Just leave it to me. I'll handle it. You want to come along?"

Mundin hesitated. Why not? His job was to stay out of sight. Until the stockholders' meeting, at least.

"Certainly," he told Bligh. "Lead the way."

BLIGH led him through the growing dusk to a vacant lot, the burned-out site of one of Belle Rave's finest 40-by-60-foot estates. And then the little man cupped his hands to his mouth and hooted mournfully into the twilight, "Wa-wa-wa-wa-wabbit twacks!"

Mundin, stupefied, said, "What…?"

A small figure oozed from the dusk. It asked suspiciously, "Who wants a Wabbit?"

Bligh proudly introduced Mundin. "This gentleman is looking for a young lady."

"Cack, buster! Us Wabbits don't—"

"No, no! A young lady who has disappeared."

Mundin added, "Norma Lavin is her name. Disappeared a week ago. Lived at 37598 Willowdale Crescent. Drove an old Caddy."

"Um. That's Gee-Gee territory," the shrill young voice informed them. "We got a Grenadier PW, though. What's in it for the Wabbits?"

Bligh whispered to Mundin, "Ten dollars."

Mundin said promptly, "Ten dollars."

"For a starter?"

"Sure."

"Come on." The Wabbit led them a desperate pace through a mile of Belly Rave. Once, a thickset brute lunged at them from a doorway. The child snarled, "Layoff. *Wabbits!*" The man slunk back. There had been a flash of jagged bottle glass in the little fist.

They moved on. Then, a mounting chorus down a street, rhythmic and menacing: "Gah-*damn!* Gah-*damn!* Gah-*damn!*"

"In here!" The Wabbit darted into a darkened house. A startled old man and woman, huddled before the cold fireplace, looked once and then didn't look at the intruders again, having seen the busted-bottle insigne. The Wabbit said to Mundin, "Patrol. This is Goddam territory."

They watched through cracks in the warped boards that covered the splintered picture window. The Goddams, still chanting, came swinging past, perhaps fifty of them, expertly twirling improvised maces. Some carried torches.

The Wabbit, frowning, muttered, "That's no patrol. War party, heading west. No noise. There'll be a rear guard."

You could barely see them. They were black-clad. Their faces and hands were darkened.

"All right," the Wabbit said at last, and they slipped out. The old man and woman, still ignoring them, were munching rations and bickering feebly about who should chop up the chair to start a fire.

THEY dived into a house like any other house, except that it was full of pale, snake-eyed kids from eight to thirteen.

"Who're these?" a girl asked the Wabbit.

"Hello, Lana," Norvie Bligh said tentatively. She shriveled him with a glance and turned again to their guide.

"Customers," he said shrilly. "Missing person. Ten bucks. And something important: War party of Goddams heading west on Livonia Boulevard, the 453-hundred block, at 7:50. Fifty of them with those hatchets of theirs. Advance guard and rear guard."

"Good," she said calmly. "Not our pigeon; looks like a cribhouse raid. Who's the missing person?"

Mundin told her.

Like the Wabbit guide before her, she said, "Um. Goering Grenadier territory. Well, we have one of them in the attic. Want us to ask him, mister—for fifty bucks?"

Mundin paid.

The Goering Grenadier in the attic was an eight-year-old scooped up in a raid on the headquarters of the Grenadiers itself. At first he would only swear and spit at them. Then Lana took over the interrogation. Charles left abruptly.

The Grenadier was still crying when Lana joined them downstairs and said, "He talked."

"Where is she?"

"Fifty bucks more."

Mundin swore and searched his pockets. He had thirty-seven dollars and eighty-five cents. Lana accepted twenty-five on account.

She said, "Seems there's a Mr. Martinson. He has jobs for the Gee-Gees now and then. He told Grosse Hermann—that's their boss—that he wanted this Lavin dame picked up and doped. They were supposed to deliver her to some place on Long Island. The kid didn't go along, so he doesn't remember just where. Says if he heard it, he'd..."

Mundin was tearing upstairs. To the weeping child, he barked, "Room 2003, Administration Building, Morristown, Long Island?"

"That's it, mister," said the kid, sniffling. "I *told* her I'd remember!"

MUNDIN went back into the living room and leaned against a wall, brooding. So Norma was being kept on tap for the stockholder's meeting. Why? More conditioning? A forced transfer of her stock? No—Don Lavin's stock; she didn't have any. She was the legatee—her brother Don had the stock, having her irrevocable proxy.

So they would knock off her brother.

Mundin said to Lana, "Listen. You saw that I have no more dough right now. But I need help. This thing is big. There are—well, thousands involved." What a fool he would have been to tell the truth and say billions! "It's big and it's complicated. First, can you throw a guard around 37598 Willowdale? I think your friends the Grenadiers are overdue to kill a young man named Don Lavin." He didn't wait for an answer, but went right on, "Second, can you get me to the Administration Building in Morristown? You'll be taken care of if this thing breaks right."

Lana measured him with her eyes. "Can do. We can haggle later."

She barked orders. A silent group of children collected their broken bottles from the mantel over the wood-burning fireplace and slipped out.

Lana said definitely, "The Gee-Gees won't get to your friend. As for Morristown—well, if the Gee-Gees can make a delivery there, I guess I can. Frankly, I don't like it. Morristown's tough. But we have an arrangement with the Itty-Bitties there. They're rats; they use guns, but..."

She shrugged helplessly. You gotta go along, her shrug said.

Mundin found himself escorted to the door. "Wait a minute," he said. "I want to hole up somewhere for the night. I'll meet you here in the morning, but what about right now?"

Bligh volunteered, "How about my place, Mr. Mundin? It isn't much, but we've got bars on the windows."

Lana nodded. "That'll do. In the morning—what now?"

One of the Wabbits had slipped in the door. "Gee-Gee scouts," he reported. "We got one of them, but there's a couple more around. Might be a raid."

"We'll fix them," Lana said grimly. "Guess they want their boy back. Come on, you two—I'll have to convoy you out of here."

She led the way. The street was black and silent. Before they had taken three steps, Lana was invisible. With some qualms, Mundin followed Bligh's confident stride.

LANA melted back out of the darkness and said, "Hold it! There's one of the Gee-Gees under that fence."

Her bottle glimmered. Bligh choked and tackled her from behind as she was about to slice into a pudgy young-girl face. Lana floundered on the ground, swearing, while Bligh snapped at his stepdaughter, "Sandy, get the hell out of here. These are friends of mine. I'll see you at home!"

Alexandra, wriggling as he clutched her arm, said philosophically, "Sorry, Norvell. That's the way the little ball bounces." She threw back her head in a barking, strangling yell: "Sieg—*heil!* Sieg—"

Norvell held off Lana with one hand and, with the other, measured the distance to Alexandra's jaw. He knocked her out, heaved her over his shoulder and said, panting, "Let's go, Mundin. You tag along, Lana."

After ten minutes, Mundin had to relieve the little man of Alexandra's weight. By the time Mundin's knees were buckling, the girl was coming to. He put her down and she trailed sulkily along with them.

Mrs. Bligh tried to raise hell when the four of them came in. "And," she screamed at Norvie, "where have *you* been? Out of here without a word—gone for hours—we could have..."

Norvell said it was none of her business. He said it in such a way that Alexandra gasped with indignation, Lana with admiration. Mundin blushed at the language, but reflected that Belly Rave was doing things to little Mr. Bligh. And the things were not all bad.

"And," Norvell concluded, "if I see any more monkey-business between that hairy ape Shep and you, there's going to be trouble!"

"*Hah!*" snorted Virginia Bligh. "I suppose you'll beat him up."

"He could break me in two. I'd wait until he went away and then I'd beat *you* up."

Lana said sweetly, "I'm going now. What about this little stinker?" She jerked a thumb at the sullen Alexandra.

"I'll take care of her," Bligh promised. "She didn't know any better, that's all."

Lana gauged him. "Okay. Be back in the morning." She was gone as Virginia Bligh, regaining her breath, started in for the second round.

Mundin said, "Please! I've got a hard day tomorrow—can I get some sleep?"

CHAPTER THIRTEEN

THEY spent the morning in Old Monmouth, Mundin and Lana and Norvie Bligh, who tagged along in a sort of vague secretarial capacity.

First, they stopped by Mundin's bank, where he plugged in his key, punched *Close Account* and scooped up the bills that rolled out.

He counted morosely. Two hundred thirty-four dollars, plus eighty-five cents in change. Lana looked hungry and Mundin recalled that he still owed her twenty-five dollars balance from the night before. He gave it to her and said, too cheerfully, "Let's get something to eat."

They ate in Hussein's. Lana said, "I've been here before. That ward-heeler Dworcas is across the street, isn't he?"

Startled, Mundin said, "That's right. What were you doing here?"

"Things. Look, here comes a friend of yours."

It appeared to be one of Mundin's Ay-rab constituents-to-be. He said, "Effendi, I confess it. I was drunk when the day came and the Judge insulted me."

Mundin said patiently, "I ought to tell you, Hamid, that I'm withdrawing from—" He stopped in time. Careful, he warned himself—better let things ride until after the stockholders' meeting. He amended it to, "I mean what's the trouble?"

"The inheritance from my father," the Ay-rab said bitterly. "It is a matter of Clark v. Allen, 91 L ed (Adv 1285), 170 ALR 953,67 S Ct 1431." He was reading off a sheet of paper. "What this means, I do not know, but the Judge insulted me."

"I'll look it up," said Mundin, taking the slip of paper with the annotation number on it. "What were you doing in court?"

"My father died," the Ay-rab explained. "There is a law that one must be a citizen to inherit, unless there is a treaty—and how can there be a treaty with Saudi Arabia, which no longer exists? I went to the court, Effendi."

"And you were drunk," said Mundin.

Hamid said gravely, "Effendi, it is even as your great poet Fitzgerald so beautifully wrote—

"Indeed the Idols I have love so long
Have done my Credit in this world much wrong:
Have drowned my Glory in a shallow Cup
And sold my Reputation for a Song,"

"Sure, Hamid, sure," said Mundin. "I'll look into it."

LUNCH continued without further interruption or much conversation. Over coffee, Lana said, brooding, "I guess the big shots'll ride out to Morristown in armored cars. Too bad we ain't rich. Well, let's get to the jumping-off place."

A taxi took them through the Bay tunnel to the Long Island Railroad terminus in Old Brooklyn. Just for the record, they tried the ticket window.

"No, sir," the man said positively. "One train a day, armored. For officials only. What the hell do you want out there, anyway?"

They canvassed the bus companies by phone, without luck. Outside the railroad station, at the head of the cab rank, Lana began to cry.

"There, little girl." One of the hackies soothed her, glaring at Mundin and Bligh. A fatherly type. "What's the matter?"

"It's my daddy," Lana bawled. "He's in that terrible place an' he's lost an' my mommy said we should go help him. Mister, just take us to the edge, please? An' Uncle Norvie and Uncle Charlie won't let anything bad happen if those bas—if those bad men in Morristown try anything. Honest!"

The hackie broke down and agreed to take them to the edge. It was a two-hour drive over bad roads. He let Lana ride next to him in the front, swinging her little handbag gaily. With the volatility of a child, she chattered, all smiles, the whole way. Uncle Norvie and

Uncle Charlie exchanged looks. They knew what was in the little handbag.

Morristown, being older, was better organized than Belly Rave. The driver stopped a couple of weed-grown blocks from the customs barrier.

"Here we are, little girl," he said tenderly.

The little girl reached into her handbag. She took out her busted bottle and conversed earnestly with the driver. He cursed and drove on.

At the gate, a couple of men looked genially inside. Lana whispered something—Mundin thought he caught the words "Wabbits" and "Itty-Bitties" —and the men waved them on. A block past the gate, on Lana's orders, the driver stopped at another checkpoint, manned by a pair of dirty-faced nine-year-olds.

They got a guide—an Itty-Bitty with a carbine. On their way through the busy brawling streets to the Administration Building, grownups got out of sight when they saw him clinging to the cab.

At the Ad Building, Lana said curtly to the driver, "Wait."

Mundin pointed to the steel-plated wheeled and tracked vehicles drawn up in the building's parking lot. "We get out of here in one of those or not at all."

Lana shrugged. "I don't get it, but all right." She told the Itty-Bitty, "Pass the cab out will you? And whenever you guys need something in Belly Rave, you know who to come to."

IT was one o'clock—the meeting was scheduled for one-thirty. The checkpoint in the lobby passed Mundin and Bligh on the strength of Mundin's stock certificate. Lana was to wait in the visitor's room.

Some twenty men filled the meeting room. Quite obviously, they were Titans. Beside these richly, quietly dressed folk, Mundin and Bligh were shabby interlopers.

They were also ridiculously young and awkward.

From here on, it gets hard, Mundin told himself. Corporate law!

The vision blinded him with its brightness.

Another new arrival was greeted cheerfully by the Titans. "Bliss, old man! Never thought you'd turn up for this nonsense. Old Arnold's going to tramp all over you again, as usual."

Bliss was thin and younger than most of them. "If a couple of you gutless wonders would back me up, we'd stop him. Anyway, what else have I got to do with my time?" Then archly, "I *did* hear something or other about a Miss Laverne..." It broke up in laughter.

Mundin dove into the breach. "How do you do, Mr. Bliss," he said breathlessly, taking the man's hand. "I'm Charles Mundin, Regular Republican candidate in the 27th District—and a small stockholder here."

The thin man gently disengaged his hand. "It's Hubble, Mr. Ermurm—Bliss Hubble. How do you do." He turned to one of the Titans and demanded with mock belligerence, "Didn't you get my wire, Job? Why haven't I got your proxy for the contract thing?"

"Because," Job said slowly, "I like old Arnold's policies so far. You'll rock the boat one of these days, Bliss—unless we kick you out of it first."

"Mr. Hubble," Mundin said insistently.

Hubble said absently, "Mr. Ermurm, I assure you I'd vote for you if I lived in the 27th District, which, thank God, I don't." His eyes were wandering. He headed across the room to buttonhole another Titan. Mundin followed him in time to hear, "...all very

idealistic, I'm sure, my dear Bliss. But many an idealistic young man has turned out to be a hard taskmaster. I mean no offense."

Bliss Hubble was off again. Mundin judged that this last Titan was angry enough to talk to him. A vein was throbbing nicely in his reddened temple. Mundin asked in tones of deep disapproval, "Same old scheme, eh?"

THE Titan said angrily, "Of course. The fool! When young Hubble's seen as many raids on management as I have, he'll think twice before he tries to pull wool over *my* eyes. The contract thing indeed! He's trying to shake the faith of all of us in the present management, stampede a board election, bribe—oh, in a gentlemanly way, of course—bribe himself onto the board and then do as much damage as he can. But, by Godfrey, it won't work! We're keeping a solid front against him..." His eyes focused. "I don't believe I know you, sir. I'm Wilcox."

"Delighted. Mundin. Attorney."

"Oh—proxies, eh? Whom do you represent? Most of the chaps seem to be here."

"Excuse me, Mr. Wilcox." Mundin followed Bliss Hubble, who had thrown himself into a chair after another rebuff. He handed him the power of attorney from Don Lavin that Ryan had prepared.

"Hey? What's this?"

"I suggest you read it," Mundin said.

There was a patter of applause as half a dozen men came in. One of them—Arnold—said, "Good afternoon, gentlemen. Let us all be seated and proceed."

Mundin sat beside Hubble, who was reading mechanically. One of the new arrivals began to drone out the minutes of the last meeting. Nobody was paying a great deal of attention.

Hubble finished reading, handed the document back to Mundin and asked with an amused smile, "Just what am I supposed to do about it?"

Mundin said sharply, "Looks foolish, doesn't it?"

Disconcerted, Hubble said, "I didn't say that. And—well, there have been rumors. Rumors to which you might have just as much access as I."

Mundin looked knowing. "We're not going to be greedy, Mr. Hubble," he said, wondering what he was talking about. "Assuming that I'm not a swindler and that isn't forged, how would you like to be on the board?"

"Very much," Hubble stated.

"We can put you there. Our twenty-five percent voting stock plus your—?"

"It's a matter of record. Five and a half percent. I vote the family holdings."

Mundin did sums in his head. Thirty and a half percent. If they could take Hubble into camp and swing twenty percent more…

He faced front. Let Hubble think it over for a while.

The minutes were accepted as read. One of the new arrivals grinned. "Now, gentlemen to business. To begin with, election of a board member to replace Mr. Fennelly."

SOMEBODY proposed Mr. Harry S. Wilcox, the gentleman with the throbbing vein in his temple. Somebody else proposed a Mr. Benyon and nominations were closed. Secretaries moved among the stockholders with ballots, which they filled out after an inspection—brief and with deferential smiles—of the stockholders' proxies and share certificates. Mundin blandly presented his one share to a secretary's horrified gaze. The man gave him his ballot as if he were passing alms to a leper.

Wilcox won and there was a social round of applause and back patting. From certain broad smiles, Mundin suspected the result of the balloting was as fixed as the morrow's sunrise.

He grinned at Hubble. Who didn't seem to think it was at all funny.

"Coming in with us?" Mundin asked.

Hubble scowled.

The chairman passed on to the matter of compensation of officers. Mundin gathered, from the reading of a long, involved statement of capital gains and tax depreciations, that the corporation officers didn't think they were making anywhere near enough money.

During the reading, stockholders chattered sociably. Mundin began to wonder why they had bothered to come, for the raise was lackadaisically approved by a unanimous voice vote.

At the next order of business, he found out why.

It was called, "Diversification of Raw Material Sources, with Special Reference to Alumina and Silicates." Mundin couldn't make head or tail of the dull technicalities, but he noticed that the sociable conversations tapered to a halt. One group, not more than four or five men, were putting their heads together with much figuring on the backs of envelopes and checking of records. Secretaries were running in and out with books and sheaves of documents as the reading droned on.

At last, the chairman said genially, "Well, gentlemen, the question. Shall we save time by asking for a unanimous vote of 'Aye'?"

A thin, gray old man rose and said, "I call for a record vote." He looked at an elaborately unconcerned man in the first row and quavered menacingly, "And let me say to you gentleman that I'm going to keep a copy of the record. And I will be guided by it in reaching future decisions, particularly during the last week of the coming quarter. I trust I have made myself entirely clear."

The chairman harrumphed and the record vote was taken.

THE proposition was defeated by a narrow margin, in an atmosphere of restrained passions. Mundin sensed dimly that there had just been a pitched battle—a corporate Gettysburg, a trial of strength between two mighty groups, with millions a year as the least part of the unseen stakes.

Hubble, beside him, was growing restless. Mundin leaned over and whispered, "You could hold the balance of power in a matter like that if you came in with us."

"I know. Let me see that paper again."

Mundin knew he had him.

The meeting continued.

There were three other clashes—Union Representation, Petition for Lowered Haulage Rates, and Committee to Study Design Improvements. Each time the struggle, while Hubble read the spots off the power of attorney and fished for information.

Mundin was noncommittal.

"Yes, they're clients of mine. No, sorry, can't tell you just where Mr. Lavin is staying at present, I'm afraid. Yes, there is a sister. Mr. Arnold up there can probably give you more information than I."

"*Arnold* is in it?"

"Up to his eye-teeth. He'll probably attempt before long to—wait, here it comes now!"

One of the colorless secretaries was mumbling, "Proposal to rectify an anomalous distribution of voting stock. Proposal is to empower board to acquire—at par—dormant stock, dormant to mean stock unvoted since issue, provided time in question be not less than ten years, stock to be deposited in company treasury." It sailed through the air of the room without raising a ripple.

Mundin whispered, "Ask him how much stock is involved. That'll be your answer."

Hubble hesitated, then firmly rose, looking grim, and put the question.

Arnold smiled. "I'm afraid we haven't the exact figures. It's more of a contingency measure, Mr. Hubble."

Hubble said, "I'd be satisfied with an estimate, Mr. Arnold."

"No doubt. But as I said, we haven't got the figures. Now to proceed—"

Hubble began to look mulish. "Is the amount by any chance twenty-five percent?"

Throughout the room, people sat up and conversations broke off short.

ARNOLD tried to laugh. Hubble snapped, "I repeat my question. Is or is not the amount of stock you are asking us to empower you to buy and deposit in the company treasury, under your control, twenty-five percent?"

As it soaked in, there was a mild uproar. Hubble ignored it. "Is it or is it not, Mr. Arnold? A very simple question, I should think! And if the answer is 'no' I shall ask to see records!"

Arnold grimaced. "Please, gentlemen! Please, Mr. Hubble! I can hardly hear myself think. Mr. Hubble, since you have objections to the proposal, we'll withdraw it. I presume I have the consent of all present for this agenda change. To pass on—"

"You do *not* have my consent to this agenda change, Mr. Arnold. I am still requesting information on the proposal."

Somebody slid into a seat beside Mundin, a big, handsome well-preserved old man. "I'm Harry Coett. What's this all about? I see you talking to Bliss and then all hell breaks loose. Say, weren't you with Green, Charlesworth? No? Thought I knew you. Well, what's up? Arnold's scared. You've got something. What is it?"

Mundin smugly asked, "What's in it for me?"

The man started. "Hell, boy, I'm *Harry Coett*. Where are you from, anyway?"

A third party joined them as the debate between Hubble and the chairman raged and spread. "You seem to have put Hubble onto something, young man. I like spirit. Somebody told me you were an attorney and it happens there's a vacancy in our law staff. Quite a vacancy. I'm Roadways, you know. George Nelson's the name."

Coett snapped, "I was here first, George!"

By then, the floor debate had escaped from Hubble's hands. Scenting blood or gold, half the stockholders present were fighting for the chance to question Arnold, who was sweating and grimly managing not to say a thing—at great length. The other half of the stockholders seemed to be clawing their way into the group around Mundin, the odd young man who seemed to know things.

Mundin, smiling politely and meeting no one's eye, heard the whispers and conjectures: "—an attorney from the S.E.C., I guess, going to throw the book at old Arnold for—" "—into camp, but how do you know it isn't Green, Charlesworth or—" "No, you ass! Proxies! They've been quietly—"

JUDGING the time to be ripe, Mundin said politely, "Excuse me, gentlemen," and stood up.

"Mr. Chairman," he called. Arnold pointedly avoided his eye and recognized somebody else—who was at once the goal of a ten-yard dash by Harry Coett. Coett whispered urgently to the man, who said, "I yield to Mr. Mundin."

"Thank you," said Mundin. "Perhaps I can clarify this confused situation. However, Mr. Arnold, first I should like to talk to one of my principals—the young lady."

"Principals?" Arnold asked distractedly. A secretary murmured something to him. "Oh, Miss Lav—oh, certainly. She'll—uh—be free to talk to you immediately after the meeting is concluded. Is that satisfactory, Mr. Urmurm?"

"Quite satisfactory."

And that was that. It was far more than he had dared hope for. Not only had he thrown an egg into the corporate electric fan, so that half the stockholders in G-M-L were swarming around him, but Arnold was returning Norma as his price for not "clarifying the situation." Arnold's raid had blown up in his face. Far less than getting the Lavin stock to vote, he would be lucky to hold his domination of the board.

Mundin sat down, comfortably—and silently—acknowledging leading questions and offers from the Titans with polite nothings.

The stockholders' rebellion began to peter out. With Mundin quieted, angry and uncertain men perceived that some sort of deal had been made under their noses. They didn't like it. They had done it themselves too often to enjoy feeling the spur on their own flesh. One of them called for unseating Arnold, but majority opinion was—wait until this Mundin tells what he knows.

The rest of the meeting went at breakneck speed.

Hubble spent much of it insisting, "Damn it, Mundin, you made *me* the first offer! The hell with these vultures. They'll use you and throw you away. I'm the only heavy stockholder in the company with an open mind and—"

"Nonsense!" Harry Coett said decisively. "I don't know what you're up to, Mundin, but whatever it is, it'll need financing. And I'm *Harry Coett.* Let me handle—"

George Nelson said, "Tell him what you did to old Crowther, why don't you? *He* needed financing, too."

MUNDIN never did find out what Harry Coett did to old Crowther. As the meeting was adjourned, he buttonholed Arnold, who gave him a wan smile. "Come and see me, Mr. Mundin. I'm sure we can get together. Don't we know each other? Weren't you with Green, Charlesworth?"

"The girl, Arnold," Mundin demanded.

"Miss Lavin is waiting for you in the reception room."

Trailing tycoons, Mundin raced outside.

Norma Lavin was there, pale and angry. "Hello, Mundin," she said, not so crisply. "You took your time about it." And then she was weeping on his chest. "I didn't sign it. I knew Don wasn't dead. I didn't sign. I—"

"Shut up, superwoman," Mundin snapped. "Stop giving things away to the eavesdroppers. Your every word is golden." But he found that he was also shaking—from the reaction to the hours of strain. And unexpectedly but emphatically, from—Norma.

He got a grip on himself as Coett, behind him, mused, "So *this* is the young lady Arnold horse-traded you, eh? Your principal, Counselor?"

"Maybe," Mundin evaded.

"Oh, come off it, Mundin," Goett said shrewdly. He turned to Norma. "My dear, can I drop you any place? You, too, of course, Counselor."

"Listen, Mundin," Nelson urged. "Get him to tell you about old Crowther."

"Damn it!" raged Hubble. "If you vultures will step aside…"

Mundin said, "I'll lay it on the line, gentlemen. Miss Lavin and I have to stop in the waiting room to pick up an—uh—a young lady. In five minutes, we will be at the front entrance. We'll go along with all three of you or with any two of you. You fight it out among yourselves."

He swept Norma out to the visitor's room. Lana was perched on the receptionist's desk, looking hostile—but not as hostile as the receptionist. Mundin asked her, "What happened to Bligh?"

"Outside," Lana replied. "He said he'd already had a bellyful of Field Days, whatever he meant by that. This your girl?"

"Yes," said Mundin. "This is my girl."

The three of them collared Norvie Bligh, sitting in the sun outside, and started toward the ranks of parked cars and halftracks. They were met by an amicable committee of three.

"All settled, Mundin," Hubble said happily. "Coett and Nelson are coming with us."

"Good. Where do we talk?"

Hubble said joyously, "Oh, my place. You'll like it—simple, quiet, but comfortable."

They made quite a procession—two cars and a half track. They didn't stop for anything, neither the Itty-Bitty checkpoint nor the customs shed. In well under five minutes, they were on the open road for Hubble's place.

CHAPTER FOURTEEN

LANA was tugging at Mundin's shoulder. "I want to go home," she told him.

Mundin said peevishly, "Sure, sure." Norma, exhausted, had fallen asleep on his arm and its circulation had been stopped for the past ten miles. The girl was a solid weight—but, he was thinking, a curiously pleasant one.

"I mean now," Lana insisted. "I got a duty to the Wabbits."

"I'd kind of like to go, too," Norvie Bligh chimed in. "If you won't be needing me, I mean."

Mundin eased Norma's head off his arm. She stirred, mumbled, "Arglebargle damn men think they're..." and was asleep again.

Mundin flexed his arm, considering. Lana and Bligh had fulfilled their bargains. There wasn't likely to be much need for bodyguards for the next little while—and not too much that Lana, for instance, could do, cut off from her gangs.

He said, "All right. I'll have the driver let you off at Old Yonkers and you can get a bus or something."

At Old Yonkers, their car stopped at an Inter-City depot. The car behind skidded to a stop beside them. Hubble, Nelson and Coett—none of whom had trusted any of the others alone with Mundin and Norma for the ride—peered out anxiously.

"Anything wrong?" Hubble yelled from a window.

Mundin shook his head and let Lana and Norvie out.

Twenty minutes later, the motor caravan reached Hubble's house.

Quiet and comfortable it was—simple it was not. It was a Charles Addams monster in a fabulous private park in Westchester. They rolled up its driveway and parked next to what appeared to be a 1928 Rolls-Royce limousine.

Bliss Hubble was already at the door of the car, holding it open for them. "My wife," he explained, indicating the limousine. "She makes a fetish of period decoration. Today, I see, it's Hoover—all last week, it was neo-Roman. Can't say I care for it, but one has one's obligations."

"And one has one's wife," said Norma Lavin, who appeared to be back to normal acid self.

"Oh, it's quite nice," Mundin said diplomatically. "So stately."

MRS. Hubble greeted them with an unbelieving look. She turned to her husband with an explain-*this*-if-you-can air. Being a thin brunette with cheekbones, she did it very well.

Hubble said hastily, "My dear, may I present Miss Lavin…"

"Just 'Lavin,' please," Norma said coldly.

"Yes, of course. Lavin, and Mr. Mundin. You know Harry and George. Mr. Mundin has been good enough to compliment the way you've fixed up the house, dear."

"Indeed," said Mrs. Hubble, ice forming on her gaze. "Thank Mr. Mundin and explain to him that his taste matches that of the housekeeper. Suggest to Mr. Mundin that he might consider employing the housekeeper, who has been out of a job since I woke up this morning and found she had set the house for *this*

unsightly, trashy piece of construction. Inform Mr. Mundin that when the housekeeper left—rapidly, I might say—she took off with *all* of the key settings, and I have been condemned to roam through these revolting rooms until my husband chose to come home with his keys so that I might change them to something resembling a human habitation."

Hubble stiffened, thrust a hand in a pocket, brought out a set of keys. His wife took them from him, turned and swept off through the vast, gaudy rooms.

"Sensitive," Hubble muttered to his guests.

Coett said eagerly, "We got a couple of things straight on the way over, Mundin. Now…"

"Harry, I insist!" Hubble said severely. "I'm the host. Let's not rush things until we've had dinner."

He led the way through a majestic corridor, keeping carefully to the middle.

He said sharply, "Watch it! Stand back!"

The others, obeying his gesture, stood clear of the walls, which were in curious, shimmering motion.

"My wife," Hubble explained with a glassy smile. "You'd think a regular bubble-house wall would be enough. No, nothing will do but full three-D illusion throughout. The expense! The stumbling home in the dark! The waking up in the middle of the night because the four-poster is changing into a Hollywood bed! She's a light sleeper, you see…"

The walls had firmed up now. The old furniture was fully re-tracted and gone, new pieces had formed to replace them. Mrs. Hubble's present preference appeared to be Early Wardroom—a satisfactory enough style for the flying bridge of a heavy cruiser, but not really Mundin's idea of how to decorate a home. He pointedly did not comment on the steel-gray walls.

The dinner seemed like a very good notion to Mundin. The tadjin ahmar he had eaten at Hussein's seemed a very long way in the past.

A SHAMBLING butler, wearing sharp dress blues, served them. His presence seemed to make Hubble jumpy. The table talk was not sparkling.

"Am I to understand," Hubble probed gently, "that Miss Lavin—that Lavin, I mean to say—was actually abducted by Mr. Arnold?"

"Doubt it very much," said Norma, chewing. "He probably just looked unhappy and said, 'Dear me, I wish something could be done about that outstanding stock.' Some foot-kisser standing by set the wheels in motion. Arnold's hands would be clean. Not *his* fault if people insist on exceeding their authority."

She took another forkful of wild rice. "They had me for about a week. God almighty, what confusion! I could go and I couldn't go. I was free to leave anytime I cared to, but temporarily they thought it would be better if they kept the door locked. Sign your residuary legatee's share of the stock to us and we'll pay you a cool million. But we don't *want* the stock, of course. It has only a certain small nuisance value. Now, lady, are you going to be reasonable or do we have to get tough? My dear girl, we wouldn't dream of harming you!"

She scowled. "Arnold came to see me once. He kept pretending *I* was trying to sell to *him*. I don't know, maybe that's what somebody told him. All I know is, I feel as if somebody hit me over the head with a lighthouse."

The shambling butler asked, "Are you at home to Mr. Arnold, sir?"

Hubble said delightedly, "No! You hear that, Coett?"

Nelson cut in, "Hold it a minute, Bliss. Are you sure you're doing the right thing? Maybe if we all get together, we could—" he looked quickly at Mundin—"that is, perhaps *all* of us could freeze out the Toledo bunch."

Coett said, "Tell him to go to hell. Tell the *butler* to tell him, so we can hear you do it. First we settle things among ourselves— then we figure who else we have to cut in. My guess is nobody."

"Tell him," Hubble said gleefully to the butler. As the man shambled off, he turned to Nelson. "Harry's right, George. Figure it out. You've got eleven percent under your thumb, counting the voting trust. I've got five and a half, solid. Harry has three of his own and he influences—how many, Harry?"

"Nine," Coett said shortly. *"Heavy* influence."

"You see? That's plenty, with these people's twenty-five percent."

Mundin kicked Norma's foot under the table, just as she was opening her mouth to ask how they had located the stock. He said rapidly, "Don't you think we should save this until dinner's over?"

Hubble cast an eye around the table. "Why, dinner's over now," he said mildly. "Let's have our coffee in the library—it'll be a little more comfortable."

HUBBLE stopped at the entrance to the library and did something with a switchbox before permitting the others to enter.

"Have my own controls, here," he said proudly. "Wife has most of the house—hah-hah—she can't begrudge me one little den of my own. Let's see if we can't get something more cheerful."

The "library"—there was nothing resembling a book or micro-film in sight—shimmered and flowed, and turned into something that looked like a restoration of a 19th Century London gentlemen's club.

Mundin tested one of the wingback chairs and found it good. Norma was still looking at him suspiciously—but she was silent.

He said cheerily, "Now, gentlemen, to work."

"Right," said Harry Coett. "Before we get too deep, I want to know how we stand on one thing. I'm sure it's just one of those crazy things that get started, but I heard somebody say something at the meeting. They said you were from Green, Charlesworth. Just for the record, are you?"

Green, Charlesworth. Ryan had mentioned them, Mundin recalled. They seemed to be something to worry about. Mundin said definitely, "We are not from Green, Charlesworth. Miss Lavin and her brother are the direct heirs of one of the founders of G-M-L. I—uh—happen to have a small amount of stock myself, as well as being their attorney."

Coett nodded briskly. "Okay. Then it's a plain and simple raid and we've got the strength to do it. I take it we are all agreed, then, that the first step is to throw the corporation into bankruptcy?"

Mundin gaped. "What?"

"*Thought* you were no expert," Coett said amiably. "What did you expect, Mundin?"

"Why," Mundin floundered, "there's your stock and our stock and—well, majority rules, doesn't it?"

He stopped. They all were enjoying a polite laugh. Coett said, "Do you seriously think we could vote our stock *outright* under the existing rules?"

"I don't know," Mundin said honestly.

"You can't. The proxies won't stand for it. A raid, yes, but handled *right.*"

Norma Lavin commented, "I suppose he's right, Mundin. They've stopped us so far, one way and another. The only real change is that now these three ghouls know we're alive and think they can easily take us to the cleaners."

"Please!" protested Hubble and Nelson.

Coett, grinning, assured her, "You are absolutely correct. For the first time, I begin to doubt that we can do it."

Mundin interrupted, "Why bankruptcy?"

They stared at him. Finally, Hubble asked, "How would you do it, Mr. Mundin?"

MUNDIN said, "Well, I'm no corporation lawyer, gentlemen— I leave that aspect of it to my colleague, Mr. Ryan, who is a member of the Big Bar. But it seems to me that our first step is, obviously, to form a stockholders' committee and request an accounting from the present board. We can back it up, if you think it necessary, with a notification to the S.E.C. I know that Arnold's group will stall and attempt to compromise, probably offer us some kind of board representation, something far less than our holdings entitle us to. But that's simple enough to handle. We simply protest and file suit in—"

"Risky," Nelson objected.

Coett said, "That won't get us to first base. I remember when the Memphis crowd tried—"

"The who?" Mundin interrupted.

"Arnold's group. They took G-M-L away from the Toledo bunch eighteen years ago through due process, the way you're talking about. But it took six years to do it—and if the Toledo bunch hadn't been caught short in Rails, Memphis never would have made it. And Toledo is still strong—you saw how Arnold had to put Wilcox on the board to please them."

Mundin said desperately, "Can't we at least try?"

"Waste of time! We have before us an immense mass of capital. It has inertia, Mundin—inertia. You can't move it with a feather—you need dynamite. It's going to take time and brains to budge it. I'll tell you how." And he did. Mundin listened in growing bewilderment and something that came close to horror. Bankruptcy! How did you put a corporation worth fourteen billion dollars, eminently solvent, unbelievably prosperous, into bankruptcy?

He didn't like the answers when he heard them. But, he told himself, you can't make an omelet without breaking a few golden eggs.

Coett, enjoying himself, was planning in broad, bright strokes. "Bliss, you get your chaps on the petition for composition and arrangement. We'll spring that one ourselves, before they think of it, arid we'll want it ready. Then…"

Mundin, grimly taking notes, stuck through it to the end. But he wasn't enjoying the practice of corporate law nearly as much as he had always thought he would. He wished urgently for the presence of old Ryan. And a nice full box of opium pills.

IT was nearly midnight. Mundin had never felt so drained in his life. Even Norma Lavin slumped in her chair. Coett, Hubble and Nelson were bright-eyed and eager, skilled technicians doing the work they best knew how to do.

But the work was done. Mundin, yawning, dragged himself to his feet. He said tiredly, "So the first thing for me to do is set up offices, eh?"

Harry Coett sighed. "Not *quite* the first thing, Mundin."

"What then?"

"Call it a matter of personal satisfaction. We've all heard rumors about young Lavin. I don't say they're true. I don't know if they are or not. But *if* they're true, we don't get off the ground."

Mundin blazed, "See here, Coett—"

"Hold on. We've all had a look at that paper of yours. It's a power of attorney, all right, and I've no doubt that it's valid. But it isn't a proxy, Mundin. It doesn't mention G-M-L stock in it anywhere, except in the affidavit at the end—and Don Lavin didn't sign that himself."

"What do you want?"

Coett said, "Let me tell a fantastic story. Mind you, I don't say it's true. But it's interesting. There are two young people, a brother and sister, for instance. One of them has some stock, but can't use it. The other is—temporarily out of circulation. Let's suppose that a smart young lawyer gets hold of them. First thing he does, he walks in on a meeting and lets it be known that the stock exists. With that as a wedge, he pries the girl loose from wherever she is.

"With the girl, he sucks in three good, dumb Joes—like Hubble, Nelson and me, for instance. With the dumb Joes in the palm of his hand, he squeezes recognition of the stock out of, for instance, Arnold. That's pretty good work—he has the girl and he has the stock. The question is, what do the dumb Joes have then?"

God! thought Mundin. *And I never believed in mind reading!* He said, "Am I supposed to take this fantasy seriously?"

"Of course not. Just for the sake of the record, before we get too far involved in any of this, let's see the stock. Will tomorrow morning be time enough?"

"Tomorrow morning will be fine," Mundin said hollowly. "Come, Norma."

Hubble's chauffeur—now driving what appeared to be an admiral's staff car—convoyed them home. The house, from outside, had become a gray stone and ivy barracks. Mundin watched it dwindle behind them.

Since he was pretty sure the chauffeur was under orders to hear anything they said, they didn't talk.

So it wasn't until they were back in Belly Rave that Norma asked bitterly. "Well, Mundin? Is tomorrow morning time enough to locate the stock?"

CHAPTER FIFTEEN

IT was a ghastly night. Norma Lavin snapped, "You could have stalled them."

"Stalled them how?" Mundin asked, needled into snapping back at her. "One hint of indecision and they'd have pulled out."

"And where did you think we'd find the stock?"

He looked hopefully at Ryan. "What about the possibility of duplicate certificates?"

"Overnight?" Ryan said. "A thing like that takes weeks—assuming there's no hitch, and G-M-L will create as many hitches as they can—and then there is still the question of Don's conditioning against remembering where the stock is and being able to vote it."

He was jittering badly, although he had doped himself almost blind during the argument. He took another yen pox pill and his eyes began to close.

"That's great," Mundin grumbled. "Now he's no help."

Norma said contemptuously, "And you are, I suppose. At least *he* didn't make any stupid promises."

"Maybe Don can give us a hint. One is all we'd need. They might not have blocked *all* his memories about—"

"Leave him alone! You said you'd produce the stock. All right, produce it, but not by tormenting him!"

Mundin knew it was desperate and cruel when he pushed past her and shook the boy awake, but at the very first question, Don Lavin's eyes stretched wide in terror and he stammered, "K-k-k-k-k—" and began to cry.

"I'm sorry," Mundin said inadequately and went back into the ramshackle living room while she glared at him and tried to calm her frightened brother. "Now what?" he asked Ryan.

The old attorney roused slightly. "Tellmtruth," he mumbled.

"What?" Mundin exclaimed. "Who? About what?"

"Hubblenthothers. 'Bou' Don. Stockenconditionnn."

Revolted, Mundin watched the drugged lawyer slide back into his opiate dream world, where problems like this could be solved magically just by telling the truth. It was idiotic and he didn't give the suggestion another thought. There *had* to be a way out. All they had to do was think of one.

But Ryan was doped and Don Lavin had fallen into an easy sleep again, protected by his conditioning as much against residual terror after questioning as from talking or doing anything about his G-M-L shares, and Norma was furious at Mundin.

When morning came, he had blearily decided to do what he should have done in the first place—somehow put off Hubble, Coett and Nelson. Ryan, however, insisted that he bring Don along just in case.

AT Hubble's house, Mundin tried to be evasive, but Coett said impatiently, "Look, this represents a huge gamble for us. If you've just been bluffing and haven't got the stock, come right out and say so, but don't try using excuses on us—we know them all."

And Mundin, knowing he was blowing the case, hating himself because he hadn't come up with *the* solution, told them the truth.

"How do we know this isn't another stall?" demanded Nelson.

"Ask Don where the stock is," Mundin said tiredly.

They did, and got the same fright reaction, and the same anger from Norma, and Hubble admitted uncomfortably, "It's real, all right. Nobody could imitate conditioning that well."

"And there's the way Arnold acted at the meeting," Coett added. "*He* knew the Lavin stock was no phony."

Mundin listened to them in bewilderment. Drugged or not, Ryan was the better lawyer; he had come up with the right answer. They had accepted the shameful truth where they had rejected excuses and delays, and now they were discussing ways and means, shrewdly, clear-headedly, as if conditioning were just another problem in finance.

"We could get duplicate certificates," Mundin offered, which was accepted as a possibility when everything else failed; they shared Ryan's belief that G-M-L would, put every obstacle in their way.

"I know a doctor," Hubble said quietly.

Coett and Nelson nodded as though a vote had been taken.

"But de-conditioning is illegal!" Mundin protested. "We can't be parties to—"

"Hah!" Norma snorted in scorn.

"Who said anything about de-conditioning?" asked Hubble. "The boy needs an operation, that's all."

So Don Lavin had himself a brain tumor. A highly reputable diagnostician analyzed it as a spongioblastoma, the commonest and most malignant of the intracranial gliomas. He recommended immediate surgery and then bought himself a new Rolls 'copter with power doors, power windows, ramp and steering.

The surgeon he suggested was in Wichita and had a private hospital. He extirpated the spongioblastoma—or at least the hospital Tissue Committee examined what he said he had removed from Don Lavin's brain, and this indisputably was spongioblastoma multiforms, consisting of round, elongated and piriform cells, characteristically recalling the varied cytological picture in osteogenic sarcoma of bone.

The surgeon then put down a sizable deposit for a new wing for his hospital.

CHRONICALLY suspicious, Norma scowled down at her brother, mumbling under the last of the anesthesia. She said to Mundin, "He might have left him an idiot. What better way to cover his tracks?"

Mundin sighed. They had, purely on her insistence, watched the surgery. The lights, the sterilizers, the hole saw. The wisp of scorched smell from the bone, the nerve-wrenching moment when the disk of skull lifted out. Insertion of anode and cathode needles, minute electroshocks that smashed this pattern, blurred that memory, shattered one or another reflex into neuronic rubble. The hours before of endless tests and questions, the strobe flickers in Don's eyes, the miles of EEG tape, the mapping of Don's brain and its workings.

Norvell Bligh, handy little man, looked in. "Doctor's coming," he said and, faithful little man, resumed his post outside the door.

Dr. Niessen asked them, "Anything yet?"

Don chose that moment to open his eyes and smile at Norma. "Hello, Sis. It feels better now." Norma burst into tears and Dr. Niessen looked mightily relieved.

"Check the blockage," the doctor suggested to Mundin. "We can find out now if we've done it."

Don said, "The stock? Safe-deposit box 27,993, Coshocton First National. Identification—picture of me, my fingerprints, code phrase, "Gray, my friend, is all theory and green life's golden tree'." He explained chattily, "Goethe. Dad used to say that one a lot after they put the boot to him. It used to cheer him up a little."

Dr. Niessen asked formally, "Is that essentially it?"

Norma choked and said, "Have you got it all back, Don? All?"

Her brother winced. "Oy, have I! Including the time they worked on me. That part I don't *want* to remember."

The doctor muttered, "Barbarous. We're all lawbreakers here, but I'm glad of it in this case. Mr. Kozloff—" That was Don's pseudonym—"are you able to verify my conjecture that flicker-feedback was the principal means employed?"

"I guess so, if flicker-feedback is them shining a light in your eyes and you go into convulsions!"

"That's it. Well, Mr. Kozloff, I think you've recovered from your tumor. One of the staff physicians will check you for traveling. Come back if there's anything new. In these spongioblastomas, there is always a slight possibility that some malignant tissue was overlooked. And if you can possibly arrange it, Mr. Kozloff, please don't bring your sister."

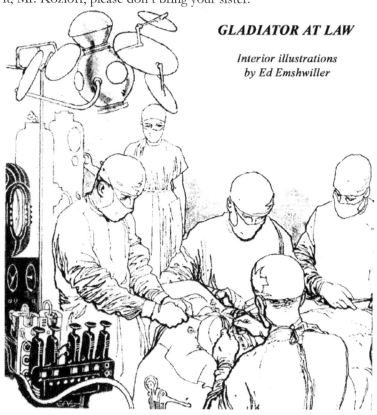

GLADIATOR AT LAW

*Interior illustrations
by Ed Emshwiller*

Bligh opened the door for him. Mundin followed him out into the corridor for a smoke and refuge from the touching reconciliation scene. But he could hear it even out there.

THE Columbus manager of Brinks-Fargo looked skeptical. "Now have I got this straight? Armored truck from here to Coshocton First National, guarded pickup of securities from there and immediate overland trip to New York, you four riding all the way. Right?"

"Right," Mundin said.

"Twelve thousand, five hundred dollars," the manager said after some scribbling. "For our biggest and best, with six guards."

It was paid.

The pickup went off smoothly. A conditioned clerk handed over the little box in which were certificates of Don Lavin's fantastic claim to 25 percent of G-M-L.

Mundin examined them wonderingly as the armored, eight-wheeled land cruiser rolled bumpily through the streets of Coshocton. Three and one-half billion dollars at par, he kept saying to himself. Three and one-half billion dollars at par. He felt numb.

Don, who had been revealed by conditioning as a happy-go-lucky kid, whispered to him, "Confidentially, I'd swap those things for a lifetime lease on a bubble house and fifty bucks a week pocket money. But Norma—you know. And maybe she's right. The responsibility and everything," he added vaguely.

Norvell Bligh, inevitably, was the one sitting uncomfortably on a couple of folded money sacks. Only three welded-steel seats in the locked middle compartment where they rode as passengers. He hoped the ride would go on forever, jolts to the spine and all. *He was working.*

Hubble said, when they arrived, "Did it work, Don?"

Coett said, "If that sawbones couldn't deliver after all his big talk—"

Nelson said, "I hope it didn't cost too much—"

"I'm all right, thanks," Don Lavin said.

"And," Mundin told them casually; "we came back through Coshocton."

They examined the stock certificates with awe, then gloating.

"We're in," Coett said decisively, "as of the next stockholders' meeting. Three months—plenty of time to shake the firm and pick up all we need for a majority. My God, a *majority!* Gentlemen, I move we now turn this operation over to Mr. Mundin. He understands us and we have, in addition to our usual activities, to pick up stock as it becomes available. Mr. Mundin, with an expense account of seven hundred and fifty thousand, will easily see to it that it *does* become available, I am sure."

COETT looked like some aged, still-ferocious jungle predator, and quite suddenly Mundin began to loathe him. The tactics, he thought, were disgusting and anti-social. Thus far, he had been persuaded by their papa-knows-best attitude and by the fact that Don Lavin, conditioned, had been his only talking point. De-conditioned and in possession of his stock certificates now…

"I've been meaning to ask you gentlemen whether, the smear against G-M-L is absolutely essential," Mundin said.

They were quite ready for him. Coett snapped, "That's a closed question, Mundin. I'm sure Mr. Lavin realizes that we're doing what's best for him. Don't you, Don?"

The boy said, "I don't really give a damn, Mr. Coett. Talk to Sis. You'll have to, anyway."

Norma was undecided. "Old Ryan says your plans are quite routine under the circumstances and I have a great deal of faith in him. I suppose—I suppose the important thing is to get it *done.*"

Coett spread his hands. "There's your answer, Mundin. Now about—"

"Hold it, please," said Mundin. "I'm still not—"

"Mundin," Coett broke in sharply, "will you, for God's sake, come to your senses? This thing is still a gamble and it's our money everybody's gambling with."

"Absurd quibbles about destroying some paper values," Nelson sniffed. "You don't understand these things. And I heartily endorse Mr. Coett's reminder that we are putting up the capital to enable Mr. Lavin to realize his claim of interest."

"Smear's the word," Mundin said, feeling heavyhearted.

"Fine," agreed young Hubble, but Mundin thought there was a twist to his mouth when he said it.

"Now," said Coett, "it is conceivable that Green, Charlesworth may take an interest in the contemplated operation. If they *should* show up, Mundin, don't try to handle it yourself. Buck it to us. They have the reputation of not dealing with intermediaries."

"Noted," Mundin said. Green, Charlesworth. Insurance and bankers' bankers. Old man Ryan had mentioned them.

"Then we're ready to rip and tear," said Coett. "Go get 'em, Mundin. You've got three months and seven hundred and fifty thousand dollars to get them with."

Mundin nodded, but he felt shaky inside. It didn't seem like much against the fourteen billion dollars G-M-L had.

CHAPTER SIXTEEN

ONE month after the go-ahead, Del Dworcas, Regular Republican county committee chairman, stood incredulously before an office door. The sign said:

RYAN & MUNDIN
ATTORNEYS AT LAW

The office occupied a solid floor through of a very good building. All he knew, standing there, was that Charles Mundin, his foredoomed candidate in the 27th ward, had first become inaccessible to him and then had moved and then had formed a partnership with somebody named Ryan and then—but there the stories became incredible. Dworcas had to check for himself.

He took several long, deep breaths before he pushed the door open and announced himself to a ripely curved blonde receptionist.

"Pleased be seated, Mr. Dworcas," the girl cooed. "Mr. Mundin asked me to tell you that you'll be the very next person he sees."

The dozen or so other individuals in the waiting room glared at Del Dworcas. However, being a professional politician, he had no difficulty in striking up a conversation with the fellows nearest him.

One was a petrochemist who understood there were consultant jobs opening up at Ryan & Mundin. Another was a publishers' bright young man who thought there must be a whale of a story in old man Ryan's sensational comeback and stood ready to sign it up. The others were easy enough to tag—a couple of crackpots, two attorneys obviously seeking affiliation with the new firm, a handful of persons who seemed to be in the market for lawyers, and had suddenly come to think that it might be a good idea to retain Ryan & Mundin.

Nobody in the waiting room seemed to have any idea of what, if anything, was going on in the remainder of the enormous suite.

Dworcas—being a professional politician—was able to absorb information, pump for more, evaluate what he had heard and speculate on its meaning. But the answers were slight and cloudy. All he could make out for sure was that Ryan & Mundin were rising like a rocket and plenty of shrewd operators were trying to hitch a ride.

At last he got the nod from the receptionist. A hard-faced young Ay-rab with a badge that said *Guide* took him in tow.

Ryan & Mundin operated the damnedest law offices that Dworcas, in a full life, had ever seen. Law offices...complete with such eccentricities as chemistry labs and kitchens, living quarters and a TV studio, rooms locked off from his view, and open rooms that he could make no sense of.

DWORCAS said tentatively, "You must be proud to be working for Mr. Mundin. Of course you know his record with our party in the 27th—right down the line for Arab rights."

"That's nice," the Ay-rab said. "Right in here, mister." He guided Dworcas into a bay. It lit up with a shimmering violet light; the Ay-rab scanned a fluoroscope screen. "You're clean. In that door."

"You searched me!" Dworcas gasped. "Me! Mr. Mundin's oldest friend!"

"That's nice," the Ay-rab said. "In that door."

Dworcas went through the door.

"Hello, Del." Mundin was abstractedly checking off items on a list.

He said, "Excuse me," and picked up an interoffice phone. Five minutes later, he put it down, glanced at Dworcas, and turned to another list.

Dworcas, in cello tones, said, "Charles..."

Mundin looked at him with annoyance on his face. "Well?"

Dworcas waved a finger at him, smiling. "Charlie, you're not treating me right. You really aren't."

"Look, Del, business has picked up," said Mundin tiredly. "I'm busy. What do you want?"

"Nice office you've got. G-M-L fix it for you?"

"What do you think?"

Dworcas retained his smile. "Remember who got you in with G-M-L?"

"You've got a point," Mundin conceded unwillingly. "It isn't going to do you much good, though. I haven't got time for favors. Some other time, I'll listen closer."

"I want you to listen now, Charlie. I want you to reconsider on the race."

Mundin stared. "Run for the *Council?*"

"I know it sounds like small potatoes. But it can lead to big ones, Charlie. You can do it. And what about us? You owe me— the Party—all of us something for putting you on to the Lavins. Is this the time to let us down? I'm not too proud to beg if I have to. Stick with the Party, boy! We can make a real race of it. Media space and time—rallies—literature—sound trucks—street meetings—we're in the running again, boy!"

"Sorry, Del," Mundin said patiently.

"Charlie!"

Mundin looked exasperated. "Del, you old crook, just what are you up to now? Suppose I did sink some time and some dough into the election—which I won't. But suppose I did. You'd be in serious trouble if we won, Del. This is the year when the Regulars take a fall in the Council and the Reforms take a fall in the Statewide. What are you going to do, break the agreement?"

THE politician leaned forward, his face completely changed. "I underestimated you, Charlie. I'll tell you the God's truth. No, normally I wouldn't break the agreement; I'd be crazy. But something's on the fire. I never miss on something like this. I feel it through the soles of my feet."

He had Mundin's full attention now. "What do you feel?"

Dworcas shrugged. "Little things. Jimmy Lyons, for instance. Remember him—the captain's man at the precinct?"

"Sure."

"He isn't any more. Captain Kowalik transferred him out to Belly Rave. Why? I don't know why, Charlie. Jimmy had it coming to him, sure. But why did it happen? And what's happening to Kowalik? He's losing weight. He can't sleep nights. I asked him why and he wouldn't tell me. So I asked somebody else and I found out. Kowalik's trouble is that Commissioner Sabbatino doesn't talk to him any more."

"And what's the matter with Sabbatino?" Mundin was playing with a pencil.

"Don't kid me, Charlie. Sabbatino's trouble is a man named Wheeler, who had a long, long talk with him one day. I don't know what about. But I know Wheeler works for Hubble and Hubble is one of your clients."

Mundin put the pencil down. "So what else is new?" he asked.

"Don't joke, Charlie. What about the Ay-rabs? There's a crazy rumor they're all going to be moved into G-M-L Homes. The old folks don't like the idea. Some of the young folks do, so there are family fights. A dozen riot calls a day in the 27th. So I asked my brother Arnie, the engineer with G-M-L. You met him, you know what a fathead he is. But even he feels something in his organization. What *do* we feel, Charlie?"

A secretary person—with a start, Dworcas recognized his brother's friend, Bligh—put his head in the door. "Excuse me, Mr. Mundin, but they phoned from the landing stage that they're holding the D.C. 'copter for you."

Mundin nodded. "Look, thank them, Norvie, and ask them if they can give me five more minutes. I'll be free shortly." He glanced at Del Dworcas.

Dworcas said, "You're busy, Charlie. I'll see you some other time. I just want you to remember that I'm leveling with you."

"Good-by, Del," Mundin said cordially.

Then to Bligh, after Dworcas was gone, he said, "Thanks, Norvie. You were very smooth. Let's walk over to Mr. Ryan's office."

Bligh said, "We can't stay too long. The 'copter really does leave in twenty minutes."

RYAN, as usual, was snoozing with great dignity at his desk. He looked good, considering. His yen pox pills were rationed to him these days and he accepted it with good grace. His confusing explanation was, "As long as you *know* you can get your hands on them, you can say 'no' most of the time. It's when you can't possibly get them that you've *got* to have them." As a consequence, his very able brain had cleared and he was able to work for as much as an intensive hour at a stretch. He had evolved personally most of the 78 basic steps of tackling G-M-L.

Mundin reported Del's conversation carefully. In effect, it was that steps one through twenty-four were clicking nicely.

"A very pleasant miasma of doubt and confusion," Ryan declared. "I am gratified, Charles. There is no public-opinion poll as sensitive as the judgment of a professional politician—but we will, of course, continue with the polling as a matter of course. You have reason to be proud."

"Have I?" Mundin asked glumly. "Spreading doubt and confusion? Knifings every night in the 27th ward?" He felt instant regret as the old man's face drooped. "Excuse me, Mr. Ryan. Perhaps I've been working too hard."

Ryan said slowly, "Yes, at the wrong things. You remember the state I was in when we first met?"

Mundin did. The old man had been disheveled, very sick with withdrawal symptoms, in a smoke-filled Belly Rave slum.

"It was partly Green, Charlesworth that brought me to that sorry state. Partly Green, Charlesworth and partly conscience. Don't strain yours too far, Charles."

Mundin found himself engaged in an elaborate justification of the role he was playing, explaining to the gently smiling, nodding old man that of course there was a good end, in sight, that he wouldn't be touching the thing if it were just for money, that they were out to end the contract-rental system in G-M-L.

Bligh touched his elbow and muttered, "I think Mr. Ryan is asleep again." He was. "And we really ought to head for the 'copter deck now."

They did, and took their seats in the big Washington-bound craft. Mundin said fretfully, "We ought to have a couple of executive ships of our own. There's going to be more and more ground to cover. Put somebody on it, will you, Norvie?"

Bligh made a note.

Mundin asked, "When do you get in touch with Del's brother? We can't stall on it any longer. We've got to have those serial numbers or today's work—and the whole buildup to it—is wasted."

"Tomorrow all right?" Bligh inquired.

"Fine, fine."

HE took a briefcase from Bligh, shuffled through reports he ought to read, memoranda he ought to sign, notes he ought to expand. He irritably stuffed them back into the case.

Incredibly, Bligh said to him, "Conscience, Charles," and winked.

"You don't know what it's like, Norvie! You don't have the responsibility, so don't try to kid me out of it. Let's just talk; I don't have to be a criminal again until we walk in on the museum. How've things been with you?"

Bligh considered. "Well," he said, "Virginia's pregnant."

Mundin was genuinely shocked. "Norvie, I *am* sorry! I hope you're not going to do anything foolish—"

Bligh grinned. "The kid's mine. First thing I did was drag her to an immunochemist and get that settled. How's *your* girl?"

"Huh?"

"Norma Lavin."

"You're dead wrong there. We can't stand each other. And on my side, there's full justification."

"Sure," said Bligh soothingly. "Say, can we boost the allowance for the Wabbits? Lana was hinting."

"Why not? But do you think it's doing any good? A bunch of kids, after all. I don't think the rumors they spread ever get over to grownups."

"We can test easily enough. Launch one through the Wabbits alone. See how it compares in the polling."

"Okay, Norvie, have it done. No raise for the Wabbits until then, though. How's your foster daughter, by the way?"

"I'm almost proud of her. Came home five days running, beaten to a pulp. Sixth day, not a mark! She's a Burrow Leader in the Wabbits now. And she closes her mouth when she chews and calls me 'sir.' Why, I practically *like* the little witch!"

Mundin felt a sudden flash of insight. "That's why you're still living in Belly Rave, isn't it?"

Bligh got defensive. "Maybe that's part of it. But there's something to be said for Belly Rave. When you can install a water tank and a generating system and fix your place up—it's kind of lively." His voice rang with civic pride. "In our block, we've organized a real volunteer police force, not one of those shakedown squads, and there's talk in the blocks around us of doing the same."

Mundin said, "One day, who knows? Norvell Bligh, first mayor of New Belly Rave!"

The little man was suddenly gray; he fiddled with the earpiece of his hearing aid. "Make it a joke if you want to," he said, hurt. "The fact is they like me. I'm doing something for them—in a small way at first—and something has got to be done for these millions of outcasts. *From the inside*, I'm a funny-looking little man and I'm deaf and you automatically thought what you did when I said Virginia was pregnant. So what are you doing for Belly Rave, big man?"

"Norvie, I'm sorry! I didn't dream you were that serious about it—"

"Doesn't matter. Here's Washington."

THE Museum of the National Association of the Builders of the American Dream had once been a proud idea, built with the contributions of businessmen and schoolchildren. But the American Dream was mere history in this G-M-L era, like Pax Romana or Brittania's rule of the waves—words that had meaning only for the dead. The Museum remained, as the Pyramids had, but with the difference that the Pyramids needed no maintenance or staff. Of all this Mundin was reminded when he entered the shabby building and found his way to the anteroom of the director's office.

The withered secretary said to the gentlemen from New York, "Dr. Proctor is a *very* busy man. You must write or telephone for an appointment."

Mundin said gently, "Please tell the director that it is in connection with a rather substantial bequest. If it isn't convenient for him to see us now, we'll be glad to come back at some other time—although we don't expect to be in the city long..."

The director came flying out of his office, beaming.

The attorney introduced himself.

"Yes, indeed, Mr. Munsen! Even here, even in our remote and dedicated corner of the world, we have heard of your firm. Might one ask the name of—"

"Sorry."

"Oh, I quite understand, Mr. Munchkin! And the—ah—amount?"

"Flexible," Mundin said firmly. "My client has commissioned me to inspect the Museum and report to him on which departments seem most deserving of additional support."

"Ah! Pray allow me to guide you, sir. Just through here is the Collection of—"

Mundin said blandly, "I think we would prefer to see the Hall of Basics first."

Dr. Proctor very nearly frowned. At the last minute, he changed and merely looked confidential. "For the general public," he said, nudging Mundin. "Gimmicks and gadgets. Not *important,* though perhaps of some limited interest to the engineer, the sociologist, that sort of person. Now our collection of Coelenterates, just through—"

"The Hall of Basics, please?"

"Mr. Monkton! A tourist trap, I assure you. On the other hand, the Coelenterata—which happen to be my specialty, I might add—"

Mundin said sadly, "Norvell, I'm afraid Dr. Proctor isn't really interested in our client's bequest."

"Too bad," Bligh said. "Well, luckily the 'copter's waiting."

DR. Proctor sputtered and led them to the Hall of Basics. They gravely studied the spinning jenny, the sewing machine, the telegraph, the telephone, the airplane, the Model T, the atomic pile.

They stopped before the G-M-L bubble house, beaming approvingly—except for Dr. Proctor. A tourist family of five was hogging the descriptive plaque. It was a minute or so before they could get close enough to read it.

No. 342371

THE FIRST G-M-L HOME

Donated by Mr. Hamilton Moffatt

"Father of the Bubble House"

This G-M-L Home, moved to the Museum from its original site in Coshocton, Ohio, was fabricated in the plastics factory of Donald Lavin. Electrical circuitry and mechanisms were designed and installed by Bernard Gorman. It has stood for more than five decades without a scar or a malfunction, Chemists and engineers estimate that, without any sort of maintenance, it will last at least 1,000 more years, standing virtually forever as a tribute to the immortal genius of

MR. HAMILTON MOFFATT

"Do tell," murmured the attorney. The director glumly started to lead them through the bubble house.

"Hell with it," said Mundin. "Let's go back to your place."

In Dr. Proctor's private office, Mundin looked at the small, dusty bottle the director exhumed from an umbrella rack. He shuddered and said decisively, "No, nothing to drink, thanks. Dr. Proctor, I think I can definitely state that my client would be interested in donating twenty thousand dollars as a fund to be divided at your discretion between the Hall of Basics and the Coelenterata collection."

"Dear me!" Dr. Proctor leaned back in his chair, fondling the bottle, his face wreathed in smiles. "Dear me! Are you sure you wouldn't care to—just a very small—no? Do you know, perhaps I will, just to celebrate. A *very* wise decision, sir! It is, believe me, *most* unusual to find a layman who, like yourself, can at once perceive the ecological significance and *thrilling* morphology of the humble Coelenterate!" He tipped the bottle into a dusty water tumbler and raised it in a toast. "The Coelenterata!" he cried.

MUNDIN was fumbling in his briefcase. He produced a check, already made out, a typed document in duplicate, and a flat can that gurgled.

"Now," he said matter-of-factly, "pay close attention, Doctor. You, personally, are to dilute the contents of this can with one quart of ordinary tap water, fill an ordinary garden sprayer with the solution, and spray the G-M-L Home in the Hall of Basics with it, covering all plastic parts from the outside. It shouldn't take more than ten minutes, if you have a good sprayer. Naturally, you will make sure nobody sees you doing it. That should be easy enough, in your position, but make absolutely sure of it. And that will be that."

Dr. Proctor, eyes bulging, coughed an ounce of tinted grain neutral spirits over his desk. Choking and wheezing, he at last got out, "My dear sir! What on *earth* are you talking about? What is in that container? Why should I do any such preposterous thing?"

"I'll take your questions in order. I am talking about twenty thousand dollars. What is in that container is something worth twenty thousand dollars. You should do it because of twenty thousand dollars."

Dr. Proctor wiped his mouth with the back of his hand, almost speechless. "But—but if you assured me that the fluid would be entirely harmless—"

"I'll do no such thing. Where I come from, you can get away with quite a lot for twenty thousand dollars," Mundin smiled frostily. "Come now, Doctor. Think of twenty thousand dollars!

Think of the ecological significance and the thrilling morphology. And then sign this receipt—and *then* take the check."

Dr. Proctor looked at the check. "It's post-dated a month," he said tremulously.

Mundin shrugged and began to repack his briefcase. "Well, if you're going to *quibble*—"

Dr. Proctor snatched the check. He scribbled his name on the receipt and, with a quick, furtive movement, dropped the flat can of fluid into his desk.

In the return 'copter, Mundin and Bligh looked at each other. "He'll do it," Norvie Bligh said gravely.

"He will. And that means we've got to have the serial numbers from the G-M-L files fast. You'd better see your friend Arnie Dworcas tonight."

Bligh choked down a protest. This part was his job.

ARNIE Dworcas let him in, for he was old Norvell, the true friend, the shy acolyte. Sitting there with Arnie, listening to Arnie's explanations of world affairs, it seemed to Norvie that Belly Rave was a nightmare and Mundin a figure from a dream. Nothing had changed, nothing would ever change, as long as he could sit and drink Arnie's beer.

But there were changes...

Arnie drained his glass of beer, wiped his mouth and dialed another.

"No, Norvell," he said meditatively, "I wouldn't say that you have succeeded. Not as we Engineers understand success. To us Engineers, a mechanism—and all of us are mechanisms, I, you, everybody—a mechanism is a success when it is functioning at maximum efficiency. Frankly, in my little experiment of suggesting that you try Belly Rave, I was attempting to perform what we call 'destructive testing'—the only way in which maximum efficiency can be determined. But what happened? By pure fortuitousness, you made a connection and are now a really able man's secretary." He sipped his beer sorrowfully. "To use an analogy, it's as if my slipstick were to take credit for the computations I make on it."

"I'm sorry, Arnie," Norvell said. It was very difficult to decide whether he wanted to laugh in Arnie's face or take out some of those front teeth with a beer glass. "Mr. Mundin thinks a great deal of you and your brother, too, you know. You impressed him very much when you met him."

"Naturally. That's one of the things you'll have to learn. Like seeks like, in human relations as well as electrostatics."

"I thought in electrostatics like *repelled*—"

"There you go!" yelled Arnie violently. "The dogmatic, argumentative layman! It's people like you that—"

"I'm sorry, Arnie!"

"All *right*. Don't get so excited. Really able people never lose control of themselves, Norvell! That was a stupid thing for you to get all upset about."

"I'm sorry, Arnie. That's what I was telling Mr. Mundin."

Arnie, raising his glass irritatedly, stopped it in mid-air. He peered suspiciously at Norvie over the rim. "What were you telling Mr. Mundin?"

"Why, that you never lost control in an emergency. That you would be a damned good man to put in charge of—oh! I shouldn't have said anything!" Norvell covered his mouth with both hands.

Arnie Dworcas said sternly, "Norvell, stop stammering and come out with it! In charge of what?"

NORVIE, who had been fighting back a tendency to retch, removed his hands from his mouth. "Well—well, it isn't as if I couldn't trust you, Arnie. It's G-M-L."

"What *about* G-M-L?"

Norvie said rapidly, "It's too soon to say anything definite and, *please*, Arnie, don't let a word of it get out. But you've heard the rumors about G-M-L, naturally."

"Naturally!" Arnie said, though he frowned blankly.

"Mr. Mundin is associated with the—uh—the Coshocton bunch, Arnie. And he's looking around—quietly, you know—for key men to replace some of the old duffers. And I took the liberty of mentioning you to him, Arnie. The only thing is, Mr. Mundin doesn't know much about the technical end, you see, and he wasn't sure just how much experience you've had."

"My record is in the professional journals, Norvell. Not that I would feel free to discuss it in this informal manner in any case, of course."

"Oh, of course! But what Mr. Mundin asked me was just what G-M-L Homes models you had worked on—serial numbers and locations and so on. And I had to tell him that all that information was locked up and you couldn't possibly get your hands on it."

Arnie shook his head wonderingly. "Laymen," he said. "Norvell, there is no reason in the world why I can't get micro-films of all that information. It's only corporate fiddle-faddle that causes all the secrecy. We Engineers are accustomed to cutting through the red tape."

Norvell looked worshipful. "You mean you *can?*"

"I have already said so, haven't I? It's just a matter of going through the records and picking out the units I've worked on myself, then making microfilms—"

"Better microfilm *everything*, Arnie," Norvell suggested. "It'll help Mr. Mundin understand the Broad Picture."

Arnie shrugged humorously. "Why not?"

"Don't forget the serial numbers," Norvell added.

"Laymen," snorted Arnie Dworcas.

CHAPTER SEVENTEEN

QUITE by chance, the Big Seven were gathered in Ryan's office on the day it happened at the Museum of the National Association of the Builders of the American Dream.

It was an ill-planned meeting, having more than one purpose. At the top level, it was a pep session and information seminar. On a lower level, three teams of auditors, one each for Hubble, Coett and Nelson, were going over the books of Ryan & Mundin. Don Lavin was amiably present and Norma had started things off right when Hubble absent-mindedly attempted to guide her to a seat.

She snapped, "I do not impose on the biological fact that I am a woman and I don't expect anybody to impose on *me*. If Mr. Hubble can't keep his hands to himself, I expect him at least to leave me alone during working hours. After hours, I can manage to avoid him."

Bliss Hubble said with a straight face, "Sorry, Lavin. It won't happen again." To the rest, he said cheerfully, "Who'd like to take charge?"

It was Coett, of course. He benignly told Mundin, "We'll just ignore the audit boys outside, shall we? I'm sure their work will be purely routine. Now, among ourselves, how are we doing? I, for one, haven't been able to pick up as much floating G-M-L stock as I'd wish, nor have the prices been right so far."

"Same here," said Hubble.

"Ah—I agree," Nelson said.

Old man Ryan raised his hand. "Up to now, it's been rumors, gentlemen. Very shortly, *things* will begin to happen. I think you'll find some dumping of G-M-L will begin within, say, a week. And with proper management and some luck, there will be as pretty a panic as you could wish within a month thereafter. There won't be time for a rally. Our group, gentlemen, will make the next meeting with a clear majority."

Hubble said abruptly, "I can't get through to Green, Charlesworth." It was a challenge, flung at Coett. "The comptroller of my publishing outfit thought it would be a good idea to renew a mortgage they hold on the transmitter tower in Sullivan County. They said no, so he paid them off in cash from our contingency fund. I thought I'd better check; it looked like a new policy. But I can't get through. When they want to be remote—*you* know."

"I find that very interesting, Bliss," Nelson said. "Ah—I, too, have had occasion to make a routine inquiry regarding insurance policies. That was six weeks ago and as yet I've had no reply. "Green, Charlesworth sometimes appears to be dilatory, of course—a natural reflection of their deeply rooted conservatism."

"They're progressives," Hubble said scornfully.

"Middle-of-the-roaders," insisted Coett.

Hubble asked Coett directly, "Having any trouble, Harry? We've bared *our* bosoms."

"Nothing you could call trouble," Coett said. "Just that I'm not—getting through. Like you gentlemen. Oh, I'm doing business with them, but no real communication."

MUNDIN was inescapably reminded of Captain Kowalik, unnerved and jittery because Commissioner Sabbatino didn't *talk* to him any more. He asked bluntly, "Is this a bad situation?"

They smiled politely and told him not to worry; it wasn't his problem. Green, Charlesworth did nothing on the operating or manufacturing end. They were finance.

Hubble said, "Frankly, I don't know where they stand on this thing. It was my opinion that they wouldn't give a damn one way or the other. Nelson agreed with me and Harry thought they'd be all for us—not that they vote my G-M-L stock, but with their moral influence. Still, they're a funny outfit, so this lapse may not mean anything."

Mundin asked, "Want me to go calling on them? Level with them? Have it out? Meet whatever terms they may have?"

Four heads swiveled and four incredulous stares drilled him. Coett spoke for all when he said gently, "No."

"My guess is that they're onto us," Hubble elaborated, "that they know every move we make and just haven't committed themselves—yet."

Mundin looked at the three Titans in turn and asked wonderingly, "When you say 'they,' whom do you mean, exactly?"

A three-cornered wrangle developed while old man Ryan dozed off. Coett believed that Green, Charlesworth were essentially the top men in the Memphis crowd plus Organic Solvents and New England utilities. He himself was most of the Southwest crowd and practically all of Inorganic Chemicals.

Nelson, who was New England and Non-Ferrous Metals, believed that Green, Charlesworth were essentially California, coal-oil-steel and mass media.

Hubble, who was mass media and New York, said that couldn't be. Unless—with a hard look at Coett and Nelson—somebody was lying like hell. Green, Charlesworth, he thought, were essentially money.

On that, everybody agreed. Worriedly.

"Look," said Mundin. "I just, want to get this straight in my mind. Would we scuttle the whole project if Green, Charlesworth came out against it?"

When somebody tells you, "Say, I've heard a rumor that two and two make four; do you put any stock in that stuff?"—that's the kind of look Mundin got.

Coett said quietly. "Why, yes, Charles. We would."

Hubble's nervous voice cut in, "I don't believe that's going to happen, Charles. It's simply a matter of getting in touch with them. After all, we're taking a step forward and Green, Charlesworth have always been on the side of progress."

"Conservatism," said Nelson.

"Middle-of-the-roaders," Coett insisted.

That, clearly, was getting them nowhere.

ANNOYED, Mundin demanded, "But who *are* they? Where are they?"

Hubble said, "Their offices are in the Empire State Building—the entire building."

Mundin's eyebrows climbed. *"In New York?* I thought the place was condemned. And are there a real Green and a real Charlesworth?"

Hubble shook his head. "They're there, all right. As for a real Mr. Green and a real Mr. Charlesworth—the firm name is a couple of hundred years old, so I'm not sure. When you go there, you never see anyone important. Clerks, junior executives, department heads. You do business with them and there are long waits—weeks, sometimes—while they're 'deciding policy questions.' I suppose that means while they're getting their instructions. Well, now you know as much about Green, Charlesworth as anybody else. Just remember, if they turn up anywhere, or you encounter anything—well, anomalous that makes you *suspect* they're turning up, blow the whistle. We'll handle it."

"But there won't be any trouble," Coett said hopefully, and Nelson nervously agreed.

Norvell Bligh popped in. "It happened!" he yelped, and dived for the television screen. "We had a guy monitoring and it just—"

"At first blamed on vibration," roared a newscaster before Norvie got the sound where he wanted it. "Experts from G-M-L, however, said that at first glance this appears unlikely. A team of G-M-L engineers is being dispatched to Washington to study the wreckage. We bring you now a picture from our library of the first bubble house. As it was—"

The slide flashed on; there stood G-M-L Unit One, dwarfed by the Hall of Basics.

"—and as it is."

A live shot this time: Same site, same hall—but instead of the gleaming bubble house, a tangle of rubbish, with antlike uniformed men crawling about the wreckage.

NORMA Lavin blubbered, "Daddy's first house!" and burst into tears. The others gave her swift, incredulous looks and went right back to staring in fascination and fear at the screen.

"Our Washington editor now brings you Dr. Henry Proctor, Director of the Museum. Dr. Proctor?" The rabbit face flashed on, squirming, scared.

"Dr. Proctor," asked the mellow tones, "what, in your opinion, might be the cause of the collapse?"

"I really—I really have no opinion. I'm—uh—completely in the—uh—dark. It's a puzzle to me. I'm afraid I can't—ah—be of the slightest—I have no opinion. Really."

"Thank you, Dr. Proctor!"

To Mundin, rapt on the screen, it seemed that all was lost; any fool could read guilt, guilt, guilt plastered on the director's quivering face and at once infer that Proctor had sprayed the bubble house with a solvent supplied by someone else; and it would be only moments until "someone else" was identified as Charles Mundin. But the newscaster was babbling on. The rabbit face flickered off the screen.

The newscaster said: "Ah, I have a statement just handed to me from G-M-L Homes. Mr. Haskell Arnold, Chairman of the Board of G-M-L Homes, announced today that the engineering staff of the firm has reached tentative conclusions regarding the partial malfunction—"

Even the newscaster stumbled over that. The listening men, recalling the pile of rubble, roared and slapped their knees in a burst of released tension.

"The—uh—partial malfunction of G-M-L Unit One. They state that highly abnormal conditions of vibration and chemical environment present in the Museum are obviously to blame. Mr. Arnold said, and I quote, 'There is no possibility whatsoever that this will happen again.' End of quote." The announcer smiled and discarded a sheet from the papers in his hand. Now chummy, he went on: "Well, ladies and gentlemen, I'm certainly glad to hear that and so, I'm sure, are all of you who also live in bubble houses.

"And now, for you sports fans, the morning line on Grosse Point Field Day. It's going to be a bang-up show produced by the veteran impresario Jim 'Blood and Guts' Hanrahan. Plenty of solid, traditional entertainment. First spectacle—"

"Turn that thing off," someone ordered Norvell. Wistfully, he did—straining to catch the last words—remembering.

Harry Coett broke the silence brutally. "Well, that's that. We're committed. Is everybody here as terrified as I am?"

THAT night, a 'copter droned west from New York, Norvie at the stick and Mundin glumly toying with a lever that would push a bowden wire that would open the cock of a pressurized belly tank full of golden fluid.

Norvie asked, "Did I tell you it's a boy? Looked through the fetuscope myself. The doctor said it's the finest forty-day embryo he's seen in twenty years of practice. I tell you, that kid's going to have every advantage I never—"

"Swell, Norvie," Mundin said with a snap in his voice.

Norvie shut up.

Mundin turned on a small pocket reader and slipped microfilm into it. Old records copied on the sneak by Norvie's friend Arnie Dworcas, brought to him proudly and furtively. Much guff about "We Engineers, Mr. Mundin" and "You won't forget this, I hope, Mr. Mundin. As We Engineers say, you brace my buttress and I'll brace yours, hah-hah-hah!"

So the records said G-M-L No. 2 was the northwest corner of the Coshocton Bubble City; proceed along the western side of the polygon, then south...

And where the golden drops rained down, Bubble House No. 2, then No. 3, then No. 4 through No. 280 would one by one crumble, leaving families naked to the foundry fumes and weather. And throughout the country, hysteria would be unleashed. G-M-L lessees would frantically hunt for the serial plate of their houses, scribble calculations, wildly phone their friends. There would be a terrific run on sporting goods stores; the morning after the night Coshocton began to crumble, not a sleeping bag or tent would be left on their shelves.

But that was all right. Hubble, Coett and Nelson had quietly bought control of the leading sporting goods companies. The rise in their stocks would constitute a nice little by-product.

Charles Mundin, attorney, checked the tanks for the dozenth time and Norvell Bligh looked rigidly at the instruments that were set on Coshocton.

CHAPTER EIGHTEEN

THE panic was as pretty as could be desired. Probably not one man-hour of work was done for days by anybody who occupied a bubble house. Hubble, Coett and Nelson flooded the New York Parimutuel Stock Exchange with agents. A satisfactory trickle of dumped G-M-L stock began to run into their portfolios, against bidding by scattered, unready, disorganized agents for the Arnold group that controlled the G-M-L Board.

Clearly, it was time for another session on the neutral ground of Ryan & Mundin, Attorneys at Law.

"Progress, gentlemen," Coett said happily after they had pooled information. "We are within sight of fifty-one percent ownership!"

Norma demanded, "Is there going to be any more wrecking?"

Nelson sniffed. "If the Arnold group firms up within, say, two days, they'll be able to hold against us. In that case, we'll have to hit them with something new."

"No wrecking," Norma said hoarsely.

"You will kindly leave such decisions to us. If we must wreck, we will."

"And so will I!" She picked a vase from Ryan's desk and threw it at Nelson. Her aim was true, but he ducked fast.

The vase exploded with an electric snarl of blue light that charred the wall. Norma's look of utter stupefaction matched any in the room. The silence lasted almost half a minute.

"Call somebody in," Coett said at last, his eyes not leaving the shards on the floor that still smoked.

Mundin phoned, his voice shaky, for the firm's top chemist.

"Not my baby," the chemist said after peering at the fragments. "Get Joe Panelli, Mr. Mundin. It seems to be electrical, whatever it is."

Panelli, communications engineer, pronounced the intact vase to have been a wonderfully clever communicator—whether one-way or two-way, he could not say yet. The crackle in its glaze had been metallic—the vase was small, but the crackle was fine—perhaps a hundred meters of antenna. There were relics of transistors, fused little lumps buried in the clay. The four medallions and the band about the shoulder of the vase might contain Chinese characters or might not. To him, the characters looked like unfamiliar printed circuits. The bell mouth of the jar suggested a non-directional mike and, yes, it could be a loud-speaker, too.

MUNDIN asked urgently, "Can you find out if there are any more of these things around?"

"Oh, sure, Mr. Mundin," said Panelli. "They put out a signal, so we just scan the bands."

"Can you do that without whoever is listening in knowing about it?" Coett insisted.

"Maybe yes, maybe no. My guess is no. Whoever designed this could—maybe would—design the receiving equipment to indicate a drop in energy received when we put a tap on."

"Then don't do it," Coett said. Panelli gave him a rebellious look.

Mundin said, "Just hold everything, Joe. I'll let you know."

There was another long silence. Hubble broke it with, "Scratch seven hundred and fifty thousand dollars, gentlemen."

"It's an idea," Coett said. He took out his fountain pen, looked wonderingly at it and put it back in his pocket. He sighed.

Old man Ryan put his face in his hands and groaned. Mundin had a fair idea of what was going through his mind. Back to Belly Rave and despair. And three days from the top.

Mundin said loudly, "Speaking for my clients, the Lavins, I don't see how I can conscientiously let you people back out of the agreement. Nor do I see any reason why you should. Somebody planted a microphone on us—so what? It happens every day."

"Quite a mike," Hubble commented. He alone of the three moneymen seemed to be unscared. Mundin decided to concentrate on him.

"Why the panic, Bliss? What's wrong with these two?"

"If you think I'm going to say one more word in your offices, Charles, you're crazy. There may be more of those things around. Until this is wrapped up, I think it would be wisest to meet in Turkish baths. I don't see how Lavin could get in on such a conference, but perhaps that's best. The fewer who know, the safer the secret."

Mundin exploded, "Damn it, this is crazy! So there's somebody spying on us. What of it? There're just people. They've got nothing but money. We're people, too, and we've also got money—plenty of it. All right, maybe they have more, but that doesn't make them God almighty. We can lick them if we have to!"

He stopped. Hubble, Coett and Nelson were wincing at every word.

Coett said faintly, "Don't talk any more, Charles. You've said too much. Some interests—well, some people would call them relentless. Not that I'm agreeing for a minute." His eyes were darting around the room.

NORMA Lavin, pale and quivering, stood up. "My father invented the bubble house for—" She began tremblingly, then caught herself. "No! Leaving Daddy out of this, one-quarter of G-M-L Homes belongs to Don and myself. It's ours, understand? *Ours!* Not yours or whoever's scaring the wits out of you. It isn't just money, you know. We got along fine without any. We can do it again. It's *people*. It's making life worth living for the poor slobs who buy their bubble houses with their life's blood! Slavery's against the law. G-M-L's been breaking the law—but *we* are taking over—and *we* are going to stop slavery. You hear me?"

They heard her—and seven people were shouting at once, even old Ryan. "—no better than a Democrat, young lady!" Nelson was howling. And "for God's sake, let her talk!" screamed Mundin. And Coett was spouting endless shushes, with gestures patting the air.

And the door opened. Mishal, the Ay-rab boy, stared in, terror on his face.

"Visitor," he told them, and disappeared.

"Oh, hell," Mundin said in the sudden silence, starting toward the door. "I told those idiots—oh, it's you." He looked irritatedly at the figure of William Choate IV, now entering. "Hello, Willie. Look, I'm awfully busy right now…"

Willie Choate's lower lip was trembling. "Hello, old man," he said dismally. "I have a—message for you."

"Later, Willie, please."

Willie stood his ground. "Now."

He handed Mundin a square white envelope. Mundin, torn between annoyance and hysteria, opened it and glanced absently at the little white card inside.

Then he glanced at it again.

Then he stared at it until Coett came to life and leaped forward to take it out of his hand. It said in crabbed handwriting:

Green, Charlesworth request the appearance of Mr. Charles Mundin and Miss Norma Lavin when convenient.

IT was a long ride. Willie Choate apologetically took out a magazine as soon as they settled down in the car. "You know what Great-great-granddaddy Rufus said, Charles—'Happy is he who has laid up in his youth, and held fast in all fortune, a genuine and passionate love for reading.' I always like to—"

"Sure, Willie," said Mundin absently. "Look, what's all this?"

"Of course, he wasn't my real Great-great-granddaddy. Grandpap just kind of took that name when he bought into the firm. It's just a way of—"

"Willie, *please.* Remember how it was in law school, the way I helped you pass the exams and all?"

Willie seemed about to cry.

"Charles, what can I say?"

"You can tell me what this is all about!"

Willie looked at Mundin. Then he looked all around him, at glowering Norma, at the fittings of the car. Then he looked at Mundin again. The implication was unmistakable.

"At least tell me what your connection is," Mundin begged.

"*Gee*, Charles!" But the answer to that one, at least, was plain, written in those soft cow eyes, spelled out in that trembling lip. Willie was what God had made him to be—an errand boy—and doubtless knew little more than Mundin about what, why or wherefore.

Mundin gave up and let Willie read his magazine, while he stared morosely at the crumbled city they were driving through. Norma's hand, startlingly, sought his for a moment, then jerked away.

The building *smelled* old. They stepped into a creaking elevator and slowly went up fifty flights. A long walk and then another elevator, even smaller, even creakier.

Then a small room with a hard bench. Willie left them there; all he said was, "See you."

Then—waiting. An hour, several hours. Norma talked about her childhood, her dedicated father, his miserable fate, her bitter disappointment that Don would not grow up to the responsibility of being that great thing, a Lavin. It was scared, compulsive babbling. Something in the air militated against logic and sense. Crawly fingers—

At last she fell silent, her eyes jerking about the room.

Mundin thought he was going to crack apart and start yelling.

Then he realized that that was what Green, Charlesworth wanted him to think, and got a grip on himself.

And, by and by, a small, quiet man came and led them into another room.

There was no place to sit and no place to hang their coats. Mundin draped his over his arm and stood staring back into the unblinking eyes of the man seated at the desk. He was an imposing figure of a man, lean-featured, dark-haired, temples shot with silver. He leaned forward, comfortably appraising. His chin was in one cupped hand, the fingers covering his lips, his eyes following

Mundin. His chest rhythmically rose and fell; otherwise, he was stock-still.

Mundin cleared his throat. "Mr.—ah—Green?"

THE man said emotionlessly, "We despise you, Mr. Mundin and Miss Lavin. We are going to destroy you."

Mundin cried, "Why?"

"You are Rocking the Boat," the man said through his fingers, the piercing eyes locked with Mundin's own.

Mundin cleared his throat. "Look, Mr. Green—you *are* Mr. Green?"

"You are Our Enemy, Mundin."

"Now wait a minute!" Mundin took a deep breath. *Please!* he silently begged his adrenal gland. *Gently!* he ordered the pounding sensation in his skull. He said temperately, "I'm sure we can get together, Mr.—sir. After all, we're not greedy."

The figure said steadily, "People like you would doom Civilization As We Know It if we let them. We do not intend to."

Mundin swept his eyes hopelessly around the room. This man was obviously mad; someone else, anyone else— But there was no one. Barring the desk and the man, there was nothing in the room but a pair of milky glass cabinets and Mundin and Norma.

He said, "Look, did you call us down here just to insult us?"

"You two put your Fingers in the Buzz Saw. They will be Lopped Off."

"Insane," Norma muttered faintly.

"Dammit!" Mundin yelled. He hurled his coat violently to the floor, but it did nothing to calm him. "If you're crazy, say so and let me get out of here! I never came across such blithering idiocy in my life!"

He stopped in the middle of a beginning tirade; stopped short.

The man wasn't looking at him any more. The same unblinking and unwavering gaze that had been on Mundin was now piercingly directed at the coat on the floor.

To the coat, the motionless man said, "We brought you two here to see Infamy with Our Own Eyes. Now we have seen it and we will Blot It Out." And then startlingly, shrilly, "Hee!"

Mundin swallowed and stepped gingerly forward. Three paces and he was at the desk, leaning over, looking at what should be the neatly tailored, trousers of the man's modest suit.

The personnel of Green, Charlesworth were not wearing trousers this year. The personnel of Green, Charlesworth were wearing bronze pedestals with thick black cables snaking out of them, and brass nameplates that read:

SLEEPLESS RECEPTIONIST
115 Volt A.C. Only

"Hee!" shrilled the motionless lips, just by Mundin's ear. "That's far enough, Mundin. You were right, I suppose, Mrs. Green."

MUNDIN leaped back as though the 115 volts of A.C. had passed through his tonsils. A flicker of light caught his eye; the two milky glass cabinets had lighted up. He looked, peripherally aware that Norma had toppled in a faint beside him.

He wished he hadn't looked.

The contents of the cabinets were Green and Charlesworth.

Green, an incredibly, impossibly ancient dumpy-looking, hairless female. Charlesworth, an incredible, impossibly ancient string-bean-looking, hairless male.

Mercifully, the lights flickered out.

Another voice said, but from the same motionless lips, "Can we kill them, Mr. Charlesworth?"

"I think not, Mrs. Green," the Sleepless Receptionist answered itself in the first voice.

Mundin said forcefully, "Now wait a minute." It was pure reflex. He came to the end of the sentence and stopped.

The female voice said sadly, "Perhaps they will commit suicide, Mr. Charlesworth. Tell him what he is Up Against."

"He knows what he is Up Against, Mrs. Green. Don't you, Mundin?"

Mundin nodded. He was obsessed by the Sleepless Receptionist's eyes, now piercingly aimed at him again—attracted, perhaps, by the movement.

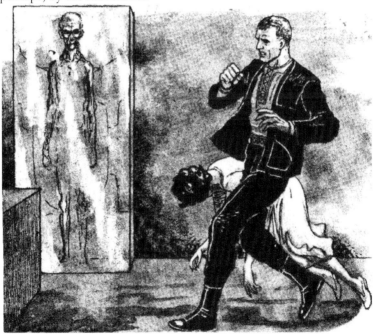

"Tell him!" shrieked Mrs. Green. "Tell him about that *boy*. Tell him what we'll do to him!"

"A Child of Evil," the male voice said mechanically. "He wants to take G-M-L away from us."

Mundin was galvanized. "Not you! Just Arnold and his crowd!"

"Are Our Fingers Us?" the female voice demanded. "Are Our Arms and Legs Us? Arnold is Us!"

The male voice piped, "The girl, Mrs. Green. The *girl!*"

"Painted Courtesan," observed the female voice. "She wants to free the slaves, she says. She talks about Mr. Lincoln!

"But you know we fixed Mr. Lincoln's Wagon, Mr. Charlesworth," chortled the female voice.

"We did, Mrs. Green. And we will fix her Wagon, too."

Mundin, thinking dazedly that he should have been more careful where he put Ryan's yen pox—it was stupid of him to get it mixed up with his vitamin pills—said feebly, "Are you *that* old?"

"Are we that old, Mrs. Green?" asked the male voice.

"Are we!" shrilled the female.

"Tell him! Tell him about the boy!"

"Perhaps not now, Mrs. Green. Perhaps later. When we have softened them up. You two may go now."

Mundin automatically put on his coat and lifted Norma to his shoulder. He turned dazedly to the door. Halfway, he stopped, staring at the milky glass. Glass, he thought. Glass and quivering, moving corpses inside that a breath of air might—

"Try it, Mundin," challenged the voice. "We wanted to see if you would."

Mundin decided against it.

"Too bad," said the voice of Charlesworth. "We hate you, Mundin. You said we were not God Almighty."

"Atheist!" hissed the voice of Mrs. Green.

CHAPTER NINETEEN

BACK in Ryan's office, Mundin said, lying, "It wasn't so bad."

Ryan had taken advantage of their absence to get coked to the eyebrows. He said dreamily, "Think of them, hundreds of years old. You know what H.G. Wells said? 'A frightful queerness is coming into life.' Nothing went right, no matter what you did. You know what Jonathan Swift called Green, Charlesworth? Struldbrugs. Those were the only people were on to them. Gulliver said they had a law that no Struldbrug could keep his money after he was a hundred. Think of them, hundreds of years old, hundreds and hundreds and hun—"

Don Lavin touched his shoulder and he stopped.

Harry Coett. Smiling affably at his own thumbnail, said gently, "How about a drink?"

Mundin poured it for him, pretending not to notice that the big man was quite soaked with sweat there in the air-conditioned room.

"We must proceed to an orderly liquidation," Nelson said, his eyes jumping from one corner to another. "Naturally, any further action along our previous lines is out of the question."

Norma appeared at the door carrying a projector. Mundin had left her in her office under the care of the company nurse.

"Is it all settled by now?" she asked grimly.

"Everybody seems to be in agreement." Mundin felt weighed down by a tremendous apathy. Four men who aggregated eight times his age, thirty times his business experience—you couldn't buck all that.

Norma opened the projector and swept papers from Ryan's desk.

"I just wanted to show you," she said. "These are the family's home movies. It's kept me going through some hard times…" She dimmed the lights and turned on the projector.

"Here's Father," she said. "In the plant."

Somebody had sneaked up with a camera, catching Lavin unaware. The "plant" looked very much like a cinder-block barn, with benches and presses. Three people working on a big bread-board electrical layout, backs to camera.

Tired, authoritative voice: "You don't seem to get the idea, Bernie. I don't just want a door. The Egyptians had doors. I don't just want a *good* door. Some doors have been pretty good in the past five thousand years. I want a *perfect* door. Hell, I guess my mistake is *calling* it a door. That creates a picture in your mind.

Now let's scrap all this junk of yours and think about entering-and-leaving devices."

An agonized protest: "Mr. Lavin, twenty-six months of work!"

LAVIN lost his temper. "Twenty-six months of work, Gorman, versus five thousand years of drafts, squeaks, sticks, slams, irritation, muscle-strain, lost keys, burglary, scuffed thresholds, scarred panels, that damned ridiculous disproportionate strain on the upper hinge that *guarantees* malfunction, the stupidity of making doors too small for furniture and too large for people! Don't come whining to me about your lousy twenty-six months of pooping around! *Think* about it, Gorman! Use your head for a change! We're trying to bring some ease and graciousness into life for everybody! Let's *do* something for people instead of whimpering about twenty-six months—"

The speaker turned, then grinned startledly at whoever the cameraman was, and waved. Gorman looked sulky and defensive as the clip ran through. It was, Mundin uneasily realized, a foretaste of his eventual suicide because of frustration and defeat.

Norma said, hushed, "A quick one of our living quarters." It was a posed shot of Lavin and his wife. The background was something that looked like a chicken coop, but was more likely a variety of pre-fab dwelling. Beaverboard walls insecurely held together by battens, a smoky oil heater, a grotesque chrome-and-formica dinette set ferociously trying to elbow the two Lavins out of the picture altogether. Mr. Lavin was smiling absently. His wife looked sour and darted uncertain looks at the smoking heater. Obviously she couldn't wait to get at it.

"The trade show," Norma said. "The awards banquet."

It was the speakers table of any grand ballroom of any downtown hotel. The debris of squab with wild rice, cups of deathly black coffee and melting, multicolored ice cream being removed by sullen banquet waiters. A toastmaster pinged on his water glass as he rose and cleared his throat into the mikes.

"Members and guests," he said fruitily, "of the Delivered Dwelling Industrial Association. It is altogether fitting and proper tonight that we have gathered to do honor to a new star in the constellation of Delivered Dwelling manufacturers. Surely, as we review the meteoric rise of Donald Lavin, there can be none here who doubts that he is a man who does credit to the industry, a competitor who fights hard and clean, a designer of striking originality and a businessman whose acumen points the way toward an entirely new concept of Delivered Dwelling finance and underwriting. Members and guests, it gives me great pleasure to present to Mr. Donald Lavin of Coshocton, Ohio, this plaque designating him the Delivered Dwelling Manufacturer of the Year!"

APPLAUSE; passing the plaque; still photographers crowding in for shots. Lavin rising. To his left, a man like an undernourished shoat—Gorman. To his right, a gaunt man who looked like an exceptionally lean gray rat—Moffatt.

Lavin fumbled the plaque for a moment and then uncertainly put it down.

He said, "Thanks. Maybe I'm accepting this thing under false pretenses—I know the title of my speech is supposed to be 'New Approaches to the Delivered Dwelling,' but first I'd like to give some credit where credit's due and to make a correction in the introductory remarks. To my left is sitting Mr. Bernard Gorman, who deserves as much credit as I for the design of the Lavin House. I may be the dynamo some people have called me, but Bernie's the detail man, the best I ever knew, and I'm not going to let him get away without taking a bow."

Gorman rose and bobbed, flushing.

"Reference was also made to me as a businessman. I decline the honor. The only businessman on our premises is our good treasurer and comptroller, Hamilton Moffatt, without whose common sense and fiscal knowhow, my company would never have got off the ground."

The thin gray rat took a precise little bow, unasked.

"And I should say that Mr. Walsh's introductory remarks about our novel policy of financing and underwriting by industrial purchase and subsequent leasing are Mr. Moffatt's idea and a darned good one, too, for a young company in need of working capital—but an idea that I hope we'll be in a position to abandon shortly.

"And now to my main heading. There's no need for me to be modest, is there? You all know the Lavin House is good or you wouldn't have given me that plaque. How did it get that way? Partly because technology is at last developed to the point where good housing is possible; partly because I realized long ago that human stupidity is nowhere so marked and so costly as in housing.

"I sat up one day in my bedroom. The floor was wooden. The walls were paint over paper, over plaster, over lath, over two-by-fours. The roof was gabled. The windows were steel-casement. The doors were hinged slabs. The stairs were stairs—and I can say nothing worse of them. The people in that house were hot in the summer, cold in the winter, assailed by pollen and every passing street noise—oh, yes, the house was, of course, equipped with central air-conditioning. The place was filthy, requiring a battery of cleaning machinery to be hauled about weekly or oftener."

LAVIN paused. "The house was a weird combination of the flexible and the rigid, which meant that there were cracks. It was a Tinker Toy structure—lots of little bits fastened to other little bits with little fastening devices, which meant that little bits were continually coming loose and falling off and having to be replaced. That house fought its occupants like a tiger—or I should say like a plague of ants. It nibbled away at its occupants' leisure and serenity instead of supplying both in copious quantities.

"I sat up in my bedroom and decided this foolishness had gone on long enough. The next day, I drew my first sketches of a better house, and I continued drawing for ten years. By then, I was ready to start on a pilot model, which took five years. After that, I was ready to start on the production problem, which we have only just licked—I say with my fingers crossed.

"Am I wandering from the subject, New Approaches to the Delivered Dwelling? I hope not. My new approach, gentlemen, was to think of the dweller in the dwelling and give him a house that helps him instead of fighting him. A house at a cost he can afford, without any disasters in the way of repairs. A house that gives him light to see by, privacy, safety for his kids, leisure for his wife and him, variety to make homecoming a happy adventure instead of a revolting daily chore.

"My New Approach to the Delivered Dwelling, gentlemen, was nothing more or less than a sincere attempt to leave the world a better and happier place for millions than it was when I found it."

The applause was sparse and dubious.

Norma flicked the machine off, but did not brighten the lights. She said broodingly, "So Moffatt sold him out, broke his heart and killed him. And today that dream is a nightmare to millions of wretched people chained to their jobs by G-M-L contract leases..."

She turned on the three financiers, figures in the gloom.

"Well?" she demanded harshly. "Don can walk into that stockholders meeting and take over with your backing. It *matters*, don't you see? It *matters.*"

Mundin cleared his throat and said, "I'm sticking with it, Norma."

She didn't flare at him for using her first name, but continued to stare her challenge.

Nelson murmured, "An orderly liquidation, under the circumstances, still seems most advisable. If you will excuse me—" He slipped discreetly from the room.

Coett, big bluff man, told her, "Ideals don't matter much when you're my age. My advice to you is to peddle your stock on the Big Board, live happily ever after—and stay away from Green, Charlesworth. Uplift doesn't pay. Now I've got to go." He went.

Hubble was gnawing his nails. He said, "I was brought up to be a sensible, dollar-fearing young man and Green, Charlesworth have more dollars than anybody else around... You know, I liked that look on your father's face when he told them about homecoming being a happy adventure... For God's sake, don't tell anybody, but I'm sticking with you as long as my nerve holds out."

Norma flung her arms around him and kissed him. Charles said, "Hey, cut that—" and then realized he had no basis whatsoever for the proprietary feeling which had suddenly overwhelmed him. But he turned up the lights, anyway.

"Where's Don?" he asked.

Norma was recovering from her elation. "Must've slipped out."

Mundin called Norvell Bligh in and asked after Don.

"Oh, yes," the little man said. "He left about three minutes ago."

"Left? Where to?"

"Well, I asked him in case, and all he said was 'High wire.' Some kind of joke, I suppose."

"High wire?" Mundin asked Norma blankly.

She shook her head.

"He seemed in high spirits," Bligh chatted. "His eyes were shining like stars. Most unusual—"

"My God!" said Norma. "A post-hypnotic command from his conditioning!"

"Does anybody," Hubble demanded, "know what a high wire may be? There could be some perfectly simple explanation."

Norvie's jaw had dropped. He said at last, faintly, "I know quite a lot about high-wire work. It's the most dangerous stunt they put on at a Field Day."

A raucous cackle filled the room.

"Absolutely, Mr. Charlesworth?"

"Positively, Mrs. Green!"

Hell broke loose. A seat cushion exploded. Then a fountain pen in Norvie's pocket. The *In* basket on Ryan's desk. There were screams from the outside offices; Mundin ran out. A diffraction grating in the chem-lab. Steno's lip-sprays. An acetate-recording blank for a dictating machine. The water cooler—that was a sloppy one. A magazine in the reception room.

Eventually things settled down.

The last hysterical filing clerk was sent home, the last of the little fires put out.

Hubble, white with rage, snapped, "Let's go to my place. They can't have that gimmicked."

Norvell Bligh said: "Excuse me, Mr. Hubble—I don't think there's time. Field Day is tomorrow at two in the afternoon."

CHAPTER TWENTY

THEY searched throughout the night. Hard. They found the cabby at dawn.

"Sure, mister, I hacked him. Right to the artist's entrance, at Monmouth. Friend of yours? Some kind of dare?"

They tried to bribe their way into the arena and almost made it. The furtive gatekeeper was on the verge of swallowing their cock-and-bull story and palming their money when the Night Supervisory Custodian showed up. He was a giant and his eyes shone.

He said politely, "I'm sorry, folks—unauthorized access is forbidden. However, lineup for bleacher seats begins in a couple of hours. Hello, Mr. Bligh. I haven't seen you around lately."

"Hello, Barnes," Norvell said. "Look, can you possibly let us through? There's a fool kid we know who signed upon a dare. It's all a silly mistake and he was muggled up, besides…"

The giant sighed regretfully. "Unauthorized access is forbidden. If you had a pass—"

The hackie said, "I don't mind waiting, folks, but don't you have better sense than to argue with a conditioned guy?"

"He's right," Norvell admitted. "Hell won't get you by Barnes without a pass or a release. Let's try Candella. He used to be my boss, the louse."

The taxi whizzed them to the amusement company's bubble city and Candella's pleasure dome. Ryan snoozed. Norma and Mundin held hands—scared. Bligh looked brightly interested, like a fox terrier. Hubble, hunched on a jump seat, mumbled worriedly to himself.

Candella awakened and came to the interviewer after five minutes of chiming. Obviously he couldn't believe his eyes. "Bligh?" he sputtered. "Norvell Bligh?"

"Yes, Mr. Candella. I'm sorry to wake you up, but it's urgent. Can you let us in?"

"Certainly not! Go away or I'll call the police!" The interviewer blinked off. Norvell leaned on the chime plate and Candella reappeared. "Damn it, Bligh, stop that. How dare you?"

Mundin elbowed Norvell from the scanner eye. "Mr. Candella, I'm Charles Mundin; attorney at law. I represent Mr. Donald Lavin. I have reason to believe that Lavin took a release and is now in the artist's quarters at Monmouth, due to appear in today's Field Day. I advise you that my client is mentally incompetent to sign a release and that therefore your organization will be subject to heavy damages, should he be harmed. I suggest that this can be quickly adjusted by you in filling out the necessary papers canceling your contract with him. Naturally, we're prepared to pay any indemnity—or, service fee." He lowered his voice. "In small bills and plenty of them."

"Come in," Candella said blandly and the door opened. He gaped as they entered. "My God, an army!"

THE house, intercom said in a female voice, "What is it, Poopsie?"

He flushed. "Business. Switch off, please, Panther Girl—I mean Prudence." There was a giggle and a click.— "Now, gentlemen and miss—no, I don't care what your names are—let me show you one of our release forms. Here, you said you were a lawyer. Have a look."

Mundin studied it for ten minutes. Ironclad? Watertight? No, tungsten-carbide-coated, braced, buttressed, riveted, welded and fire-polished. Airtight, hard vacuum proof, guaranteed not to wilt, shrink, sag, wrinkle, tear or bag at the clauses under any conceivable legal assault.

Candella was enjoying Mundin's expression. "Think you're the first?" he snickered. "If there's been one, there have been a million. But there hasn't been a successful suit for thirty years, Mr. Attorney."

Mundin said, "Hang the law, Mr. Candella. Hang the bribe, too, if you don't want it. It's a humanitarian matter. The kid's got no business in there—"

Candella turned righteous. "I'm protecting my company and its stockholders, Mr. Whoever-you-are. As a policy matter, we can allow no exceptions. Our Field Days would be a chaos if every drunken bum—"

Mundin was about to clobber him when Norvell unexpectedly caught his arm. "No use, Charles. I never realized it before—he's a sadist. Of course. Who else could hold that job and enjoy it? You're interfering with his love life when you try to get one of his victims away from him. We'll go higher."

Candella snorted and showed them pointedly to the door.

In the taxi again, Mundin said to Hubble, "I guess this is where you take over, Bliss."

The financier flipped through a notecase and reached for the phone as they rolled back toward the Park. He dialed and snapped, "Sam? Mr. Hubble here. Good morning to *you*. Sam, who's in charge of the outfit that puts on the Monmouth Field Days? I'll wait." He waited and then said, "Oh—thanks, Sam," and hung up the phone. He told them, looking out the window, "Trustee stock. Held by the Choate firm. And we know who they run errands for, don't we?" He drummed his fingers. "Bligh, you must know *some* way in. You worked there, after all."

Norvell said, "The only way in is with a release."

Norma urged with dry hysteria, "Then let's sign releases." They stared. "I'm not crazy. We want to find Don, don't we? And when we find him, we restrain him—with a club, if we have to. We can sign for crowd extras or something like that, can't we, Norvie? It's all volunteer, isn't it?"

Norvell said, "Remember, I wasn't a pit boss. I was on the planning end. And from the planning end, it was all supposed to be volunteer. But maybe it's not such a bad idea. I'll go in alone. I know the ropes—"

"Not you," Mundin said. "He won't *want* to be found. He'll fight. I'll go—"

They would all go. And then Norvell had a bright idea and it took a lot of small bills to get the hackie to take them to Belly Rave and an hour to find Lana of the Wabbits.

"We'll be there," she promised casually.

THE briefing room beneath the stands was huge and crowded. About a quarter of the occupants were obvious rumdums, another quarter were professionals, another quarter swaggering youngsters in for a one-shot that they'd brag about the rest of their lives. The rest seemed to be just people. It was twelve-thirty and everybody had been given an excellent hot lunch in the adjoining cafeteria.

One professional had noticed Mundin hungrily wolfing down his and suggested, "Better not, stranger. Belly wounds." Mundin had abruptly stopped.

There was no sign so far of Don Lavin, which was not odd. It was easy enough to lose yourself in that crowd. Their hopes were pinned on twenty Wabbits whom Lavin would have—he'd think—no reason to avoid.

Somebody on the rostrum said, "May I have your attention, please? You stumblebums in the corner there—that means you, too. Thanks, all." He was a distraught young man who ran his fingers through his hair.

Norvie whispered to Mundin. "Wilkes. He'll have a nervous breakdown by tonight. Every year. But—" wistfully— "he's a good MC."

Wilkes went on, "You know this is the show of the year, ladies and gentlemen. Double fees and survivor's insurance for this one. And in return, ladies and gentlemen, we expect you all to do your absolute best for Monmouth Park.

"Now let's get on with the casting. First, a comedy number. We need some old gentlemen and ladies—nothing violent; padded clubs in a battle-royal to the finish. The last surviving lady gets five hundred dollars; the surviving gentlemen gets one thousand. Let's see some hands there! No, not you, buster—you can't be a day over seventy."

"Take it," Bligh told Ryan. "Go with them and keep your eyes open for Don."

Ryan got the nod and tottered away with the other old ladies and gentlemen.

"Now are there two good men who fancy themselves as knife-fighters, Scandinavian style? Don't waste my time if you have a pot-belly." Scandinavian style meant being fastened together by a belt with two feet of slack. "One thousand? Anybody at one thousand? All right, I'll make it twelve-fifty and if there isn't a rising ovation, we drop the number, you yellow crumbs!" Perhaps a dozen pros hopped up, grinning. "Fine response! Let's make it six matches simultaneous. Take 'em away, boys."

The casting went on. Mickey's Inferno; Lions and Tigers and Bears; Kiddie Kutups, which scooped in all the Wabbits. Lana shot Mundin a glance and shrug. No Don Lavin—but the crowd was thinning.

"Roller Derby!" Wilkes called. "Spiked elbows, no armor. Five hundred a point to contestants, twenty flat to audience, a hundred to audience members if a contestant lands on him or her and draws blood."

Norvell gathered the eyes of Mundin, Norma and Hubble. They rose, were accepted for "audience" and hustled out of the briefing room, still vainly peering about for Don. Only after the glass door closed behind them did they see him. He was rising—with glazed, shining eyes—for High Wire with Piranha. Price, ten thousand dollars. And he was the only volunteer.

Norma struggled with the immovable door until two matrons yanked her away and shoved her in the direction of the ready room.

"I'll think of something," Norvie kept saying. "I'll think of something."

CHAPTER TWENTY-ONE

NORVELL tried the chummy approach with the ready room manager. He was brushed off. Norvell tried entreaties and then threats. He was brushed off. The ready-room manager droned: "You made yer bed, now lie in it. Alluva sudden you an' ya frenns get yella, no skin off a my nose. Derby audience ya stood up for, derby audience yer gonna be."

"What's the trouble, Campo?" a fussy and familiar voice suddenly demanded.

It was Stimmens, Norvie's skunk of an ex-assistant who had quietly and competently betrayed his boss into Belly Rave. It would have been pure delight, to bawl him out, but the stakes were, too high.

"Mr. Stimmens," Norvie said humbly.

"Why, Mr. Bluh—why, Norvie! What are you doing here?"

Norvie brutishly wiped his nose on his sleeve. "Trying to make a buck, Mr. Stimmens," he whined. "You know how it is in Belly Rave. I stood up for the Roller Derby audience, but Mr. Campo here says I got yellow. Maybe I did, but I want a switch—from Derby Audience to Highwire Heckler. I know it's only ten bucks, but you don't get one of those spiked-elbow gals in your lap. Can you do it for me, Mr. Stimmens? And a couple of friends of mine? *Please?*"

Stimmens basked. "It's unusual, Norvie. It creates confusion. But for an old employee, we can bend some rules. See that he's switched, Campo."

"And my friends, please, Mr. Stimmens?"

Stimmens shrugged tolerantly.

"And his friends, Campo." He sauntered on, glowing with the consciousness of a favor done that humiliated his ex-boss and caused himself no trouble at all.

"You heard him," Norvell said. "Switch!"

Campo growled and reached for his cards.

Back on the bench, Norvell told Hubble, Mundin and Norma briefly, "We're in. It ups Don's chances plenty. You have any cash on you, Mr. Hubble? Pass it around to the other High-wire Hecklers when we go on."

And then there was nothing to do but watch through the glass wall. The Old-timers' Battle Royal was on; they saw Ryan laid out by a vicious swipe to the groin from an octogenarian lady. The clubs were padded, but there was a lot in knowing how to use them. He was carried past the wall, groaning, to the infirmary.

IT was a responsive audience, Norvie noted with pure technical interest, laughing, howling and throwing things at the right time. He heard, in memory, the familiar chant of the, vendors, "Gitcha rocks, gitcha brickbats, ya ca-a-an't hit the artists without a brickbat!"

Click, click, and the Scandinavian knife-fighters were on. Snip, snap, the knives flashed and the blood flowed. There were two double-kills out of the six pairs and the band blared from Grieg to Gershwin for the Roller Derby, which would last a good ten minutes.

It was gory. Repeatedly, skaters shot off the banked boards into the "audience" of old stew-bums and thrill-seekers rather than get a razor-sharp elbow spike, and their own spikes wreaked havoc. Almost us, Norvie thought numbly. At a hundred a lapful, almost us.

For the first time in his life, he found himself wondering when and where it all had started. Bone-crushing football? Those hockey games featured by concussions? Impatient sidewalk crowds that roared "Go-go-go" to a poor crazed ledge-sitter? Those fans who flipped lighted firecrackers at the visiting team's outfielders racing for a fly? "We don't take no prisoners in this outfit, kid"? White phosphorus grenades? Buchenwald? Napalm?

And then, before he knew it, Campo was shaking his shoulder and growling, "All right, ya yella punk. You an' yer frenns, yer on. Take yer basket."

He took the basket numbly and looked at the noisemakers and gravel. He followed the section as it moved out onto the field. He became aware that Hubble and Mundin were half carrying him.

"Don't cork out, Norvie," Mundin begged him. "We need every man."

Norvie gave him a pale grin and thought: Maybe I won't have to. Maybe I won't have to. That's the thing to stick with. Maybe I won't have to. But if I do—

"Ladies and gentlemen," the MC roared as they assumed their places around the tank, while the riggers hastily set up the two towers and strung the wire, "Monmouth Park is proud and happy to present, for the first time in this arena's distinguished history, a novel feat of courage and dexterity."

Don had been hustled atop one of the towers. Norma was weeping. Hubble and Mundin were passing among the hecklers; handing out bills.

"No heckling, understand? Just keep quiet. You'll get this much more after it's over. Anybody crosses us up, we'll throw him to the fish. No heckling, understand?"

"This young man, ladies and gentlemen, utterly without previous experience in the gymnastic art, will attempt to cross the fifteen feet from tower to tower against the simultaneous opposition of sixteen opponents. They will be permitted to jeer, threaten, sound horns and cast gravel, but not to shake the towers!"

AUDIENCE identification, thought Norvie. The sixteen "opponents" would be there to do exactly what the audience wanted to do, but was too far away to do. Still, a good strong arm with a favoring wind and a brick—

"The special feature of this performance, ladies and gentlemen, lies in the tank above which this young man will traverse. At enormous expense, the Monmouth Park Association has imported from the headwaters of the Amazon River a school of the deadliest fish known to man, the famed piranha. Your binoculars, ladies and gentlemen! I am about to drop a fifty-pound sheep into the tank. Kindly watch the result!"

In went the bleating, terrified animal—shaved and with a few nicks on its side for the scent of blood. Then they pulled on the rope and hauled out—bloody bones. There were still ghastly little things flopping and wriggling, dangling from the skeleton. They beat them off into the water with sticks as the crowd shrieked in delight.

Just like you, you swine, Norvie thought. But maybe I won't have to do it—

The earpiece of his hearing aid had slipped a trifle. He looked shyly around and pulled it out preparatory to readjusting it. Then he didn't readjust it. The shrieking crowd, the gloating, smacking language of the MC, the faint creak in the wind of the tower guys—all of it came through.

It was the decision, he told himself, not quite knowing what he meant. He hadn't *wanted* to hear any of it; he hadn't *dared* hear any of it. Not as long as he was a part of the horror.

He went to Norma Lavin and put his thin arm around her shaking shoulders. "It's going to be all right," he said.

She cowered against him, wordlessly.

"I've got a boy coming, you know," he told her.

She gave him a distracted nod, her eyes on the tower.

"And if anything happens," he went on, "it's only fair they should be taken care of—Sandy, Virginia and the boy. You'll remember in case anything happens?" She nodded. "There was this time in Bay City," he chattered. "High wire with piranha. A judge—" She wasn't paying attention.

He got up and joined Mundin. "If anything happens," he said, "it's only fair that Sandy and Virginia and the boy should be taken care of."

"What are you talking about, Norvie?"

"Just remember. *Please* remember."

THE drumroll began and the MC set fire to the platform on which Don Lavin stood. The crowd howled as the flames licked up and the boy hopped convulsively forward, his balancing pole swaying.

The MC yelled angrily at the hecklers, "What's the matter with you people? Toot! Chuck gravel! What do you think you're getting paid for?"

One of them, a young tough, began to swing his rattle, glancing nervously at Hubble. Hubble snapped at him, "A hundred more, buster. Now calm down." The tough calmed down and gaped at the wirewalker.

A foot, two feet, the pole swaying. He has special slippers on, Norvell thought. Maybe it'll be all right, I won't have to do anything and then I can be comfortably deaf again, buying batteries for a penance, turning this nausea off at will.

Three feet, four feet, and the MC howling with rage: "Get in there and fight! Take out your horns! Plaster him!"

Five feet, six feet, and the crowd-noise was ugly, ugly as blood. In one section, a chant had started, one of those footstomping, hand-clapping things.

Six feet, seven, and the MC was breaking down into sobs. "We paid you and this is the way you treat us! These fine people in the stands. Aren't you *ashamed?*"

Eight feet, nine feet, ten feet, two-thirds of the way to the second tower. Somebody with a mighty arm and a following wind had found the range. The half-brick at the end of its journey sailed feebly, *plop*, into the tank and white-bellied little things tore at it and bled themselves and tore at one another. The water boiled.

Suddenly ice-cold, all business, Norvie said dryly to Mundin, "Be ready to haul him out fast. They'll have him in a minute. Remember what I said."

He strolled over to Wilkes, who was watching the stubbornly silent hecklers in numb despair.

Another half-brick and this one hit the tower. Much maneuvering of the balancing pole and a shriek from Norma.

"No nervous breakdown this year, Wilkes," Norvell said to the MC.

"What? Bligh, they won't *listen* to me!"

Thirteen feet, and then the brick, unseen, that tapped Don Lavin between the shoulder blades and made him flail the pole too hard.

One last agonized look around the arena was all Norvell could take. There was nothing, no chair, no cushion, nothing but—

He grabbed the sobbing Wilkes in his arms and lunged into the tank for an eternal instant, before he could see Don Lavin topple and fall. First the water was cool and then boiling.

FOR ten minutes, there was not a sane person in the stadium. The critics would remember that moment all their lives. It was greatness, the ultimate masterpiece of Field Day emotion.

While the piranhas seethed at the far end of the tank, Mundin yanked Don Lavin out in one heave. Not a soul molested the four of them as they walked slowly over the bloody sand. They passed Candella, who stared at them with blind, streaming eyes and said, "Masterpiece! Masterpiece! And I knew him! I walked and talked with *Norvell Bligh!* Art can go no further. M*asterpiece!*"

They picked up Lana and her Wabbits from a deserted ready room.

"I saw it," she said. "Good little man, wasn't he?" She broke off into sobs. "I'll tell his wife and kid," she sniffed at last. "Only—which way should I tell it?"

Mundin thought. Blessed simplicity. Which way? There were undoubtedly a hundred ways, a thousand ways, all true and all intertwined, of telling about that frightful, horrifying, noble moment.

Outside the stadium, the Wabbits were paid and formed fours, stumping grimly off toward the Belly Rave that Norvell Bligh had come to love and serve.

"I think," Don Lavin said slowly, "I'm awake. All the way. And I think I know what woke me up. Sis, Charles, Mr. Hubble—are we going to give those bottled ghouls—Green, Charlesworth—the business? I say we are!"

"First," said Hubble practically, "let me call Sam. His orders were to grab up anything Coett and Nelson dumped on the Exchange. Even if we don't have our majority for tomorrow, we should have enough to Rock the Boat and Monkey with the Buzz Saw, as your two marinated friends put it."

This incurable levity of mine, he thought, and sighed. He noted how Norma Lavin was leaning on Mundin's arm and how she glanced at him.

He thought of how his wife glanced at him and sighed again, this time enviously.

EPILOGUE

From TYCOON, The Magazine for Tycoons:
After a savagely efficient management raid on the gigantic G-M-L Corporation conducted last week during its regular stockholders' meeting, the winners and new champions, Messrs. Hubble and Lavin, issued a terse joint statement promising far-reaching, deep-rooted policy changes.

From the BELLY RAVE TIMES:
Now that we enter our second year, it is time to pause and take stock. I think most of us will be pleased by what we see around us. The Belly Rave Municipal Association launched by my late husband, and of which I now have the honor to be president, is flourishing. Membership now covers eighteen blocks and our Organized Area covers ten. Progress is slow but sure. The re-establishment of sewer mains proceeds at a gratifying pace and everywhere one sees busy hands and happy faces. Truly, as my revered husband used to say, "Self-help is the only kind that sticks."

From the MONMOUTH NEWS:
Newly elected Senator Mundin left for Washington today in his private 'copter after reaffirming his election pledge to raze Old New York to the ground. "We need the metals," he said, "and we need the room. I cannot understand why this condemned slum has been tolerated for many years past the legal date for its extinction. Esthetically speaking, it is also a dreadful eyesore—particularly the old Empire State Building. It must and will be destroyed." The Senator's attractive wife, nee Norma Lavin, accompanied him…

From The FIELD DAY FAN:

The cranks are at it again. Those mysteriously financed leaflets and broadcasts and lobbies for compulsory hours of anti-Field Day "education" in the public schools have again flared up. *Your* legal, rational, traditional entertainment is again under attack. For the third time in as many months, this magazine is compelled to solicit contributions that will offset its declining circulation. Attendance figures are down across the nation. But this is not a gloomy picture. The Field Day fans have been stripped to their hard core of true enthusiasts...sincerity...artistic triumph. Vapid reformers and their bloodless ilk...utter inability to comprehend such moments of truth, such avalanches of emotion as were unleashed in the great old days upon the stunned spectator. In this context, we need no more than mention with due reverence the great name *Norvell Bligh!*

THE END

If you've enjoyed this book, you will not want to miss these terrific titles…

ARMCHAIR SCI-FI & HORROR DOUBLE NOVELS, $12.95 each

D-191 **GLADIATOR AT LAW** by Frederik Pohl & C. M. Kornbluth
       THE JACK OF PLANETS by Paul W. Fairman

D-192 **THE NAKED GODDESS** by S. J. Byrne
       THE GOD BUSINESS by Phillip Jose Farmer

D-193 **BATTLE FOR THE STARS** by Edmond Hamilton
       BORDER, BREED, NOR BIRTH by Mack Reynolds

D-194 **THE SENTINEL STARS** by Louis Charbonneau
       WARRIOR MAID OF MARS by Alfred Coppel

D-195 **ORPHAN OF ATLANS** by William L. Hamling
       THE ILLUSION SEEKERS by P. F. Costello

D-196 **PHANTOM OUT OF TIME** by Nelson S. Bond
       MYSHKIN by David V. Reed

D-197 **THE SOUL SNATCHERS** by Lee Francis
       DOOMSDAY EVE by Robert Moore Williams

D-198 **MONARCH OF MARS** by John Pollard
       THE ONSLAUGHT FROM RIGEL by Fletcher Pratt

D-199 **ESCAPE FROM DOOM** by John Wilstach
       BEYOND BEDLAM by Wayman Guinn

D-200 **BARON MUNCHAUSEN'S SCIENTIFIC ADVENTURES** Hugo Gernsback
       THE REVOLUTION OF 1950 Stanley Weinbaum & Ralph Milne Farley

ARMCHAIR MYSTERY-CRIME DOUBLE NOVELS, $12.95 each

B-35 **DEAD IN BED** by Day Keene
      BONES WILL TELL by Bruno Fischer

B-36 **GANG MOLL** by Albert L. Quandt
      TIP YOUR HAT TO DEATH by H. B. Hickey

B-37 **THE MOURNING AFTER** by Frank Kane
      THE CONFESSION by Mary Roberts Rinehart

B-38 **RUN IF YOU CAN** by Owen Dudley
      THE SCENTED FLESH by Milton Ozaki

B-39 **THE CORPSE IN THE PICTURE WINDOW** by Bruce Cassiday
      THERE'S DEATH IN THE HEIR by Larry Holden

A PUZZLING MYSTERY ON THE SANDS OF MARS

It was something that the bigwigs at the U. S. Space program couldn't seem to figure out. Over the past twenty years two different interplanetary flights, Voyager One and Voyager Two, had blasted off for Mars. It was assumed they had landed there, successfully, each with a four-person crew. But after each ship had arced toward the planet's surface…nothing. They had never been heard from again. No communications, no distress calls, not a peep. Both missions were eventually written off as failures. However, now the space program was poised for another try: This time the equipment was newer, more durable, and the crew more thoroughly trained. But all the training in the world would do no good against a Martian landscape fraught with peril and not one, but two races of creatures bound and determined to make sure Earth's explorers never saw home again.

CAST OF CHARACTERS

JORGMAN
This older guy (from Florida) was gentle, bright, cheery, and liked to talk—yet he never really gave you concrete answers.

LEE TARP
It's amazing how a little bit of unrequited love can have such a destructive effect on a fellow's common sense.

JENNIFER KANE
This attractive female doctor had a big problem: two of the three male crewmen on her 10-month trip to Mars had the hots for her!

SAM WALDEN
An exceptional commanding officer in that he fully recognized his own superior abilities but was entirely without conceit.

BARRY CARTER
He was the brainy engineer type—good with gauges, hyper-drives, and spaceship engines, but not necessarily with women.

COLONEL SWAIN
He was in charge of prepping the crew of Voyager Three for their trip to Mars, and what he had to say was perplexing to say the least!

THE JACK OF
PLANETS

By
PAUL W. FAIRMAN

ARMCHAIR FICTION
PO Box 4369, Medford, Oregon 97504

*For more information about Armchair Books and products, visit our
website at…*

www.armchairfiction.com

Or email us at…

armchairfiction@yahoo.com

CHAPTER ONE

THE SHIP came down out of the sky in a great flaming arc; down out of space toward Mars. It marked a great circle around one hemisphere of the planet, half of which was under the blaze of the sun, the other half in a semi-darkness through which two moons raced each other toward the horizon.

The arc of the ship grew smaller after the manner of a diminishing corkscrew; lessening and tightening until, with one last swift run, the silver shell found a landing on the surface of the planet. The jet fire died; the jet smoke hung for a time in a sullen cloud formation, before it dissolved and became nothing.

For an hour the ship sat on the brooding plain; on the plain where no living thing moved.

Now a port opened in the side of the ship. A ramp went out like the tongue of some hungry space animal. A single figure appeared on the ramp; the figure of a man, pale, weak, emaciated. His eyes were bloodshot and sunken, his jowls fish-belly pale with black stubble contrasting with rather than hiding the pallor.

The man came to the foot of the ramp and allowed his eyes to roam over the scene before him. They had just settled upon the peculiar structure flanking the western side of the landing area, when the man winced suddenly and a look of wonder came into his face.

He slapped sharply at a spot on his neck. Almost immediately he cried out in sudden pain. He placed both hands over his face and crouched as from the onslaught of a swarm of hornets, then turned and staggered, whimpering, back into the bowels of the ship. The ramp was pulled in; the port closed.

Another hour passed before the man again dared the surface of the planet. This time he resembled a huge, clumsy, grotesque doll, the heavy gray folds of his spacesuit protecting his flesh, his

The Jack of Planets

Lee was lucky to find an Earthman like Jorgman on Mars. Especially when he got in trouble and Jorgman had him killed!

The Martian screamed as the pellet from Lee's gun tore a jagged opening in his chest

bloodshot eyes peering from a helmet through a section of heavy glass.

The man turned westward and began walking, each step an effort, each movement a studied thing. The half-mile walk

Interior
Illustrations
by Lawrence

By Paul W. Fairman

consumed another hour, after which the man veered slightly on his course to arrive at what he hoped was a means of entrance into the building ahead. His hopes were fulfilled. As he stepped on the threshold, a door opened before him. He moved inside, slowing, each step a great effort. The door closed.

The moons raced; the planet turned; time passed. One year—two years—four—seven—twelve. The door never reopened. The man never reappeared.

Out on the open plain, the ship changed form. Six months and its hull was no longer silvery. A year, and that same hull corroded, rusted, dropped away in small flakes. In five years the first hole appeared, and from that time on disintegration set in even more swiftly; until the bowels of the great space master were open to the lonesome sky; until the shell fell away completely; until the ship became one of a dozen of such rotted and unidentifiable hulks dotting the great plain.

Fifteen years and another space queen arced down from the sky. It too described the preliminary gyrations before it settled to rest on the plain. Again a ramp opened—a tongue ran out. This time four people emerged from the hull to go through the same hornet-swatting motions that had occupied their predecessor years before.

And they did what he had done: returned to the ship to re-emerge in the weird spacesuits. This time the suits were not so bulky. Fifteen years had brought improvements.

As though drawn by some weird, prefabricated pattern, they too directed their steps westward toward the building; they too walked to the waiting threshold and placed their feet thereon.

The door opened. They entered. The door closed upon them.

Outside the ship waited endlessly, but the four—like the one—never came back again. Years—two—four—six. Years of silence, corrosion, emptiness.

*　　*　　*

"AT THIS stage of your training," Colonel Swain said, "you no doubt feel yourselves to be entirely familiar with the history of space travel to date."

The group of four seated about Swain believed they had every right so to feel. But there was something in Swain's tone—a mixture of amusement and anticipation—that caused them to exchange glances of uncertainty. Sam Walden—the young man who had won the astrogation competition, who had a grin built into both his face and his disposition said, "You people been holding out on us, Colonel?"

Colonel Swain smiled fleetingly. "I'm afraid we have." He directed his attention to Jennifer Kane, twenty-two-year-old whizz kid; neurologist, physician, bacteriologist; the ablest exponent of these sciences whose age qualified her for space travel. "Tell me, Miss Kane, what is the past history of our efforts in that direction?"

The girl hesitated, sensing some sort of trap in the question. Then she shrugged. "After the Lunar bridgehead was established in 1978, a ship was built and outfitted for the Mars run."

"*Voyager One,*" Barry Carter, the drive specialist, muttered.

Jennifer Kane favored him with a slight frown. "Of course. *Voyager One* blasted off in 1981. It was never heard of again."

Lee Tarp was fidgeting. "The first of two disasters."

Jennifer said, "Stop prompting me. Later, in 1996, *Voyager Two* cleared atmosphere on the same mission. The world is still wondering what became of her."

"Admirably put," Colonel Swain smiled. "And most accurate. Up to a point."

LEE TARP, the nervous one, leaned forward sharply. "What do you mean, sir—up to a point?"

"There were details of both flights that the high brass saw fit not to reveal. The international situation was touchy at the times of both flights. They reasoned the censored details, if publicized, might make us...somewhat of a laughing stock."

"I don't understand," Jennifer said.

"I'll be as brief as possible." Swain's eyes narrowed as he went back into memory. "*Voyager One* carried a crew of four. Among them was an astrogator named Taylor. Taylor, along with the other three crewmembers, entered the ship under the eyes of twenty thousand people. He did not leave the ship before it blasted off into space."

Swain's half-smile was in evidence again. He obviously enjoyed the role of storyteller. "The situation relative to *Voyager Two* was basically the same; four crew members, one of whom bore the name of Gardner."

Sam Walden's precise mind resented partial details. "That leaves six names—"

"The names of the other six aren't important in this briefing," Colonel Swain said. "We are interested only in Taylor and Gardner. They blasted off, remember, beyond all doubt."

"So they blasted off," Lee Tarp admitted with a frown.

"But, three months after *Voyager One* was lost to our instruments, Taylor was found in Chicago, working in a commercial jet factory."

The group blinked in unison.

"And four months after *Voyager Two* vanished into space, Gardner turned up in a New Orleans night club playing a piano."

"Then both flights were duds," Barry Carter said. "Tell me—how did the high brass construe that as ridiculous?"

Colonel Swain's smile faded as he himself became engrossed in the mystery of the affair. "That isn't quite how it was. At least, not to our knowledge. Exhaustive search was made for the ships. They were never found. We have no proof they returned to Earth.

"No proof? Then the men you called Gardner and Taylor—the ones you found later—were imposters?"

"No. They were the same men who entered the two ships; that beyond all doubt."

"Then you had your proof. The ships certainly returned."

Colonel Swain sighed. "It would appear so. But there was another bewildering point. Both Gardner and Taylor swore they had never boarded spaceships in their lives; they both denied, emphatically, their roles in the first two attempts at space travel."

"They were lying, of course."

"A logical supposition, but in this day and age it's almost impossible for a man to conceal the truth. We didn't take their words for it. They were subjected to exhaustive tests. The radial lie detector—the hypnotic-twilight examination—the several derivatives—the chemico-bio basic—" Swain shrugged, though not as gracefully as had Jennifer Kane. "There was no possibility of falsehood. We discovered, however, a blank spot in the minds of each of them. These blanks were identical in pattern. They covered periods beginning a month before each flight and ending roughly five months afterward. Both men remembered vaguely of having *planned* to go to Mars, but their memories were confused and vague. Gardner insisted the memory was a vivid dream he'd experienced and had not quite forgotten. Taylor was entirely unable to explain the memory.

THE FOURSOME slated to take *Voyager Three* into void not twenty-four hours hence glanced at one another with some misgivings. Lee Tarp spoke first, "I don't like this. I don't like it at all. The basis of Project Space should be pure mathematics. Up to this point it has been. I'm at home with mathematics, but not with daydreams out of the bowl of someone's pipe."

Swain pocketed a memo book he'd been fingering. "What I've told you is entirely true. It sounds utterly fantastic, of course, but let's not become alarmed. Excellent human specimens such as yourselves..." Swain let his eyes mirror admiration and what could have been envy, "...should approach the thing with calm logic. You should reason instinctively that nothing springs from other than a sound basis; that the seeming fantasy in this affair comes of our not having all the facts. We have only some seemingly impossible end-results. When the basic data are found, the presence of Gardner and Taylor on Earth—where they apparently had no right to be—will not seem at all astounding."

This rather comfortless advice brought no reply, and Swain went on, "Also, we suggest you have no fears of *Voyager Three's* sharing the fate of its predecessors. Much has been learned in the last five years. Neither of the previous ships may have reached the projected destination, but your ship will. Several important corrections have been made. So have no fear. You will reach Mars safely."

Swain got up from his chair. The four arose also and Swain shook hands all around. He smiled again. "I didn't tell you all that just to bewilder you. It's in the nature of another assignment. On top of all the other things you are to discover and record, we'd like you to keep an eye out for the facts bridging the gap between the previous blast-offs and the discovery of Taylor and Gardner back here on Earth. The complete story should be most interesting."

"I'm sure of that," Lee Tarp said.

Sam Walden grinned. "I'm not bad with a flute, Colonel. If we don't show on schedule, look me up in one of the symphony orchestras."

It was not a good joke, but it rated a few smiles. It drew a smile only from Colonel Swain. The Colonel clapped Walden on the back. "Very good—very good. And now you people better get some sleep. I'll see you at the blasting range tomorrow."

"I THINK I've got it figured out," Lee Tarp said.

The others, lounging at ease in the social room of *Voyager Three,* waited politely to learn what he was talking about. The men wore sports attire, as that was what had been prescribed for these hours of relaxation. Jennifer Kane wore a most becoming dress of bright green. The gown had a high-cut neck and a hem showing only a few inches of calf. This had also been prescribed.

"I think I've got it figured out," Tarp repeated, and Barry Carter set down his drink and said, "If you're waiting for someone to act as straight man, I'm your boy. What have you figured out, Mr. Bones?"

Lee Tarp, not noted for his sense of humor, frowned slightly. "That yarn Colonel Swain gave us during the last briefing. Looking at it one way, it's quite simple."

"Tell us," Jennifer said. "Make it good and you rate an extra Scotch."

"Well, there's obviously a lie involved in it somewhere. Taylor and Gardner couldn't return to Earth without a ship. If no ship was found, they did not return. So—either the ships *were* found, or the two men did not turn up in Chicago and New Orleans."

"Which do you think is the lie?"

"Both."

Sam Walden was puzzled, as were the rest of the group. But even though deeply interested in Tarp's words, Sam never let his eyes travel far from the dials and gauges on the walls of the social room. Captain of the expedition, Walden kept half his mind on the ship at all times. He never quite trusted the automatic controls even though they were foolproof, and none of the movements of the dozen or so dials was missed.

"Yes, both," Lee Tarp said. "I think there is an ulterior motive involved."

"But what motive could there possibly be…" Jennifer smoothed her dress and crossed her ankles demurely.

"Consider the time and thought that went into the routine they laid out for us. They realized, and rightly so, the grave danger of four people crowded together in a ship for ten weeks far beyond other human contact." Lee Tarp stopped to regard Jennifer gravely. "I happen to know, Jen, that you came within an ace of staying home."

The girl looked startled. "Why—I—"

"You won out in the competition—that's true—"

"And the psychological value of a woman aboard was—"

"—was put forward by a fraction that almost got voted down."

"Never mind all that," Barry Carter said. "Get on with your thesis."

"I was leading up to it. One of our great dangers, they felt, would be boredom. They had no data on the mental pressures of weeks of imprisonment out here in space."

"Then you think that story was just something to—?"

"Exactly. A fairy tale to help us wile away the hours. It was admirably suited for such a purpose. It created within each of us an anticipation of the future we would not have otherwise."

"It was a pretty fishy yarn," Carter conceded doubtfully.

"You win the extra drink, Lee," Jennifer said. "I'll mix it for you."

Lee Tarp's reaction surprised them.

He got to his feet suddenly, scowling. Then his mouth twisted sullenly. "I think you're playing with me—laughing at me," he said. "All of you."

Jennifer turned quickly from the miniature bar. "Why, Lee!"

Sam Walden's grin turned into a look of concern. "Now look here, old man—"

But Lee Tarp had quitted the social room, his footsteps echoing up the companionway.

CHAPTER TWO

ALONE IN his own cabin, Tarp gave vent to his frustration by slamming a fist hard against the steel door panel. The sharp pain that shot up his arm was refreshing. He sat down on the edge of his bunk, nursed his knuckles, and called himself eight different kinds of a fool.

He didn't belong in this ship; should never have competed for the honor. Grimly, he realized it took more than a sharp mind, a talent for difficult and complicated sciences, to fit a man for space travel. But he'd wanted the berth of cosmologist and had fought hard to secure it, for but one reason: He was in love with Jennifer Kane and he could not live with the knowledge of her being space-bound with three men, himself excluded.

He had prayed for Jennifer's disqualification even while battling for his own position in the crew. When rumor came of her possible elimination because of her sex, Lee had been joyful. But the objection had been voted down and the final tests given.

Lee knew full well of his own personal shortcomings; his inferiority complex; his lack of emotional stability. But it had not been difficult to hide them from the examining board. Lee had full knowledge of these drawbacks, and knowledge is a powerful ally.

Slowly he stripped off his clothes and climbed up into the bunk. Why, he wondered, couldn't he control his abnormalities and instabilities? He'd been highly successful in hiding them. Sadly, he realized that if he had the answer to that question, he would also have the basic key to all human behavior; a key no individual or group of individuals possesses.

He went to sleep, finally, and dreamed of Jennifer Kane clad, not in the fetching green gown, but in a costume more suited to the chorus line in a nightclub.

THE RECREATION period in the social room did not break up merely because one of the crew had walked out, exceptional as the Tarp incident was. The minutes following Lee's exit were somewhat uncomfortable, but the incident was not discussed. The group finished their drinks, and Sam Walden suggested a rubber or two of three-handed bridge; suggested it even though he'd much rather have retired to his cabin and felt the others would have preferred the same.

The rules of conduct, however, stated the get-together should be held every twenty-four hours as a lift to morale, so the table was set up and the game begun.

But Sam played with only a portion of his mind. The rest of it was divided between the wall dials and his personal thoughts. Why in hell, Sam wondered, had Lee Tarp gone off half-cocked that way? He had revealed an obvious instability. Then why hadn't the board spotted it?

Sam Walden had a machine-gun mind. It checked his hand in a matter of seconds and Sam said, "Two no-trump."

Walden was an exceptional man in that he fully recognized his own superior abilities but was entirely without conceit. He knew beyond all doubt he was not only the smartest and most able person on the ship, but also head and shoulders above more than ninety-nine per cent of Earth's population.

But Sam accepted this more as a responsibility than an honor and thus realized Lee Tarp was his personal problem. Realizing also that he'd gotten the bid at four spades and had made it, Sam experienced a natural satisfaction. As he gathered up the cards, however, he could remember no single detail of the play.

Blast it all! Only two weeks out and complications already forming. Then his natural good humor and optimism took over. Maybe things would work out all right. No use facing trouble until it got in your way.

The clock said five minutes to twenty-three when the second rubber was finished, so Jennifer boxed the cards while Barry Carter folded the table. Jennifer yawned. "It's embarrassing to admit I'm sleepy," she said. "The person with the lightest duties should be the most alert."

"Don't apologize, please," Barry Carter said. "You may have few routine duties, but yours is probably the most important job aboard. What if we got sick? What if an epidemic broke out? Without health, you know, we'd have nothing."

"Well spoken," Sam Walden laughed. "And so long as it's your turn on watch, I'm going to hit the sack. Call me at seven hours."

IT WAS NOT Jennifer's fault that neither man had seen the look of genuine affection in her eyes at Barry Carter's words. She hadn't tried to hide the look. In fact she'd scarcely been aware of it herself. She'd turned to put the cards into a drawer and when she straightened again Sam Walden had left.

The instant the door closed, Barry Carter made a complete and thorough check of the wall gauges. Jennifer watched him as he circled the room to stand before each gauge, even though he could have read them all clearly from the center of the room. Her smile deepened. She said, "Good night, Barry."

"Good night," he answered. "Sleep well. I'm going to make the rounds and then finish that mystery story I started. It's quite a puzzle."

Jennifer went to her cabin thinking of Barry Carter. He was like a little boy in so many ways. So much so that one wanted to hug him or spank him, as the mood dictated. So hopelessly and wonderfully methodical. One thing at a time. Finish it. Make it absolutely perfect. Then go on to the next thing with your whole heart, your whole soul. Complete each job, no matter how unimportant, as though the future of the world depended upon it.

Jennifer slipped out of her clothing and took a leisurely, invigorating chemical bath. As she did so, she mused upon the anticipated pleasure of getting back to Earth where one didn't have to spend time deliberately and continuously denying one was a woman. And a rather beautiful and well-put-together woman at that, Jennifer conceded as she toweled herself before the mirror.

As she slipped into her nightgown, she laughed aloud. It was all so silly. She knew more about men—their tissues, their emotions, their libidos—than they knew themselves. Yet she continued to marvel at their immaturity, their inability to regard things in the proper light.

Although she meticulously obeyed all the rules as to dress and personal conduct, she was still annoyed at not being allowed more comfort and freedom. A pair of shorts, for, instance. No garment was as comfortable as a pair of shorts. Why on earth couldn't men look at a girl's legs, admire them, enjoy them, but realize at the same time that this was neither the place nor the moment?

Jennifer got into her bunk and was asleep in two minutes flat.

Barry Carter went over the ship with a fine-tooth comb. When he finished the two-hour job, every grease cup had been looked into, every plastic oil line meticulously checked, all readings were down in the book, and the jet spectrum double-checked for accuracy.

ONLY THEN did Barry retire to the pilothouse and sit down with his murder mystery. But after ten minutes he'd spotted the killer and his interest dragged. He lowered the book and sat staring at the black observation panel. Under him was the steady vibration of the well-shielded atomic pile deep in the bowels of the ship. Barry felt a thrill of pride at the thought of *Voyager Three,* sturdy, safe, dependable, thundering on through the void. Good ship, he thought. You'll get us there.

His thoughts drifted to the demonstration of Lee Tarp in the social room. He wondered about it, but let it slip quickly from his mind because that same mind worked under perfect discipline and complete control. Possibly Lee Tarp would go off his rocker, but Sam Walden was in command. Therefore, it would be Sam's problem and Barry knew Sam would handle it. Barry blandly refused to worry about the problems of other people.

But Colonel Swain's yarn about the two men reappearing back on Earth—that one was open to everybody. Had Lee been right about the reason for its telling? A rather infantile conclusion, Barry thought. And how stupid of the board to worry about boredom on this flight! How could anyone become bored in the midst of this greatest of all adventures? The ten weeks of its duration was scarcely long enough to get acquainted with this greatest of all ships.

So far as he was concerned, Barry would have been happy to spend ten months inside her mighty shell.

Barry's thoughts now drifted lower—to Jennifer Kane's legs. That was another fool ruling. Why shouldn't a girl show her legs—if she had nice ones, like Jennifer's—on a spaceship as well as anywhere else?

Barry glanced at the clock. He was entitled now to a fifteen-minute nap. He set the signal bell and went dutifully to sleep.

Down below, the atomic pile shattered billions of microscopic worlds per second in its seemingly endless, mad fury. Rearward, the jets roared and sent long flaming tails into the void. *Voyager Third,* proud queen of the spaceways that she was, hurled herself down the sky toward the pinpoint at which she would rendezvous with another proud queen—the planet Mars.

ON THE WALL of his cabin, safe from questioning eyes, Sam Walden had an old-fashioned calendar. Also a stub pencil hanging by a string. Every revolution, at precisely twelve o'clock, he took the stub pencil and crossed out another day. This was of course a rather absurd way of keeping time, but Sam got a secret satisfaction from it.

Up now, bathed, dressed, and shaved, he crossed out a day and realized with pleasure that only a single week of allotted time remained. He thought immediately of Lee Tarp. Lee had done an excellent job in getting hold of himself. The scene in the social room had not been repeated. Of course the other members of the crew, from that time on, had handled Lee with kid gloves, probably without realizing it themselves. Such procedure had helped greatly. Sam combed his hair, hoping fervently that Lee wouldn't upset the apple cart with success almost at arm's reach.

He left his cabin wondering what there would be for breakfast. Damn the examining board! Rotten blunder they'd made in Lee Tarp's case.

Four revolutions later, Sam preambled breakfast with the statement: "I think it would be a good idea to start talking over the landing routine."

"Good idea," Barry Carter said. "It might save us from *boredom.*" Barry tried to bite the word off, but too late. He shot a glance at Lee Tarp and was relieved to discover no reaction. "First Lee makes the atmosphere and temperature checks— right?" Barry added hurriedly.

"That's right, although we're pretty sure as to what he'll find. An hour's survey from the ports is then in order as a safeguard against hostile action. If any active life is discovered, we don't land until we've ascertained its true nature. Then we—"

"—open the ports and put our feet on the soil of Mars," Jennifer said dreamily.

Lee Tarp picked nervously at his food. He was frowning. When he spoke, he directed his words at Sam. "Don't you think Jennifer should stay aboard, in any case? At least until we've checked things outside at first hand?"

Jennifer appeared startled by the suggestion. Sam turned thoughtful. "You may have something there," he said. "There's nothing in the project book covering the point, but—"

"In a pig's eye!" Jennifer snapped. "When you three get ready to step off this ship I'll be right in line, and don't you forget it!"

Lee Tarp flushed. "I—I'm sorry. I didn't mean to offend you. It's just that—"

"I know...I'm a woman. But remember this, I won my spurs in tough competition, and I plan to use them."

"Maybe we'd better drop the subject," Sam Walden said with a grin. "I go first. You can draw straws to see who follows me in what order."

LEE TARP dropped his fork suddenly. Getting to his feet, he muttered, "Sorry. Guess I was born to say the wrong thing," and hurried from the dining room.

Jennifer said, "Darn! I thought he was going to hold up nicely."

"Let's not bet against it," Sam Walden said. "Wish we could figure out what's eating his hide. Maybe I should have a talk with him."

"I wouldn't advise it," Jennifer replied. "Might do more harm than good. Let's just wear the silk gloves and try to muddle through."

This was possibly good advice. At any rate, Lee Tarp managed to reestablish a grip on himself and the time passed agreeably and smoothly until the day, hour, and moment Sam Walden announced to the group then assembled in the pilot room, "Roughly an hour, I'd say. Take the observation chair, Barry."

Jennifer Kane and Lee Tarp stood shoulder-to-shoulder looking down at the planet beneath them. Barry Carter dropped into the observation chair and adjusted the glasses. "All set," he said.

Sam Walden, seated at the control board, did not answer. A distinct tension had settled over the room. An electric silence reigned until Barry Carter, having computed swiftly after checking several instruments, said, "Three hundred miles."

"Cutting the wing-jets," Sam replied. "Watch it."

"In the arc and holding."

Suddenly the port went black. Jennifer gasped. She grasped Lee's shoulder. "Look! Look at the two moons!"

Crackling minutes passed after which daylight flashed up instantaneously.

"Large mountain range on the portside," Barry Carter announced. "Landing possibilities to starboard. Level country. Plenty of room."

"We're being pulled to starboard," Sam said. "Must be tremendous iron deposits underneath." Then he followed with, "Keep the prime jet on quarter power. We're going in."

Barry Carter became nothing more than a brain—checking instruments, staring out the observation port. "O-nine-two—drag five—eleven and a quarter degrees."

After thirty seconds of silence, Sam snapped, "What else! Come awake, man!"

Barry shrugged. "Nothing else. It's flat as a pancake. Go on in."

Lee and Jennifer did not have to be ordered into the chairs. As the ship scraped bottom they sat deep in sponge rubber. The shock was negligible. A few moments later, Sam said, "Cut the jet," and they all sat waiting for possible stopsickness. None came.

Sam Walden got up from his chair, grinning. He said, "Well, kids, you can dial long distance now and tell the folks. We're on Mars."

BARRY CARTER towered the glasses and handed them to Sam Walden. "That's some kind of a long building over there, but look at those brown piles to the left. If they aren't spaceships I'll eat my hat."

Sam took the glasses and studied the piles in question. "Ships of some sort, at any rate. That one about a mile out still has its form."

"But good lord!" Barry said. "They must be thousands of years old! Durilium is practically corrosion proof."

"Maybe they aren't made of durilium."

"Then they can't be spaceships."

Sam gave the glasses back to Barry, after which he crossed the room, got another pair out of a drawer, and returned to the window.

"There are over a dozen of them," Barry said. "This looks to be a graveyard of spacecraft."

"There are only two that I'd swear are the real McCoy. The others could be the remains of—anything."

Barry turned quickly to his skipper. "Sam, I've got a hunch we're going to run into a lot of things that don't make sense."

Sam Walden grinned. "I'm surprised at you, chum. Remember what Colonel Swain said? Everything makes sense if you have the facts."

"Yeah—even two guys turning up on Earth after twenty thousand people saw them leave on a one-way trip."

"Temperature okay," Lee Tarp said. "We won't even need overcoats."

"And the air?"

"Excellent. Only a trifle lighter than we expected it to be." Lee turned suddenly upon Jennifer; so suddenly the girl was startled. He said, "Jen! I love you! I'm so head-over-heels gone on you I can't eat or sleep. I can only go around acting like an idiot." His arms were around her and his lips pressed to hers before the surprised Jennifer could react.

Her mind reacted first, controlled her reflexes, and she freed herself from the desperate grip with a marked gentleness. "Lee, please! I'm honored—and flattered. Flattered indeed. But this isn't the time or the place for such things."

Jennifer stepped back, hoping she could kill, or at least retard, this utterly absurd proposition without bringing on a crisis. She smiled and patted her hair. "It isn't in the rule book, Lee. You know that. Love and jets don't mix."

"You're making fun of me."

"Lee, stop it. I'm not… But can't you see we have no time for—"

"Of course, darling! I know that. But promise you'll keep it in mind—think about it—until I have the opportunity to plead my case with you more—"

Jennifer risked reaching out and patting his cheek. "Of course I will, Lee. But let's get back to the pilot room with the reports. They'll be waiting."

"Of course."

It was with great relief that Jennifer hurried down the companionway, Lee tagging silently at her heels. And it was with some misgiving that she thought of the future.

CHAPTER THREE

"I BELIEVE," Sam Walden said, grinning, "that all the rules have been complied with. You may unbar the door, Mr. Carter."

Barry released the air valve and the four stood waiting while the slow release lifted the double safety bars from their sockets and cleared the lock mechanism.

"Weapons ready?" Sam asked.

Each of them carried a small handgun loaded with thirty-eight death-dealing pellets of negligible size.

"All ready," Jennifer said.

The port opened with maddening deliberation. Then they had to wait until the ramps made up its mind to push out and set its outer edge down on Martian soil. It touched finally, ending the sound of escaping air. "An historic moment," Sam said as he placed his foot on the ramp.

"Oh, get on, with it," Jennifer snapped. "We aren't the first. Other people have been here before."

They filed out—Walden first, then Jennifer and Lee Tarp, Barry Carter bringing up the rear.

Around them lay a silent, waiting land with a strange mood all its own. A fine, fuzzy plant growth carpeted the soil, its color scheme an uninspiring mixture of green and sickly yellow. The sun, far sharper of outline than when viewed from the Earth's surface, seemed more subdued, less friendly, than the sun they had known.

Westward lay a peculiar structure obviously built by hands—human or otherwise. It was of dirty yellow stone, low-roofed, and comparatively narrow. It began at a point within view and stretched away into the distance, remindful of the Great Wall of China. The plain was surprisingly level, and dotted here and there with the melancholy, rusted hulks Barry and Sam had studied through glasses.

"A dying planet," Jennifer murmured.

Sam squinted at the building that flanked the plain. "Possibly—but not dead yet. I think—what the hell...!"

Sam slapped his cheek sharply as he whirled to spot the insect that had stung him. He could not discover the pest, but now the other three were also dodging the invisible hornets. Jennifer cried out and brushed desperately at the flesh of her right wrist.

Now the attack from the invisible swarm increased in violence. Lee Tarp dropped his weapon in a frenzied effort to ward off what no one could see. Sam Walden scooped up the gun. "Back inside," he barked. "Quick! Something's wrong here."

They re-entered the ship with far less dignity and speed than they had quitted her. Sam hit the valve and the door swung too.

"That was murder!" Jennifer gasped. "What do you make of that?"

BARRY CARTER wiped his throat hard, then closely studied the palm of his hand. This gave no clue. The hand was clean.

Sam Walden rubbed his jaw as he turned to Lee Tarp. "I thought you checked the atmosphere."

"I did. It was entirely clear of poisons or gasses. It gave no clue whatever to—"

"The stuff comes down from above—like rain," Barry said. "The intake valve is low down—protected by the bulge of the hull. Better make a note to have that changed in future ships."

Jennifer was ruefully massaging her neck. "You'd think the brains of Project Space would have had the sense to put a valve in the right place!"

"One of those things," Sam said. "It looks like spacesuits and oxygen for us."

Fifteen minutes elapsed during the sojourn to the equipment room, after which the group again assembled at the exit port.

"Radio okay?" Sam asked from inside his helmet. He got three okays in return and turned the port valve. Again they marched out onto Martian soil.

"We'd better head straight for that building over there—if that's what it is."

"We'll certainly find it deserted. The racket we made coming in would have brought out even dead men."

"That's hardly a safe supposition. They may be cautious."

A distance of approximately two miles separated the ship from the strange building. But the going was easy, what with the dead level topography and the springy undergrowth. It was a little like walking on a huge bedspring.

The distance narrowed swiftly and the hike was uneventful. Until Lee Tarp whirled and brought up his gun. "For God's sake! "Look!"

Lee's gun spat a dozen times before Sam was able to knock it down.

"Why did you do that?" Lee flared.

"Don't be so trigger-happy. He—or it—is going away. Scared to death. Fortunate you fired wild."

They stood staring at the strange creature kiting off across the plain. For want of more information, the thing could have been tentatively classed as humanoid. It was apparently naked and its color corresponded almost exactly to that of the fuzzy plant-growth carpeting the plain.

"It—I almost stepped on it," Lee Tarp marveled. "It was completely camouflaged. It could have killed us in our tracks!"

THE CREATURE had faded from sight now, blending again with the protective coloration of the fuzz-bush.

"There are points worthy of note," Barry said. "It was evidently impervious to the stinging rain. That means its hide is shell-like in quality."

Jennifer shuddered inside her light spacesuit. "Did you see its eyes?"

"Yes," Sam Walden said. "Glassy. They appeared to be covered with windshields. Some sort of a transparent protective device probably."

Lee Tarp had turned again, uneasily, toward the building. "Do you suppose that's a door?"

"Looks like it. Let's find out."

They marched single file across the short intervening distance. They found a suggestively shaped inset in the smooth stone wall, but nothing in the way of a knob, a knocker, or a signal bell to indicate the rectilinear indentation as a means of entrance to the building.

A small step had been placed at its base, however, and as Sam Walden set his foot on it, the door opened as silently as the cover of a coffin.

The four stood motionless, somewhat startled by the promptness of this robot hospitality. "Shall we go in?" Lee Tarp asked.

What with the angle of outdoor lighting, it was impossible to see inside. Only a rectangle of gray darkness met their eyes.

"It certainly seems the logical thing to do," Jennifer said. "We can't stand out here all day."

"It shouldn't be too dangerous," Barry said. "We're all armed."

Sam Walden said, "Let's go. Single file. Close together."

They marched, on tiptoe, through the mysterious door. It closed behind them so silently it was moments before they realized they were cut off from escape.

But the fact was not alarming. They appeared to face nothing dangerous. The building—about forty feet wide—was nothing more than an endless corridor, a hall with no termination, and furnished in a mood and with a grandeur that was indeed remarkable.

The floor was yellow and shining, constructed of a stone akin to the marble found on Earth. A single design—a black-bordered square—was set into the floor at regular intervals as it stretched off into a distance; which defied the eye.

THE WALLS were of the same shining material, but done in gleaming white, and against which, at regular intervals, stood huge, highly polished black stone statues, done with a brilliant craftsmanship. In various poses the stone men stood, crouched, and sat in eternal silence, as though waiting patiently for some far-distant day of judgment.

"They're—they're magnificent," Jennifer breathed.

"Masterpieces beyond doubt," Sam Walden said. "But I'm more interested in finding out where the light comes from."

It was a soft, shadowless radiance that apparently had no point of source.

"The walls," Barry said. "It's a glow that comes from the walls. Some sort of fluorescent material is mixed with the stone—or laid over it."

"I think you're right. We mustn't fail to get data on that. The secret of this lighting alone is worth the trip."

"Well," Lee Tarp asked. "What do we do? Start walking?"

"I'm not quite sure," Sam admitted. "It would certainly be a long walk, and I wonder if we'd get anywhere."

"Seeing it from upstairs I'd say this building stretches over four hundred miles. And there were others."

Jennifer laid a hand impulsively on Sam's arm. A gesture not overlooked by Lee Tarp. "The canals!" she exclaimed. "The famous canals of Mars. Why, they're long, narrow, endless buildings. Who would have dreamed it?"

"Not our astronomers, at any rate." Sam Walden's mind went off on another track. "Those ships out there—do you suppose the two *Voyagers* are among them?"

"Possibly," Barry Carter replied.

"But if so, where did the others come from? Only two ships left Earth for Mars, but a hell of a lot more seem to have arrived,"

"You're assuming again that they *are* ships," Sam said. "Let's wait for more—"

His words were cut off by a scream from Lee Tarp. They whirled around to find Lee entangled in as weird a predicament as they had yet come upon.

LEE HAD wandered some fifty feet up the corridor and had paused in front of an imposing black statue. Now he appeared to have become embroiled with a mass of writhing metal snakes. They had come up out of the floor—a dozen of them—to wind themselves around his body. They were headless, each one terminating in a flat metal disc not unlike the nozzle of a shower-bath fixture.

Lee, struggling with a loop around his throat, screamed again. The rest of the group ran swiftly to his aid. But as they moved along the corridor, new action synchronized into the scene. The statue in front of which Lee had stopped swung inward, toward the wall, on a pivot. Then the entire structure of the niche in which the statue had been placed followed suit, went back into an arc out of sight, and a doorway was revealed.

The tall figure of a man stood in the center of the opening, and at that moment the metal snakes began uncoiling themselves and proceeded rapidly back into the floor whence they had come. The man spoke. His voice was clear, resonant, somewhat like a tolling bell. He said, "My most abject apologies. I should have gotten here sooner. I regret most sincerely this disturbing experience."

The eyes of the group were held by this striking individual. Even Lee Tarp seemed to have forgotten his terrifying experience. The man was tall—well over six feet—slim as a reed. He was clad in an olive-green cassock, belted at the waist with a black sash. His face bore a healthy tan, highlighting the pure white of his hair.

There was a first impression among the group of great age in this individual. A closer inspection, however, did not bear this out. His face was entirely free of wrinkles. His eyes were clear blue, bright, and guileless as those of a child. A gentle smile revealed white, even teeth, and the flesh of his hands bore no marks of age.

"I am Jorgman," the man said. "I welcome you to Mars, the life-source of the worlds, the jack of planets, the ancestral home of Man. Won't you come in?"

It occurred to Sam Walden, as he moved forward with the rest, that the speech should have sounded flowery, bombastic. Yet it did not. This he could attribute only to its ring of sincerity; to the imposing personality, of the man who made it.

It was only after the hidden door had swung to, that the group realized they had entered an unknown and possibly dangerous place without protest, with their guns hanging impotent and forgotten in their hands.

BUT THERE was the voice of Jorgman to drive away instinctive doubts. "The mechanism in which you became entangled was not lethal," he said, speaking to Lee Tarp. "It would have merely imprisoned you—as it did—until I arrived. It is the way we defend our inner door from possible marauders. An ancient device, which hasn't really been a necessity for thousands of years."

Jorgman smiled brightly, spreading his attention now over the entire group. "And now," he asked, "which of you is the leader?"

Sam Walden reddened. He felt somewhat like a schoolchild caught in a forbidden place by the master. "My name is Sam Walden," he said, and swiftly gave the names of the others. "We are the members of an expedition from the planet Earth."

"I know," Jorgman said. "We observed your arrival and have anxiously been awaiting your appearance in the hall."

"It seems you could have been a little more hospitable," Lee Tarp said, glancing around uneasily. "We sat out there for over an hour. You could have come—"

"Lee—" Jennifer said sharply.

But the smiling Jorgman was already explaining. "Perhaps an apology *is* in order, but you see, we never leave the hall except under direst emergency, and no emergency existed. You would automatically land where you did because of the great iron deposits under the plain. And once landed, there was no place for you to go except here. You see, you had to come to us."

"Just who is *us?*" Sam Wald asked.

Jorgman's eyes twinkled. "Why, the people of Mars, of course. You see, most of us live underground, what with the untenable conditions on the surface of the planet."

"But we saw someone out there," Lee said. "A man—or was it a man? He ran away."

"There are some who live on the surface. The true Martians, as it were. They correspond in some degree to the American Indian. Not in intelligence, necessarily, but let us say in circumstance. They are an excellent example of how evolution struggles to protect existing life. We must go into it deeper sometime."

It occurred to Sam Walden that there were a great many things to be gone into, but he recognized the impossibility of doing it immediately.

Jorgman said, "And now, you must all be rather tired. If you will walk along with me I will show you to your apartments. This way please." And their host led them down a long flight of stairs.

THE HALLWAY *motif* had vanished with the closing of the door. They stood now in a large high-ceilinged room built of the same shining, marble-like material, but decorated and furnished in a more intimate manner. There were sprawling easy chairs, huge oil paintings, and overall an aura of such wealth and quiet dignity as to be breathtaking. There were many other rooms such as this one; rooms that completely held the interest of the group as they passed from one to the other.

Only Barry Carter seemed preoccupied. "Would you mind telling us something about your atmosphere?" he asked. "When we left the ship it seemed we were stung by invisible hornets—"

Jorgman's laugh was gentle, musical. "It's a surprise all visitors encounter when they come by spaceship. An interesting phenomenon. You see, the atmosphere on Mars is very thin and, as you no doubt know, the atmosphere of a planet is its only shield against bombardments from space. It was a condition you encountered in a far more violent state when you set foot on your moon."

"Of course," Jennifer said.

"Here, the atmosphere has reached a point where it can almost, but not quite, protect the surface of the planet by burning the meteorite bombardments through friction. It eliminates them to all intents and purposes, but microscopic fragments, supercharged with tremendous heat, are just in the process of cooling off when they drift to the surface of the planet. It is such a finely drawn matter that the particles sting severely at a distance of four feet from the surface of the surrounding plain. On the surface itself, they are found to have burned out at the time of contact."

"But what about higher or lower ground?"

"The principle holds. If one were to lie face up in a shallow trench on the plain one would not get stung. But this is the lowest point on the surface of the planet, so the burning ash cannot very well be avoided. On the higher ground—up in the ridges—exposure is fatal. Even the Martians do not go there."

"The Martians?" Jennifer asked. "I don't quite understand. Aren't you a—?"

"A Martian? No. I was born in St. Petersburg, Florida, a very long time ago. The Martians are distinguished by their—well, somewhat different appearance and the armor-like quality of their skin."

Jorgman turned, his manner, while not in the least offensive, signaling an end of the subject. "These are your quarters," he said cheerfully. "Your meals will be served by Martian attendants—except for the sugar. You will find that in a wall safe behind that picture. Here is the combination. Please return any sugar you do not use to the safe." After this bewildering statement, Jorgman bid them goodnight.

They watched in silence as he passed from the room and disappeared from sight. A full minute of complete silence passed. A silence broken finally by Lee Tarp. "There's a note of insanity about all this. I don't like it."

"All I've got to say," Barry Carter stated, "is that it's better than outdoors. Let's get out of these rigs. And I'm damn hungry. I wonder when they serve dinner?"

Jennifer smiled at him tenderly. Lee Tarp caught the smile, and it engendered a misery in his heart almost akin to physical sickness.

CHAPTER FOUR

"IT WOULD seem," Sam Walden said, "that we must change our preconceived ideas about Mars."

"True," Barry Carter replied, "but just what are we going to change them to? I'd say we still have damned few facts."

The group was seated before the remains of as fine a meal as they had ever eaten. The dishes, while not identifiable, did not differ greatly in taste from those found on Earth. The meat had been roasted and could easily have been beef, but the Earthlings did not think so. The vegetables were more tangy than they were used to, but highly delightful. And the appointments—the silverware, chinaware—would not have been out of place in the finest hotels of Earth cities.

"We know Mars is inhabited," Sam said.

"We were pretty sure of that before." Barry lighted a cigarette and frowned. "Oh, I'll grant you my statement sounded somewhat exaggerated, but you'll have to admit we haven't even begun to get answers."

"But you've got to admit," Sam said, smiling, "that we've been pretty comfortable while we've waited for them."

"I think it's about time to go hunting for Jorgman," Lee said. "I don't like this. I don't like it at all. There's something decadent about all this ease—this softness."

Jennifer smiled. "Catch up on your sleep while you can. It's a long way back to Earth and you didn't do so well on the ship."

Lee scowled. "Just the same—three days of this waiting. Maybe this is some sort of a trap. Maybe he doesn't intend to show up."

Jennifer's smile faded. "The only thing that makes me uneasy is these Martians—the ones that wear the shell-skins," Jennifer shuddered slightly. "The way they look at you through those windshields. And sugar locked in the sa—"

She stopped speaking as the sound of soft footsteps broke in. They turned to see Jorgman coming toward them through the broad portal leading into the suite. He approached the table, smiling. "It wasn't eavesdropping, Miss Kane, but I couldn't help overhearing you, and I hasten to put you at your ease. You need have no fear of the Martians. They feel it an honor to serve on the staff indoors and would do nothing to lose the privilege."

Sam Walden got to his feet. "It's been quite a while, sir. Won't you sit down?"

"Thank you," Jorgman said softly. "I'll take this chair."

"We were wondering," Barry said, "if we'd been deserted."

"I really must apologize. It was an error in judgment. I wanted to give you ample time to become acclimated to the atmosphere and general conditions." Jorgman smiled equally upon the group. "And now I suppose you have many questions. I am at your service."

"I have a question," Lee said. "Will you cooperate with us in gathering the data we came for? We'd like to blast off for Earth as soon as possible."

JORGMAN considered, his head tilted in a birdlike attitude. "Just what data did you have in mind?"

"That should be self-apparent. We're from Earth. We want to know about your ways—your customs—there are any number of things—"

Sam Walden raised a hand. "I think if you'd let our host talk, Lee. He just offered to answer questions."

Lee frowned angrily. "I'm afraid I don't like your manner, Sam. Since setting foot on this planet you've become so—so casual—so lackadaisical. You act as if you *enjoyed* all this."

"I do," Sam Walden said. Then, pointedly turning away from Lee, he spoke to Jorgman, "There are so many questions, sir—"

"Please omit the *sir*. Your formality makes me somewhat uncomfortable. You are entirely at liberty to call me Jorgman."

"Thank you. As I said, there are so many questions, it might be wise to start at the beginning—with your words of greeting. You said, if I remember rightly, 'Welcome to Mars—life-source of worlds...' Exactly what did you mean?"

"Precisely what I said," Jorgman smiled. "In the beginning, Mars was the only inhabited planet. Its recorded history goes back over 600,000 years—somewhat longer than that of Earth. I'm sure you will agree. Mars' science, when in its glory, reached developments not yet even conceived by Earth scientists."

"You are saying there were intelligent beings on Mars before Earth was populated?"

"My dear boy, you yourself—all of you—are descendents of Martians. There is no such thing as a native Earthling. Four hundred thousand years ago—a mere afternoon in cosmic time—the Martians built spaceships and inspected the various planets of our little family. They discovered, to their sorrow, that only one—that which you call Earth—existed under conditions favorable to intelligent life. Venus is entirely without water—a hot, dry, incredibly violent globe. Mercury is without atmosphere. The outer planets are enveloped in poisonous gasses, ice, and desolation.

"But Earth was ideal, so the Martians sent a colony there long before Atlantis sank beneath the waves. The cosmic pattern of rise and fall, the mighty mould of evolution, began the slow but sure work laid out in the Master Pattern far above our conception. My son—dozens of civilizations rose and fell on your planet thousands of years before your pyramids were built—hundreds of centuries before your California redwoods were tiny seedlings."

SAM WALDEN interlaced his fingers and sat staring at them. "You can imagine, sir—Jorgman—information such as this, thrown broadside, is rather stunning."

"Beyond doubt. And I suggest you verify it at your leisure. We have several huge libraries here on Mars. I will be glad to place at your disposal books dating back four hundred thousand years—and still in excellent condition. One's greatest regret is the shortness of a lifetime. One can but scratch the surface of recorded knowledge in the few short years given one."

"A hundred civilizations," Jennifer breathed. It's—it's astounding…"

"It sounds like a lot of nonsense to me," Lee Tarp said bluntly. "I suggest we keep our feet on the ground and not swallow every fish thrown at us."

Jorgman ignored the outburst. The others seemed scarcely to hear it.

"How large is the population of Mars?" Barry asked.

Jorgman considered. "No one knows the census of the Shell People, as we call them. Underground there are close to ten thousand, I'd say."

"Ten thousand! On the whole globe?"

"Yes. You see, Mars is a dying planet." Jorgman waved a delicate hand. "All this will die soon."

"Soon?" Jennifer asked. "How soon?"

"We estimate that in a matter of twenty-five thousand years the end will be signaled. By that time all but a small portion of our atmosphere will have escaped into space."

"How about creating an artificial atmosphere?" Barry asked.

Jorgman shook his head. "Theoretically it sounds feasible, but the practical application would prove otherwise. There are limits to what man can do. The task is beyond human capacities."

"But even twenty-five thousand years," Jennifer said. "That's a long time."

"It is but a moment in the life of a planet. This world is even now on its deathbed. So we feel an attempt to repopulate it would be rather futile."

"I take it there is a sharp dividing line between the—well, the inner and the outer Martians."

Lee Tarp sprang to his feet. "I think I've had enough of this," he snapped. "I'm going to bed."

"I hope you sleep well," Jorgman murmured, but Lee was already out of earshot.

There was the silence of deep embarrassment, broken finally by Jennifer. "I hope you'll forgive Lee," she said. "He has not been feeling well. It was a long, hard trip."

"I quite understand. Let us hope the restful conditions here will mend him somewhat."

"I'm sure they will," Barry said, as though anxious to get on with the discussion. "I've been sitting here sorting out questions—trying to classify them in order of importance."

JORGMAN smiled and bowed from the waist, a gesture few men can accomplish gracefully while sitting down. "Don't feel that you will tire me," he assured. "I am quite at your service."

"Thank you. When we crossed the plain we saw a great number of rusted-out hulks. Tell me—are they remains of spaceships?"

Jorgman nodded. "It's sad they are not in better condition. You would no doubt be interested in looking them over."

"How old are they?"

Jorgman studied the ceiling. "Their ages vary. The oldest— mere rust spots on the prairie now, and long grown over—date back almost half a million years. Others are of more recent vintage. The most recent of them are perhaps one hundred thousand years old."

"None more recent than that?" Sam Walden asked, leaning forward in his chair.

Jorgman raised a finger as though correcting himself. "Oh— I'm glad you pressed the point. I am in error. The ships used by the two previous units of your expedition are there also. It quite slipped my mind."

"Then they did get through!" Barry said.

"Yes. The first arrival was somewhat sad. Three of the four crewmen died of a rare malady en route. The fourth man was in a pitiable condition. The second group was more successful. They arrived in the bloom of health."

"Then they are here? In this building?"

"Not here in these apartments, but certainly somewhere in the underground city. You see, the structure above ground is a sort of projecting spine, so to speak, of what lies beneath the ground. All the entrances to the outer world are located in the Great Corridors. Our race, moved underground several thousand years ago. There is a great deal of dwelling space."

Barry tried to interject a question, but Jorgman was ahead of him. He smiled at Jennifer and said, "Miss Kane inquired about the Shell Folk when we were interrupted. It was rude of me to overlook her question."

Jennifer held up a protesting hand.

"It's quite all right. I think our questions are tiring you. We've been very rude to grill you this way."

Jorgman's smile was unchanging. "It has been a pleasure, I assure you." But he was obviously fatigued, as he took advantage of the loophole Jennifer offered. "Suppose I can upon you tomorrow and we will continue our most pleasant exchanges? Would that be satisfactory?"

"We'll look forward to it."

Jorgman bowed. "A very good night to you all," he said. He turned and walked away; disappeared without looking backward.

There was a minute of silence after Jorgman's exit. Then Barry Carter asked, "What do you make of it?"

"Blessed if I know," Sam Walden sighed. "I can only think of the important questions that want asking."

"It wasn't his fault," Jennifer protested. "He was certainly agreeable, but the man's not made of iron."

"He said he was born in Florida. What about that?"

"Why were those spaceships allowed to rot away?"

"Taylor and Gardner showed up back on Earth—or Swain claimed they did. How did they get there?"

"He said those people with the hard shells outside are the true Martians. If that's the case, what are the ones who live indoors—Arabians?"

"How do we go about contacting the crews of the first two *Voyagers*?"

"And why are they still on Mars?"

"That's right? Why didn't they return to Earth?"

Walden stood up. "This is a waste of time—asking each other questions. Let's save our ammo until the oracle comes again."

"You're right," Barry said, "but there's something we should discuss—Lee. What are we going to do about him?"

"I wish I knew," Sam said slowly. "That examining board and their tests! I'll have something to say to them when we get back."

"And another thing, how soon does that rusting process set in? I'd hate to go out some morning and find holes in the ship. We'll have to check with Jorgman on that."

"Right. Good night." Sam left the room, leaving Barry and Jennifer alone. Jennifer smiled. "This is a pretty big place. Want to walk me home?"

"Certainly. You're in the left-hand hallway, aren't you?"

"That's right. Five blocks down. I found the sweetest little gray and gold room. Where do you suppose all this came from?"

Jennifer hooked her arm into that of Barry. He said, "Damned if I know. But half a million years—they certainly had plenty of time."

"With only a few thousand population, I'd say it was a matter of the people being over-housed. The next U.S. presidential candidate ought to take that for a slogan, 'Twenty rooms for every voter.' "

Barry grinned, and looked down at Jennifer's pert face. "This is it," she laughed. "I suppose the gal should invite the boy in for a drink, but I haven't located the liquor cabinet yet."

"If the boy isn't a cad, he should refuse."

Jennifer stood rather close. "Are you a cad?"

"I could be, with a little practice."

"What does a gal have to say to get kissed?"

"Not another word."

At that second, down the hall, Lee came softly through a door. He saw the kiss, the embrace, the second kiss. Lee turned pale. Perspiration sprang from his forehead; his knees trembled. It was an effort to get back to the doorway and inside without being seen.

CHAPTER FIVE

"I TELL you we're in a trap," Lee Tarp said.

Two days had passed since Jorgman's last visit. Jennifer, Barry, and Sam had been seated in one corner of the huge drawing room which was a part of their living quarters, when Lee Tarp came hurrying in, showing every sign of extreme agitation.

"Lee—where have you been all day? We were beginning to worry."

"And there's plenty of cause to worry. I can't for the life of me understand the complacency with which you three take all this!"

Walden glanced up quickly. Lee's words bringing the situation sharply into focus. Possibly, Sam thought, complacency *was* the term to describe his attitude of the past several days.

He frankly admitted to himself that never in his life had he felt so completely at home. Had the deep peace of this place, the sense of brooding timelessness, wrought some swift change in his personality? He felt completely severed from any life he had ever known. Even the ship, sitting on the plain not two miles away, seemed as distant as the stars. And Earth—was there such a place? The work, the discipline, the drudgery that had preceded the trip to Mars was no longer a part of him. It was some vague and ill-formed dream.

Clear realization of all this brought a sense of guilt to Sam Walden. "You spoke of a trap, Lee. What did you mean?"

"Just this," Lee Tarp said in a tone of triumph. "Jen asked me where I've been all day. Well, I've been investigating— hunting for the guy in the green nightgown. I must have walked thirty miles."

"And what did you discover?"

"That we're locked in."

"Locked in?" Jennifer frowned and crossed her legs with a quick movement. "That's absurd."

"Far from it. I never did find Jorgman. He must sink into the floor after he leaves us. But I discovered a perimeter of locked doors! This trap of ours is a great circle about two miles in diameter. There is room after room after room. You walk on and on, through suites, hallways, huge and complicated floor plans, until your head reels and you feel like something out of *Alice in Wonderland.*"

"That's what you've been doing all day—walking through the house?" Barry asked.

Lee scowled. "I can do without your humor," he snapped.

"Sorry."

"This place staggers the imagination. Then you come finally to a closed door that won't open. A heavy door no ten men could smash through. That's what happened to me—I came to this door and found it locked. So I began circling, trying to get around it. I found other doors, locked and bolted. There are thirty or forty of them, trapping us like squirrels in a cage."

SAM WALDEN was studying the strange pack of cards he'd picked up from one of the tables. The pack was somewhat larger than the standard bridge decks used on Earth. But the faces of any bridge deck Sam had ever seen bore no resemblance whatever to the cards he held in his hands.

Beyond doubt there was a sequence to them. There seemed to be seven suits, and all the cards in the deck were picture cards. He ruffled the deck through his fingers, his eyes on Lee Tarp. "What would you recommend?" he asked.

"That from *you?*" Lee gasped.

"I don't understand."

"Why, Sam! You're supposed to be the leader of this group. You hold the responsibility for our safety. I come to you and tell you we're in danger. And you ask what do I recommend!"

"I'm still asking," Sam said quietly, "although I can't see why you're upset. We aren't trapped and you know it. All we have to do is walk out the way we came in."

"And that's what I recommend. We've gained our objective! We made the Mars run. Let's get into the ship and blast off. Next time we'll come with a fleet, and if any doors bar our way we'll blast them down,"

"We didn't come here as warlords," Barry said. "We came in peace, and so far we've been received in peace. We came seeking information about this world."

"And what information have we gained?" Lee demanded heatedly. "A cock and bull story by an old character who crawls out of the woodwork now and again to charm us with his manners. If we repeated what he's told us—repeated it on Earth—we'd be laughed off the planet."

Sam Walden silently conceded that Lee had something. It was true that Jorgman's enlightenments took on the stamp of wildest fantasy when considered outside the aura of Jorgman's own remarkable personality. "We'll ask a few pointed questions when he comes again, Lee. Does that satisfy you?"

"No. I don't think we should be here when he comes again."

Sam put down the deck of cards, his manner turning slightly hostile. "No one has lit any firecrackers under us. I see no reason to run screaming to the ship and blast off."

Lee's lips quivered. He turned his eyes on each of them singly. "You're all against me," he said. "All three of you. You're laughing at me."

"Lee!" Jennifer exclaimed. "Stop saying that..."

He regarded her grimly. "I know why *you* want to get rid of me. I'm not exactly blind."

Jennifer's eyes widened as she sought words with which to reply. But before answer could be made, Lee whirled on his heels and rushed from the room.

"Why does he always do that?" Barry asked.

"Run away, you mean?" Sam asked. "You're the neurologist, Jennifer. Possibly you can answer the question."

JENNIFER, her eyes on the doorway through which Lee had made his exit, spoke without thinking, "It's the clue to what ails him; the fear of facing any situation he can't dominate. He strikes out blindly, and when the going gets tough, he runs away."

"Good evening," Jorgman said. As the trio turned to see him standing just inside the, room, he said, "I must apologize for apparent eavesdropping. It sprang from a natural hesitancy.

I didn't want to walk in on what appeared to be a private family quarrel."

Jorgman smiled brightly and approached the seated Earthlings. There was about him the attitude of the perfect host.

"We expected you back sooner," Sam said, and was immediately ashamed of the chill in his voice.

Smiling cheerfully, Jorgman ignored both the words and the chill. He glanced brightly at the strange deck Sam was again fingering. "Oh, I see you've found the bible of the Shell Folk. There is some interesting data concerning those cards. They are the oldest mediums of chance in existence. Their surfaces have not been changed one iota in half a million years."

"I don't quite understand," Jennifer said, frowning slightly. "You called them the bible of the Shell Folk."

Jorgman was seated comfortably in an easy chair. "They are an amazing people, even to we who know them. To you, their customs, heritage, and backgrounds will be even more astounding."

Each of the trio had formed questions to throw at Jorgman as soon as he appeared. But now, lulled possibly by the music of his voice, the magic of his gentle personality, the questions were momentarily forgotten…

"Their whole existence is based upon gambling," Jorgman said. "Their history has hinged, literally, upon the turn of a card. They have no family life because the more attractive females are constantly changing hands. Any work necessary for their existence is done by those who lose working hours to others. A man may win enough working hours with the cards to have a dwelling place constructed for himself. But likely as not, it will have changed hands a dozen times before the house is completed. No Shell Man will work of his own accord. All he ever gets comes from gambling, or does not come at all."

"You mean gambling is actually a religion with them?"

"The only religion they have, and there is a strict moral code concerning it. Cheating is unheard of."

"Are they a warlike people?"

"They fight among themselves, but there has been no war between the inner and the outer races for many hundreds of years."

"Are you so much more powerful?"

JORGMAN smiled. "Two factors contribute to the continued peace. Any of the Shell Folk who are temporarily running in bad luck can get food from any of several stations near our chemical food plants and underground gardens. Also, while certain of them are allowed to enter the buildings and serve us, there are areas in which they are never allowed to enter. That makes for mystery, and mystery makes for fear." Jorgman's smile deepened, as though what he was about to say amused him. "Also, their representatives are permitted to witness some of our…ah…magic, shall we say? Certain of these ceremonies are most impressive."

"What ceremonies?"

Jorgman appeared pensive. "Well, for instance, our executions."

Sam's eyes widened. "You have capital punishment here?"

Jorgman smiled again, brightly. "It is necessary to maintain a certain discipline at times," he said. "And now possibly you'd like me to show you the game the Shell Folk play with the cards."

"There are other things we are more interested in," Sam Walden said. "For instance, we would like to contact the members of our two previous expeditions."

"Certainly, but that might take a little time. I have no way of knowing where they are. A search would have to be made."

"Are we at liberty to make that search?"

"Of course, but I would insist upon procuring you a guide. This underworld is a vast, sprawling area. With so few inhabitants, a stranger could easily get lost."

"When could you arrange for the guide?"

"In a few days. Let us say a week at the latest."

Sam glanced at his two companions and Barry shot a question at Jorgman: "You told us you were born in Florida. I presume by that you meant the state on Earth?"

"Quite true."

"Then would you mind telling us how you got to Mars?"

"Not at all. We have quite a number of representatives on Earth who are always on the lookout for likely prospects for residence here. You see, while we don't augment our population, a certain number of replacements are sometimes necessary. We seek the highest type of individuals; people whose desires and temperament suit them for life among us. When such persons are found we invite them to come here.

"I was contacted some forty years ago. It took months to convince my sponsor I was suited to come to Mars. But I was finally admitted and..." Jorgman's placid face wore its eternal smile, "...that was that."

"But couldn't you be a little more specific? The means of transportation. Are there hidden spaceports on Earth?"

Jorgman thought very carefully before he replied, "Yes—and no. But there is something I want to mention before I forget it. It concerns your friend Lee Tarp. It has been brought to my attention that he leaves the building and fraternizes with the Shell People."

THE TRIO looked at one another in surprise. "You must be mistaken," Jennifer said. "He's made no mention of it to any of us. I'm sure he hasn't been out of the building."

"My information is usually correct," Jorgman said gently. "And not knowing their ways, I fear he could become badly involved. Situations could arise whereby we would be powerless to help him."

"But what possible reason could he have for—"

This time Jorgman's tone was hard. "There could be only one possible reason. And now I must bid you good day. I will arrange for a guide to take you through the underworld as soon as one can be located."

Jorgman always vanished with a speed not indicated in his leisurely stride. Thus he always left questions hanging on the lips of his guests.

But this time they scarcely noticed his departure. All questions were forgotten in view of the startling news.

"What do you suppose Lee is up to?" Sam asked.

Barry shook his head in bewilderment. "Do you think Jorgman is right about his leaving the building? Where would Jorgman get his information?"

"From the Shell People who work in here. The ones that bring our meals and make our beds."

Jennifer said, "They're the most elusive creatures I've ever encountered. I haven't been able to get within speaking distance of one since we've been here." She shuddered slightly. "Not that I've cared to particularly."

"They're certainly timid," Barry said. "At least, in here."

"I wonder if they aren't following orders from Jorgman? Lee may have been right about him, at that. I get the impression he doesn't want us to know too much."

"That yes and no business about how he got here was very enlightening," Barry said wryly.

Jennifer said, "You think then that the help avoids us to keep us from asking questions?"

"I don't know what to think, but I'm worried about Lee. What do you think we ought to do? Ask him about it?"

After a pause, Jennifer said, "I don't believe he'd tell us the truth."

"Then we've got to watch him. You and I, Barry—tonight."

"If he goes out tonight."

"We'll have to watch until he does. It's the only way we'll find out what's behind it."

"Couldn't you order him to stay inside?" Jennifer asked. "You're the skipper."

Sam frowned. "It would mean putting a guard on him night and day. That's impossible. We haven't enough people."

"We'd better lay for him in the corridor behind a couple of those statues. It's the only way he could get out."

"Then we won't say anything to him until we've got something definite to go on."

"I don't like being left out of this," Jennifer said.

Barry grinned. "You don't think I'd let you go out among all those beautiful Martians, do you?"

Jennifer tried to keep from blushing, but she knew it was impossible. "Afraid of competition? See if you can sort a bridge deck out of those cards. We didn't bring any from the ship."

CHAPTER SIX

IT WAS warm clad in a spacesuit crouching behind the brooding black statue. Sam fought the desire to scratch his nose, and glanced three statues down the line to where Barry was probably in the same predicament. They'd been waiting over half an hour; ever since Jennifer reported that Lee had entered his room.

Faced with the discomfort and uncertainty of this procedure, Sam debated the wisdom of confronting Lee and demanding an explanation. He vetoed the idea again, however, because he was sure he wouldn't get the explanation.

With time on his hands, he went back to scanning the general situation, and felt again that strange peace and contentment which seemed to charge the very air of the spacious apartments. He frankly admitted it had wrought a change in him. There were things to be learned, certainly, but why the need of hurry? Details had to be worked out for the return trip. Normally, Sam Walden would have been true to his training—sharp, alert, efficient. But now...

His mind drifted into another track. After all, what was normalcy and what was the abnormal? Possibly the keen, driving Sam Walden was the truly abnormal person. Maybe there was far more to life than—

Sam tensed as the key statue, down toward the exit, swung slowly backward. The door opened and Lee Tarp appeared, carrying a bulky package.

Lee waited for the statue to swing back, then started down the corridor, taking a flashlight from a pocket of his spacesuit as he walked. He obviously had no idea he was being watched.

Sam Walden waited until Lee went out of the corridor into the black Martian night. Then he came from behind his statue and motioned to Barry. Together they went to the door and waited for several minutes before risking an exit. Sam tested the radio by saying, "We'll be able to follow his flashlight."

"Right," Barry replied. "Shall we go?"

There were no moons in the sky at this hour, and the plain was as black as the inside of a closet. But out across the fuzz-growth, the beam from Lee Tarp's flashlight could be seen jerking through the darkness.

Barry raised his arm and opened his mouth to speak. He closed it before any damage was done, remembering Lee's radio would pick up his words. He felt the pressure of Sam's hand on his shoulder, and they moved side by side after the dancing light.

FOR TWENTY minutes they pushed on through the night, hand in hand so they would not lose each other. Then little Phobos dived up over the horizon and Sam Walden flung himself to the springy fuzz-bush, hauling Barry down with him.

The delay was short-lived, however, because they soon discovered the little moon did not shed enough light to give them away.

Barry felt Sam's helmet touch his own. Muffled words. "Turn off your radio."

"It's off."

"Let's get going. Be ready to duck, though. That other moon should be along in a minute."

"Where in all hell's he going?" Barry grunted.

But he got no reply because Sam was already up and moving. Barry clambered erect and trotted after his companion—landed beside him in one long stride as his bunched muscles defied the light gravity of the planet.

Ten more minutes with only Phobos giving scant illumination. Then Lee's flash disappeared. Simultaneously, Sam grabbed Barry's arm and leaned over to touch helmets.

"Can you still see it?"

"Nope."

"He's either spotted us or ducked in somewhere or both. Maybe we'd better stall a minute."

They fell prone and lay in the fuzz-bush for several minutes. Finally Barry said, "Look—why all this pussy-footing? You'd think we were the sneaks in this deal. Let's get up there and find out what's going on. If he sees us—okay—he sees us."

"All right. But don't turn your radio on. I think maybe we can find out more if we don't pass out any calling cards."

They got up and continued their trek—walked until Barry leaned over and sharply banged helmets. "You see that? That glow?"

"Uh-huh. It's about where Lee's light disappeared. The light's on again, but it's behind something."

"That isn't Lee's light. It's got a greenish cast."

They spotted the ruins of the spaceship simultaneously, signaled in a common motion, and said nothing. Now they went forward slowly, bringing each foot down with care.

"I still say barge in and find out," Barry grumbled.

"Take it easy. I've got a hunch he isn't alone."

The greenish glow increased as they approached the ship. It was a huge rusted hulk, now half-gone from the swift corrosion prevalent on the planet.

Sam Walden took Barry's arm and drew him quietly toward one end of the skeleton where Sam had spotted a jagged break in the lower arc. They went in under the break and cautiously raised their heads.

IT WAS a strange scene, remindful, in the greenish glow, of a color painting out of some book on demonology. On what had been the forward deck of the ship—and protected by resistant sections of overhead metal—twenty or so of the Shell Men squatted in a circle. In the center of the circle was another of these true Martians, and as Sam and Barry raised their heads to peer in, he was dealing cards to the waiting players.

Barry leaned close to Sam. "Good Lord! A card game! The damn fool comes clear out here to play cards."

"Lee's got his helmet off. Turn on your radio," Sam said.

Tarp sat in the far side of the circle, his eyes glued on the dealer. His eyes, with the eyes of the other players, watched each card as it was flung out. The dealer was an expert. Every card he shucked off the deck spun ten feet through the air to land squarely in front of the player for whom it was destined. The players sat with their hands folded until the deal was completed, each player receiving ten cards.

"They sure use a whale of a deck," Barry said.

"You notice something else?"

"What?"

"Lee isn't playing. He hasn't any cards."

"Then he just came to watch. I'm beginning to feel like a fool."

"That package he was carrying. It's beside him there and it's open. Let's wait a little while. I still want to see what goes."

The deal now complete, the Martian who seemed to be running the game from the center of the circle made a signal and the players picked up their cards.

The scene tightened. Both Barry and Sam could feel the tension as the players sorted their cards. The dealer gave another signal and—starting at a point determined in some manner, and moving clockwise—the players each threw a card back at the dealer, who carefully laid each on top of the one before until all the players were represented.

A pregnant pause, the players sitting motionless, waiting. Then the dealer gathered up the trick, carried it to the perimeter of the circle, and handed it to the winner.

This broke the tension. The favored player immediately got to his feet and approached Lee Tarp. Eagerly the Martian took a handful of small objects from a sack he had swung to his arm. He handed the objects to Lee Tarp, who inspected them critically. Then Tarp dropped them on a pile of similar objects in front of him and reached into the package by his side. He brought out a handful of what appeared to be white powder and poured it into the hands of the eagerly waiting Martian who transferred it to his sack and returned to his place in the circle.

NOW THE process was repeated. A second winner approached Lee and the same ritual was enacted.

"That's sugar he's giving them," Sam said.

"And if I'm not wrong, they're paying him gold nuggets in return. Or at least some kind of metal that looks like gold."

"I don't get it."

"Evidently they play cards for the privilege of making a trade with Lee. Screwy as it sounds, that must be it. Jorgman told us gambling was their life and their religion, but this looks insane."

"When Jorgman said everything they do hinges on gambling, he must have meant what he said."

"But it's still off-center. Why are they so hot to get a handful of sugar?"

"I don't know, but I'll bet it ties in some way with the sugar being kept under lock and key back in the apartment. Evidently it's locked up so the Martians working in there can't get at it."

"But what's so precious about sugar?"

"Under the circumstances, I think I can guess. We know nothing whatever about their diet, their metabolism, or even their physical makeup. "I'll bet—"

"One thing's certain. Lee's been talking to the Martians working inside. He found out a few things and got himself invited to the game. If that stuff is gold they're giving him, he's getting to be a very rich man."

The dealer had all the cards again and was shuffling the thick deck with a skill any Earth gambler would have envied.

"Well, what do we do?" Barry asked.

"Go back where we came from, I think, and wait for Lee. I've got a feeling it wouldn't be smart to barge in there and upset the *status quo*. When Lee comes back, I lay down the law. For all we know, this could lead to trouble."

It led to trouble before the words were out of Sam's mouth. The deal had scarcely begun when one of the players sprang to his feet with a high-pitched shriek that carried even through the helmets of the eavesdropping Earthmen. They stared dumbfounded as the Shell Man hurtled straight across the circle, knocked the dealer sprawling, and dived at the package on the floor beside Lee.

THE MARTIAN had obviously gone berserk. His hand snaked into the package to come out filled with sugar. Like one driven to complete desperation, he crammed the stuff into his mouth, ignoring Lee, ignoring the other players, ignoring all save the ecstasy afforded by mouthing the sugar.

Lee Tarp was the first to react. The two Earthmen saw his lips form an oath as he sprang up and jerked a gun from the pocket of his space garb. He turned the weapon on the Martian and pressed the trigger. The tiny pellet smashed against the creature's shell with a force that tore a jagged opening in his chest armor, and knocked him ten feet across the deck.

A roar went up from the assembled Martians, and both Sam and Barry were amazed at the speed with which they moved. A half dozen of them swarmed over Lee before the sound of the gun had died. They tore the weapon from his hand and locked his arms securely behind him.

Barry acted upon instinct—certainly without thought. The merits of the situation were lost upon him as he brought out his own gun and vaulted into the ship. He heard Sam's warning cry: "Barry! Hold it! Take it easy!"

It was too late to hold it, however, and Barry, from the corner of his eye, caught sight of Sam following him into the ship.

They didn't have a chance. Even armed as they were, they didn't have a chance. This became starkly apparent as the Martians, reacting with bewildering speed, overwhelmed them even as Barry sought to press the trigger of his gun.

The Martians were talking among themselves and seemed to look for leadership to the one who had been dealing from the center of the circle. The Earthlings saw his stiff lips move; saw his arm gesture authoritatively.

Then Barry and Sam felt themselves lifted—lifted easily, as though their weight was of little consequence—by a single Martian holding each of their arms.

But the real surprise was yet to come. It came after the Martians filed out of the ruined spaceship. There they waited, as though for another signal from their leader. The signal came and the Martians began to run.

Even with their minds filled with the urgency of the situation, Sam and Barry could not help but marvel. Two of these Shell Folk holding each of them off the ground and running as teams, with a speed that would have compared favorably to that of an Earth horse in full gallop. And doing it as though it were the most natural thing imaginable.

Speechless, Barry glanced back to see Lee Tarp struggling in the grip of another pair. Lee appeared to be screaming from more than mental anguish. He turned and twisted his head as though facing an icy sleet storm, and Barry remembered the hot ash—visualized it stinging Lee's exposed head and face.

It was indeed a strange spectacle. Twenty or so Shell People flying over the level Martian plain as though all hell followed after.

"I don't know where we're going," Barry heard Sam say. "But I'll bet it doesn't take us long to get there."

CHAPTER SEVEN

JORGMAN stepped into the room and took off his helmet; a much lighter one than those the Earthmen had. Sam and Barry, seated on a rude bench, the only piece of furniture in the place, got wearily to their feet. Their helmets lay on the rough dirt floor of their prison, but they had not removed their suits.

Jorgman regarded them pensively; neither with condemnation nor cordiality, but as if they were a source of trouble that had to be eliminated quickly. "Good day, gentlemen. You appear to have fallen into an unfortunate situation."

"You're most observant," Sam said drily. "If you can get us out of here, we'll be much obliged."

Barry was still marveling. "Those are the damndest people I've ever seen! They *ran* here. They lit out over the plain like a bunch of wild horses. They ran for an hour without stopping for breath. We must have come forty miles."

"Forty-four, to be exact," Jorgman said. "You are learning things about the Shell Folk. It pains me that you aren't learning under pleasanter circumstances."

"But they have no reason for holding us. It was natural that we went to Lee's rescue."

"I'm sure your offenses are not of grave import," Jorgman said gently.

"And Lee?"

Jorgman shook his head. "I'm afraid I can do nothing for your friend. They might possibly turn him over to me for trial and then execution if he is found guilty—"

"Trial and execution! But the Martian didn't die! Or did he? He was standing up and walking around back at the spaceship!"

"No, I understand his wound was painful, but superficial."

"Then what's this absurd talk about execution?" Sam Walden demanded.

"Not absurd so far as the Shell Folk are concerned." Jorgman smiled gently, sadly. "You have no doubt heard that Earth expression: When in Rome, do as the Romans do?"

"Of course, but—"

"It also applies to Mars. You see, the Shell Folk consider violence as the most hideous crime. It is of such rare occurrence as to be—well, I suppose you would call it sensational."

"But the death penalty—"

"THEY LOOK upon the intent rather than the result. A most admirable trait in many ways. They consider Lee's attack entirely apart from its consequence."

"But you can certainly do something!"

"I doubt if I could prevail, even if I were inclined to try."

"You mean youwon't even attempt to intercede?"

"I wouldn't dream of it, and my attitude must also be your attitude. You see, the law of the Shell Folk is just—in their own eyes. It has the dignity of an age-old heritage. We who dwell with them on this planet have learned wisdom from them. We have never sought favor for one of ours, and time has proven the wisdom of our restraints."

"By the way," Sam Walden said, "we never did find out what it was all about. Lee was giving them sugar for gold."

Jorgman shook his head with some sadness. "It is partially my fault. There was so much to explain that I quite overlooked telling you about the sugar—the reason we keep it under lock and key. You see, sugar acts upon the Shell Folk in the same manner as certain drugs and narcotics act upon Earth people; sometimes even more violently. The Shell Folk have a physical makeup all their own. They live mainly on *parzwan*, the bushy vegetation that grows on the plain. Sometimes they cook it, sometimes eat it raw, thus making them entirely vegetarian, but in a somewhat different sense from vegetarian mammals upon Earth. There is no sugar whatsoever in the Shell Folk's diet. The majority of them avoid it as the average Earthman avoids heroin or morphine. But, sadly, a few of them have a weakness. Your compatriot learned of it and turned it to his own uses."

"That *was* gold they gave him?"

"Yes. It is comparatively common on Mars and has little value. Lee Tarp must have inquired, as it would not have occurred to the Shell Folk to offer it as payment. They get it from the ancient ruins up in the higher country."

Sam sighed in perplexity. "You leave me to make a hard decision," he said. "To see a countryman executed for—"

"He has not been executed yet," Jorgman reminded. "He may be freed at the trial."

"That's possible, Sam," Barry said.

"In the meantime," Jorgman said, with more cheer in his voice, "I discussed your case with the leaders and you are free to accompany me. It seems you were seized before absolute proof, by action, that you were intent upon violence."

"Can we see Lee before we go?"

Jorgman shook his head. "I'm afraid not. A law-breaker is kept in isolation until he is executed or proven fit to associate again with others."

Barry got to his feet. "We'd better go with Jorgman, Sam. Maybe we can think of some way to help Lee but, regardless, we've got to remember Jen. She's our responsibility too."

"A very sensible attitude," Jorgman said.

He led them out into the street of the shabby village and they noted the respect with which Jorgman was regarded. He spoke in a rapid, guttural tongue and immediately a half dozen of the Shell Men came forward. They picked up their three guests in the usual manner and sped off across the plain at the speed of galloping horses.

CHAPTER EIGHT

JENNIFER said, "I think you've gone completely mad, Lee." She sat up in bed, the sheet drawn about her shoulders, and regarded Tarp in sad appraisal.

Lee replied with bitterness, "You don't believe that. It's just that you're against me. You're siding with the others. All three of you have discriminated against me from the first—banded together—left me out of things—"

"Lee!"

Tarp's eyes fell in quick confusion at the sincerity of Jennifer's protest. But they were quick to narrow again—his face quick to harden. "Even now—this minute. Are you glad to see me? Did you congratulate me on escaping from a band of barbarians? Your only comment is, 'Lee, you're insane!'"

Jennifer sought words, but Lee Tarp went swiftly on, "But don't worry, darling. I'm not criticizing you. It's not your fault. It's the influence of Walden and Carter." He stepped to the side of the bed, leaned forward. "I love you, Jen. I love you deeply and sincerely, and..." He glanced over his shoulder, his manner suddenly crafty, as though he sensed eavesdroppers, "...and I can give you tangible proof of my love."

Lee's eyes were burning now, his voice husky. "A great thing has happened, darling! A great, great thing for you and me! While Sam and Barry have been content to lounge around, I've made investigations—bestirred myself!"

"Really, Lee—"

"Wait until I tell you. I found one thing on this stupid planet that is of value to us. Gold, Jen! These hideous Shell People—"

"I heard about that. Gambling with the Martians—shooting one of them..."

"Of course they told you. And put me in a bad light. But Jen, Sam and Barry don't know the truth—what I have in mind. You and me, darling—just the two of us going back to Earth with a ship full of gold. Enough to buy mansions—untold wealth—"

"You mean *leave Sam and Barry?*"

"Of course! They seem to like it here from what I've been able to see. And besides, this is the chance of a lifetime. We can't afford to be sentimental. You know they'd never let us take back a shipload of gold." Lee straightened and sneered. "They're too deeply immersed in the *scientific* aspects of this jaunt. They'd refuse to be practical."

"Lee! Stop it. Up to this point I've felt sorry for you. I didn't think you were beyond help. But—"

His manner changed again. He froze. There was the suggestion of flintiness in his eyes. "You don't mean that, Jen."

"Of course I mean it!"

"You don't love me?"

"That's absurd. Of course I don't."

He did not explode into protestations of his own love. He did not plead. A slight smile twisted his lips.

"You don't love me," Jen said evenly. "You are incapable of true love. What you feel is only salve for your overweening ego; merely a reflection of self-love—the only emotion that stirs you."

"Just you and me," Lee said. "Alone in the ship on the trip back to Earth. I think I could change your views. I'm willing to wager you'd end up loving me."

"I've had about enough of this!"

Lee moved with the speed of a cat. Jennifer was unable to react before his hands were upon her; before the small drug-cap he took from his pocket settled tightly over her nostrils.

Then it was too late to react.

JENNIFER WAS wearing a spacesuit when she regained consciousness. The helmet lay on the ground beside her and the strange green glow made her blink—made her feel she'd come into a dream world of some sort; a world tenanted by grotesque phantoms.

Then her eyes focused somewhat more clearly, and she recognized the crouching figures as brothers, at least, to the servants she'd glimpsed in the sumptuous apartments.

A gag had been drawn tightly over her mouth and she lay partially against a rough, metal wall. As she strove to draw herself into a more comfortable position, Lee glanced in her direction. But there was nothing of tenderness in his look. His eyes were hot, feverish, and he turned immediately back to the business at hand.

There were perhaps a dozen Shell men present, and as Jennifer awoke they were in the process of passing before one of their kind who squatted stolidly on the open deck of the ancient spaceship. Each of the Shell Men deposited a large handful of nuggets on the fast-growing pile before the seated one.

Now the donations to the common heap had been completed, and the Shell Men stood back to form a rough circle around Lee and the keeper of the gold hoard.

Finding that struggle against her bonds and against the gag was useless, Jennifer turned her attention to the tableau before her. The squatting Martian was now fingering a large deck of cards, shuffling, passing them from one hand to another with amazing skill. He eyed the sack between Lee's knees and grunted an unintelligible word.

Lee evidently knew the meaning of the word, because he pushed the bag forward into a position beside the sack of nuggets. Now the Martian shuffled the cards for a final time and laid them on the floor. The circle broke into a line, each Martian passing by to stoop and solemnly cut the deck.

The final cut was reserved for Lee. The cutting, Jennifer thought, seemed of great importance; almost a ritual, so carefully and deliberately was it accomplished.

THE MARTIAN began to deal two hands. Lee snatched up his cards eagerly, and the light from the green lamp sitting nearby reflected a glitter in his bright eyes. His tension, his nervousness, showed in every movement.

The Shell Man was more deliberate, giving equal attention to his hand and to Lee's face, as though the study of his opponent was fully as important to him as the study of the cards.

Each player held thirteen of the thin purple rectangles upon which every Martian action was based. The Shell Man selected a card and laid it out. Lee played in turn, whereupon both players picked up their cards and returned them to their hands.

This process was repeated, after which several variations of the same basic process were performed, and Jennifer, despite her untenable position, found herself wondering about the game. At one stage of the play, Lee had only one card in his hand, the Martian holding all the rest. But whether this was good or bad Jennifer could not determine, because neither player gave any sign.

Then the process reversed itself and the twenty-six cards save two, were repossessed by Lee.

Jennifer found herself almost admiring the man. Neurotic, unstable, without ethics though he was, Lee had a brilliant mind. This game had all the earmarks of complexity. Several times the Martian paused to study carefully before he made a play. But Lee Tarp was never at any great loss. He played quickly and, Jennifer suspected, brilliantly.

The watching Shell Men followed the game in tense silence. Short exclamations—words in an alien tongue—escaped at times from the lips of the least self-contained of the waiting circle.

Time passed. The game—whatever manner of game it was—seesawed back and forth. But always, Jennifer sensed, with the Martian on the defensive.

But now Jennifer lost interest in the game. This occurred when two of the Martians left the circle and came slowly in her direction. A pinch of panic touched her mind. The Martians came closer, squatted on their shell-covered haunches, and peered into her face.

Her panic brightened now. Trussed and gagged as she was, with her ankles bound and her wrists tied behind her back, she was helpless to put up any show of resistance. Only her heels were free, and these she beat on the steel of the corroding floor.

But no results were achieved, because one of the Shell Men reached out with a horny hand and put a stop to the beating. Jennifer screamed, agonizingly, silently, deep in her muffled throat. But she could not pierce the aura of deep attention surrounding the card game. She was entirely at the mercy of the two Shell Men.

They did not appear to be bent on any harm, however, and Jennifer came to the conclusion their actions were motivated by sheer curiosity. They were incapable of expression, the immovable shell of their faces acting as perfect masks.

Hard, plate-like hands passed over her hair as she stared into the yellow eyes behind the plastic shields. Martian fingers pushed and probed at the flesh of her face. Her ears came in for a fair share of inspection and one of the Martians became bent upon investigating the shape of her leg beneath the bulky spacesuit.

JUST HOW far the manual inspection would have gone Jennifer was never to discover, because at that moment a cry of triumph from Lee turned all attention back to the game. The two inquisitive Shell Men hurried back to the circle where Lee was giving every indication of having won.

Jennifer breathed a sigh of relief. She turned her own attention back to the gamblers and wondered by what process Lee had won. He now held thirteen cards, as did his Martian opponent.

But both players threw in their hands. "Twelve portals," Lee crooned in his native tongue and—reaching forth—he drew both his own stake and those of the Martians to his side of the circle.

But the game, it seemed, was not over. From incredibly well hidden pockets, the Martians came forth with another pile of nuggets—a pile almost double the size of the one now in Lee's possession. Lee grinned and pushed forth his own original stake.

The Martians demurred. Whether Lee understood the rapid gutturals shot at him from all sides, Jennifer could not tell. He frowned, indicated his bag, and pushed it forth with what was almost a belligerent gesture.

The Shell Man with whom he had played cards, came erect and reminded Jennifer, in passing, of the ancient prints she had seen depicting the American Indian, that long-gone first citizen of the North American continent. Such was the Martian's stolid dignity as he stood there with folded arms.

Lee got up also and gestured his question by turning palms up and shrugging his shoulders.

The Martian spokesman had evidently been told the decision of his followers. And that decision had no doubt been arrived at by the two Shell Men who had inquiringly prodded Jennifer's physical being. The Martian turned and pointed a finger at her; then back at Lee's original stake; He made himself entirely clear. They wanted both items placed against the larger pile of nuggets.

Lee scowled and spoke with indignation, "Nagat! Nagat! Nagat!" His manner indicated the word meant the negative; that he refused the bet.

The Martian shrugged. He made a sign to his followers and they silently formed a line and began retrieving their nuggets.

A WAVE of thankfulness swept over Jennifer. But her gratitude began slowly to congeal as she caught Lee's eye. She saw him look with eagerness at the pile of nuggets; saw the sullenness, the regret, with which he watched the pile diminish.

Then he turned his eyes upon Jennifer and she could sense the avaricious workings of his mind.

No—no.

But it was only desperate wishful thinking on her part. With a revulsion almost akin to sickness, she watched Lee gesture toward the silent Martian leader. His motion of acceptance was fully as eloquent as had been that of his first refusal.

The Martian nodded, emitted several gutturals, and the line reversed itself. In a matter of moments, the game was under way.

In order to occupy her agonized mind, to keep down the waves of sickness, Jennifer sought to follow the game. It progressed in crackling silence, and she believed she discovered the method of acquiring what Lee had termed a portal. Like a miser counting pennies, she kept track of the portals gain by Lee Tarp; she balanced them against the ones gotten by the Martian. She prayed as the tide of fortune swung back and forth.

But gradually Lee gained an edge. Then it came. The moment of triumph. Lee's twelfth portal! Jennifer went weak from relief. Now, if the Shell Men had been divested of their last nuggets...

But the sickness and terror welled anew in Jennifer's heart. She had been wrong. She had not divined the intricacies of the game at all. The look of bitter frustration on Lee's face—the glad gutturals of the Shell Men—told her the awful truth.

Lee had lost the game.

JENNIFER'S world came to an abrupt end as the Martians—having finished dividing the bag of sugar and retrieving their nuggets—gathered around to inspect their human prize. Inquisitive and appraising fingers probed at the flesh under her heavy suit. Remarks were passed back and forth, and Jennifer was grateful for her lack of understanding.

But now she gained a respite, however brief it would be, when Lee pushed into the group of Shell Men; and addressed the leader. His harangue was done mainly in pantomime with a few words of both languages thrown in. Not enough words, however, to give Jennifer any inkling of Lee's subject.

She got the impression, from both his manner and that of the Martian, that Lee was reminding the latter of some obligation unfulfilled. The Martian finally got Lee's meaning and addressed his own people in the guttural which was becoming familiar to Jennifer,

There was a chorus of agreement from the Shell Men, who went into immediate action. A pair of them lifted the now-helmeted Lee, who clung tightly to his bag of nuggets; another team did the same with the apprehensive Jennifer, and the group went flying off across the dark plain.

As they traveled, the two moons came up into the Martian sky, giving light to the weird group that sailed over the short fuzz-bush.

Jennifer, dazed by the abruptness of the affair, became conscious of Lee's voice speaking through her radio. "It's all right, darling. There's nothing to be afraid of. I have a plan; a plan that will win us freedom and wealth. We're going back to Earth, Jen. You and I! And we're taking enough gold with us to buy half a city. Trust me, darling…"

But Jennifer, beaten down mentally and physically, didn't care anymore. Nothing much mattered except that this mad nightmare have an ending. Any kind of an ending. Just so this madness be finished.

Where was Barry? Where was Sam? Was she beyond reach of their aid? Evidently she was. Now only two possibilities remained for her. A trip to disaster in a spaceship with a madman, or some horrible obscene fate with a group of bulge-eyed monstrosities.

There was only one consolation. She wouldn't be called upon to make a choice. She would not be consulted.

Time passed, with her sated mind unable to marvel at the speed and ease with which the Shell Men flew across the plain. Then the form of a bright new spaceship loomed ahead. *Voyager Three*, waiting where they'd left it; waiting to carry someone into the sky. And *Voyager Three* didn't care who.

IDLY, JENNIFER sought to define this action of being carried across the plain. Evidently, she surmised, the Shell Men had agreed to deposit Lee at the spaceship, regardless of the outcome of the weird card game. They were keeping their promise.

Jennifer's mind wandered further. In case Lee's plan failed, would she become the wife of a single Shell Man? Or the playmate of a dozen? It was no use wondering. Only time would tell.

The mad race ended as abruptly as it had begun when the group came abreast *Voyager Three* and stopped on the port side of the tail assembly. Lee Tarp snapped open a small niche, flush with the hull, and released the outer port-lock. The port swung silently inward. The ramp came down like a tongue bent upon tasting the fuzz-bush.

Now Lee moved swiftly. He caught Jennifer's arm, turned her sharply, and pushed her toward the ramp. "Inside the ship, quick! You didn't think I was going to leave you with these monsters, did you?"

The Shell Men seemed puzzled; but only momentarily. With Lee and Jennifer halfway up the ramp, they sprang forward in concerted movement. Guttural words of surprise and anger filled the air...

Lee had thrown off his helmet and he now had a gun trained on the Shell Men. "Stand back, you stupid idiots!" His words were not understood, but the Shell Men associated the handgun with violence. Some of them had been present at the gambling where violence had been done. Their reluctance to move forward had its effect on the others.

Lee grinned. "I knew you'd be smart about it. You saw what this gun did before. Anybody like to try for more?"

Jennifer, though dazed, got the impression Lee would have liked an attempt at interference from the Shell Men. There was a baiting tone in his voice as he pushed her back through the port.

The Shell Men did not come forward. They stood talking among themselves in low gutturals. They watched Lee push backward into the ship after Jennifer.

"So long, suckers," Lee Tarp sneered.

CHAPTER NINE

"A NEW AND rather picturesque appellation," Jorgman said. "I never heard it before."

Both Lee and Jennifer whirled to see Jorgman, the two Earthmen, and several Martians waiting inside the ship. Now there was quick, decisive action. Two Shell Men leaped forth to disarm Lee, Sam and Barry sprang from the group also, but to catch Jennifer, who seemed ready to fall; to remove her helmet, the gag, the thongs from her wrists.

Barry glowered—darkly at Lee—a look not missed by Jorgman, who said, "I would suggest you restrain your natural impulse to do your compatriot bodily harm. Violence is shunned on this planet and there has been far too much of it already."

Lee was struggling in the grip of Shell Men. "What kind of rotten trickery is this? You've got no authority to hold me." He directed his words at Jorgman, who dominated the scene by merely standing with his arms folded. "You have no right to restrain any of us. It will be taken as an unfriendly act by our government."

"I'm afraid," Jorgman said gently, "that too much credence cannot be given to your statement. An alien is required to obey the laws of the land he enters into."

"What are you doing here anyhow?"

"After you kidnapped your female companion, we felt this was the point at which you would eventually arrive."

Jennifer was in Barry's arms, crying softly, her head on his shoulder. "He—he used me as a—a stake in a card game," she sobbed, "He lost me to the Shell Men."

Sam took a menacing step forward. "Good Lord..."

"An unfortunate thing for Mr. Tarp to do," Jorgman said, "Pardon me a moment."

Jorgman turned to a duo of the Shell Men who stood a little apart from the others. This pair had no distinguishing marks other than possibly the haughty tilt of their heads. Jorgman spoke to them in the low, swift guttural of the race.

The Shell Men held up their end of the conversation, their blank expressionless faces upon Lee Tarp. After a few moments, one of these leaders addressed his fellow Martians in a louder tone.

Jorgman turned to Jennifer, smiling gently. "You may consider the incident closed, my dear. I explained that Mr. Tarp had no right to put your person up as a gaming unit. You do not belong to him. The Martians took it for granted you were his wife. Your status is now cleared—but I'm afraid that of Mr. Tarp has worsened."

"What will happen to him?" Jennifer asked.

"They are more determined than ever that he answer for his crimes. The worst of these, of course, was the violence. But to gamble with property not your own is almost as grave an offense."

SAM WALDEN spoke for the first time, "You don't actually mean Lee will be killed! It's hard to conceive of a race so vindictive—"

"Mars is almost entirely free from crime," Jorgman said. "Perhaps that is the reason."

"But you said something about a trial," Barry reminded.

Jorgman sighed. "Yes. The Shell People recognize the principal that a man should be punished by his own race. Therefore, they have turned the prisoner over to me for trial— and possible execution."

"What sort of a trial will be staged?"

"A game of cards," Jorgman murmured. "I will engage your Mr. Tarp in a set of *gannota*. If he wins, the Martians will agree to give him his liberty."

The Earthlings stared incredulously. Sam Walden voiced their sentiments, "A method so crude! It's—"

"Amazing?" Jorgman asked. "You are on Mars now. This method of trial has gone on for hundreds of thousands of years. In the long run, I imagine, it averages out."

Already, the Shell Men had formed the circle. Lee's guards hauled him across the floor and pushed him down opposite the already seated Jorgman. Lee grinned. "You could have relieved my mind by telling me about this sooner. I knew there'd be some sort of a trial, but—"

"Do not allow your confidence the upper hand," Jorgman said. "It is the contention of the Martians that the gods of justice now rule the cards. "Also," he added, "I am considered an excellent *gannota* player."

Lee's face darkened. "You don't mean you'd actually try to beat me—"

"I will assist the gods by playing to the best of my ability."

A dealer had been appointed by the Shell Men. He shuffled the deck and allowed each player a cut. He dealt two hands of thirteen cards, then laid the deck out in plain sight and folded his arms.

"In the case of a trial game," Jorgman said, addressing Lee Tarp, "each play is called orally. It is the custom. Are you familiar with all the plays? Are you able to interpret them into your own language? If not, I am at liberty to appoint—"

"Let's get on with it," Lee said. "I've learned my way around."

"In that case, please select your channel."

LEE STUDIED his hand. He had a choice of eleven different channels. Each channel gave a different set of values; even names to the cards. By correctly evaluating his hand, and transposing the values, he could gain a possible advantage in strength.

"Planets," he said.

"Thank you."

"I advance toward the fourth portal."

Jorgman raised his eyebrows. This was a daring move at the beginning of the game. "I am required to warn you," Jorgman said, "that your life is the stake in this game."

"Play cards!" Lee snapped.

"Very well. I introduce the three of Saturn." He laid a card on the steel floor.

Lee smiled—a smile of confidence. "I intercept with the jack of planets." He laid down a card also, whereupon Jorgman placed another card from his hand onto the floor and Lee picked up all three.

"You realize, of course," Jorgman said gently, "that you have lost the game."

Lee jerked his eyes upward, startled. "That's absurd. In three more meetings I gain my portal."

"But in eight meetings you will have advanced only to the sixth. Your strength will have been used. You will remain at six while I defeat you."

"Play," Lee said grimly.

"I return with a Venus meeting. The nine. I declare for one portal."

In this exchange, Lee's hand increased by four cards.

A deep silence had fallen over the game, broken only by the brief declarations of the players. The cards moved, back and forth, none of the Earthlings, save Lee, able to draw the vaguest conclusion as to which player fortune favored.

Not until, sometime later, they saw the beads of sweat on Lee's forehead; heard him mutter, "You can save me. Only a small slip they wouldn't notice. In God's name, don't send a countryman to die."

"Cheating of any sort," Jorgman said, "is a despicable crime on Mars."

"But it isn't fair. You play better than I do. I didn't have a chance."

"On the contrary, you have a brilliant mind. We are evenly matched. My experience—your genius. We differ only in that you risk all on one card. I play cautiously."

LEE'S JAW tightened. "And I'll still gamble. Select your card."

Jorgman nodded. This, one way or another, would be the finish. He drew a card from his hand. Lee studied its back as though striving to see through it.

"I advance to the ninth portal," he said. My weapon is lord-card of the seventh planet." He laid forth a card.

"The gate is closed," Jorgman replied sadly. "Your jack of planets, like an old sin, returns to confound you," He laid a card on the floor. "I enter the twelfth portal."

Lee appeared to be choking. He raised stricken eyes to Jorgman. "Do not close the gate," he whispered. "Do not take a countryman's life."

Jorgman sighed deeply. "The gate is closed."

"You devil!" Lee lunged across the intervening space toward Jorgman, hands clutching at his throat. Two Shell Men dragged him back and to his feet. Jorgman came erect, smiling with his eternal gentleness. "I think our affairs here are completed."

"When and how does the execution take place?" Lee asked quietly. He had quit struggling with the Shell Men. The spirit seemed to have gone out of him.

Jorgman's answer was only a partial one. "Immediately. The execution chamber is underground, beyond your apartments."

"Who—performs—?"

"I do," Jorgman said. He sighed. "I have become quite adept at it."

Jennifer was still within Barry's encircling arm. "You mean you have executed other—Earthlings."

"Yes. But now I suggest we go on our way."

As they hauled Lee from the ship, he turned with a snarl on Sam Walden. "You're going to let them do this to me? What kind of a friend are you? What kind of a leader?"

"Just a moment," Sam said, speaking to Jorgman. "There are certain points in Lee's favor in this matter. One in particular that you yourself have accepted."

Jorgman's smile was bright—questioning. Sam went on, "The Shell Men have turned Lee over to you for the carrying out of the sentence on the theory that he is of your people. On that same basis, I ask that you turn him over to me. We will return to Earth and see that he is tried in Earth courts."

"Do you *wish* to return to Earth?" Jorgman asked the question suddenly, catching Sam off balance. The latter hesitated for several moments. "That is neither here nor there."

"I take it," Jorgman pursued, "that you don't think the sentence just."

"I think it's too severe."

Jorgman sighed. "I'm afraid I must over-rule you. I must take into consideration the Shell People and their ancient laws. I must not disturb the *status quo*. I will do nothing to risk disturbing our admirable relationship with them."

"In that case—" Sam never finished his sentence. Nor did he get the gun from his pocket. Two of the Shell Men moved with the speed that characterized them. Another pair took swift charge of Barry, and the two Earthmen were helpless.

"I must apologize for the seemingly inhospitable actions," Jorgman said, "but I may have saved you from an error you would regret. Shall we leave now, gentlemen?"

THE SIX Shell Men handling the Earthmen constituted also the representative witnesses of the execution. In grim silence, the cavalcade entered the spine-like building, passed through the apartments given the foursome upon their arrival, and retired to a small, bare room beyond.

Jorgman crossed the room and opened the door to a small booth. They saw what was inside and Jennifer, pale and shaken, exclaimed, "An electric chair!"

"A form of one," Jorgman said, and they watched as the Shell Men strapped Lee into it.

Lee had dredged up a surprising amount of moral strength. He was silent, grim, unbegging, as the strapping down was completed.

"It's wrong—wrong!" Jennifer whispered. Barry reached out and took her hand. "Maybe we can even things up later," he muttered.

With surprising callousness, Jorgman closed the door of the chair-cell and threw a switch on the wall.

"Wait—wait! Let him say a prayer, at least," Jennifer pleaded.

But it was apparently too late. A high keening noise was heard, after which Jorgman opened the door. Lee hung loosely against his bonds. The Shell Men, on a motion from Jorgman, gathered around the chair. Then, satisfied, they stalked silently away.

Jorgman, alone with his Earth guests, smiled brightly. The callous execution had numbed them. They stood frozen as Jorgman again closed the door and threw the switch. The high whine of hidden mechanisms was heard again. Now Jorgman again opened the door.

Lee had vanished. The chair was empty.

"Your compatriot is not dead," Jorgman smiled. "He has been back on Earth for several months now."

The three Earthlings stared. "A space-time machine!"

"Exactly. And I know you'll pardon an old man his little dramatics. This is of course the reason we allow the spaceships to rot away."

LATER, Jorgman said, "I was miserly with my information—because I wanted a chance to watch and study you. We need recruits for our Martian world, but they must be the right type; that is important. Lee Tarp obviously was not the right type. So his deportation served two purposes: it satisfied the Shell People of his death, and got him back to his planet."

"We haven't indicated that we wish to stay here," Sam said.

"Nor would I ask any hasty decision. There is plenty of time." Jorgman paused to smile. "And now, are there any questions?"

THE FOUR space candidates selected for the Martian trip on *Voyager Four* were receiving a final briefing from Colonel Hardy.

"And in the case of *Voyager Three*," Hardy stated, "I must tell you this: One member of the crew was found, six months after the blastoff, dealing poker in an Arizona gambling house. He, like the others before him, had no recollection of ever riding a spaceship.

"Now, one of your important jobs will be to find out."

THE END

Printed in Great Britain
by Amazon

14656327R00133